THE BULL APE...

Almost upon the man and woman, rolling toward them in his awkward gait, was an enormous bull ape, the largest that Old Timer had ever seen. The man glanced quickly sideways and was horrified to see the girl still standing there near him.

He started to order her away; but the words were never spoken, for it was then that the ape charged. Old Timer struck with his club, and the girl rushed in and struck with hers. Utter futility! The beast grasped the man's weapon, tore it from his hand, and flung it aside. With his other hand he sent the girl spinning with a blow that might have felled an ox had not the man broken its force by seizing the shaggy arm. Then the great ape picked Old Timer up as one might a rag doll and rolled off toward the jungle!

The *Authorized Editions* of
Edgar Rice Burroughs'
TARZAN NOVELS
available in Ballantine Books Editions
at your local bookstore:

COMPLETE AND UNABRIDGED!

TARZAN AND THE LEOPARD MEN

Edgar Rice Burroughs

BALLANTINE BOOKS • NEW YORK

ISBN 0-345-28687-1

Manufactured in the United States of America

This authorized edition published by arrangement with
Edgar Rice Burroughs, Inc.

First U.S. Edition: March 1964
Seventh U.S. Printing: March 1981

First Canadian Printing: June 1964

Cover art by Neal Adams

CHAPTERS

1

Storm

THE girl turned uneasily upon her cot. The fly, bellying in the rising wind, beat noisily against the roof of the tent. The guy ropes creaked as they tugged against their stakes. The unfastened flaps of the tent whipped angrily. Yet in the midst of this growing pandemonium, the sleeper did not fully awaken. The day had been a trying one. The long, monotonous march through the sweltering jungle had left her exhausted, as had each of the weary marches that had preceded it through the terrible, grueling days since she had left rail-head in that dim past that seemed now a dull eternity of suffering.

Perhaps she was less exhausted physically than before, as she was gradually becoming inured to the hardships; but the nervous strain of the past few days had taken its toll of energy since she had become aware of the growing insubordination of the native men who were her only companions on this rashly conceived and illy ordered safari.

Young, slight of build, accustomed to no sustained physical effort more gruelling than a round of golf, a few sets of tennis, or a morning canter on the back of a well-mannered mount, she had embarked upon this mad adventure without the slightest conception of the hardships and dangers that it would impose. Convinced almost from the first day that her endurance might not be equal to the heavy tax placed upon it, urged by her better judgment to turn back before it became too late, she had sturdily, and perhaps stubbornly, pushed on deeper and deeper into the grim jungle from which she had long since practically given up hope of extricating herself. Physically frail she might be for such an adventure, but no paladin of the Round Table could have boasted a sturdier will.

How compelling must be the exigency that urged her on!
What necessity drove her from the paths of luxury and ease
into the primeval forest and this unaccustomed life of danger,
exposure, and fatigue? What ungovernable urge denied her
the right of self-preservation now that she was convinced
that her only chance of survival lay in turning back? Why
had she come? Not to hunt; she had killed only under the
pressure of necessity for food. Not to photograph the wild
life of the African hinterland; she possessed no camera.
Not in the interests of scientific research; if she had ever
had any scientific interest it had been directed principally
upon the field of cosmetics, but even that had languished and
expired in the face of the fierce equatorial sun and before
an audience consisting exclusively of low browed, West Afri-
cans. The riddle, then, remains a riddle as unfathomable
and inscrutable as the level gaze of her brave grey eyes.

The forest bent beneath the heavy hand of Usha, the
wind. Dark clouds obscured the heavens. The voices of the
jungle were silenced. Not even the greatest of the savage
beasts risked calling the attention of the mighty forces of
Nature to their presence. Only the sudden flares of the wind-
swept beast-fires illumined the camp in fitful bursts that
wrought grotesquely dancing shadow-shapes from the prosaic
impedimenta of the safari, scattered upon the ground.

A lone and sleepy askari, bracing his back against the
growing gale, stood careless guard. The camp slept, except
for him and one other; a great hulking native, who crept
stealthily toward the tent of the sleeping girl.

Then the fury of the storm broke upon the crouching forest. Lightning flashed. Thunder boomed, and rolled, and
boomed again. Rain fell. At first in great drops and then in
solid, wind-sped sheets it enveloped the camp.

Even the sleep of utter exhaustion could not withstand
this final assault of Nature. The girl awoke. In the vivid and
almost incessant flashes of lightning she saw a man entering
the tent. Instantly she recognized him. The great, hulking
figure of Golato the headman might not easily be mistaken
for another. The girl raised herself upon an elbow.

"Is there something wrong, Golato?" she asked. "What
do you want?"

"You, Kali Bwana," answered the man huskily.

So it had come at last! For two days she had been dreading it, her fears aroused by the changed attitude of the man toward her; a change that was reflected in the thinly veiled contempt of the other members of her party for her orders, in the growing familiarities of their speech and actions. She had seen it in the man's eyes.

From a holster at the side of her cot she drew a revolver. "Get out of here," she said, "or I'll kill you."

For answer the man leaped toward her. Then she fired.

* * * * * * *

Moving from west to east, the storm cut a swath through the forest. In its wake lay a trail of torn and twisted branches, here and there an uprooted tree. It sped on, leaving the camp of the girl far behind.

In the dark a man crouched in the shelter of a great tree, protected from the full fury of the wind by its hoary bole. In the hollow of one of his arms something cuddled close to his naked hide for warmth. Occasionally he spoke to it and caressed it with his free hand. His gentle solicitude for it suggested that it might be a child, but it was not. It was a small, terrified, wholly miserable little monkey. Born into a world peopled by large, savage creatures with a predilection for tender monkey meat he had early developed, perhaps inherited, an inferiority feeling that had reduced his activities to a series of screaming flights from dangers either real or imaginary.

His agility, however, often imparted a certain appearance of reckless bravado in the presence of corporeal enemies from whom experience had taught him he could easily escape; but in the face of Usha, the wind, Ara, the lightning, and Pand, the thunder, from whom none might escape, he was reduced to the nadir of trembling hopelessness. Not even the sanctuary of the mighty arms of his master from whose safe embrace he had often thrown insults into the face of Numa, the lion, could impart more than a fleeting sense of security.

He cowered and whimpered to each new gust of wind, each flash of lightning, each stunning burst of thunder. Suddenly the fury of the storm rose to the pinnacle of its Titanic might; there was the sound of rending wood from the ancient fibers of the jungle patriarch at whose foot the two had sought shelter. Catlike, from his squatting position, the man leaped to one side even as the great tree crashed to earth, carrying a half dozen of its neighbors with it. As he jumped he tossed the monkey from him, free of the branches of the fallen monarch. He, himself, was less fortunate. A far spreading limb struck him heavily upon the head and, as he fell, pinned him to the ground.

Whimpering, the little monkey crouched in an agony of terror while the tornado, seemingly having wrought its worst, trailed off toward the east and new conquests. Presently, sensing the departure of the storm, he crept fearfully in search of his master, calling to him plaintively from time to time. It was dark. He could see nothing beyond a few feet from the end of his generous, sensitive nose. His master did not answer and that filled the little monkey with dire forebodings; but presently he found him beneath the fallen tree, silent and lifeless.

*   *   *   *   *   *   *

Nyamwegi had been the life of the party in the little thatched village of Kibbu, where he had gone from his own village of Tumbai to court a dusky belle. His vanity flattered by the apparent progress of his suit and by the very evident impression that his wit and personality had made upon the company of young people before whom he had capered and boasted, he had ignored the passage of time until the sudden fall of the equatorial night had warned him that he had long overstayed the time allowed him by considerations of personal safety.

Several miles of grim and forbidding forest separated the villages of Kibbu and Tumbai. They were miles fraught by night with many dangers, not the least of which to Nyamwegi were the most unreal, including, as they did, the ghosts of departed enemies and the countless demons that direct the destinies of human life, usually with malign intent.

He would have preferred to remain the night in Kibbu as had been suggested by his inamorata; but there was a most excellent reason why he could not, a reason that transcended in potency even the soft blandishments of a sweetheart or the terrors of the jungle night. It was a tabu that had been placed upon him by the witch-doctor of Tumbai for some slight transgression when the latter had discovered that, above all things, Nyamwegi would doubtless wish to spend many nights in Kibbu village. For a price the tabu might be lifted, a fact which doubtless had more to do with its imposition than the sin it purported to punish; but then, of course, the church must live—in Africa as elsewhere. The tragedy lay in the fact that Nyamwegi did not have the price; and tragedy indeed it proved for poor Nyamwegi.

On silent feet the young warrior followed the familiar trail toward Tumbai. Lightly he carried his spear and shield, at his hip swung a heavy knife; but of what potency were such weapons against the demons of the night? Much more efficacious was the amulet suspended about his neck, which he fingered often as he mumbled prayers to his *muzimo*, the protecting spirit of the ancestor for whom he had been named.

He wondered if the girl were worth the risk, and decided that she was not.

Kibbu village lay a mile behind when the storm overtook Nyamwegi. At first his anxiety to reach Tumbai and his fear of the night urged him on despite the buffetings of the gale; but at last he was forced to seek what shelter he could beneath a giant tree, where he remained until the greatest fury of the elements had subsided, though the lightning was still illuminating the forest as he pushed on. Thus the storm became his undoing, for where he might have passed unnoticed in the darkness the lightning revealed his presence to whatever enemy might be lurking along the trail.

He was already congratulating himself that half the journey had been accomplished when, without warning, he was seized from behind. He felt sharp talons sink into his flesh. With a scream of pain and terror he wheeled to extricate himself from the clutches of the thing that had seized him, the terrifying, voiceless thing that made no sound. For an instant he succeeded in breaking the hold upon his shoulders and as he turned, reaching for his knife, the lightning flashed, revealing to his horrified eyes a hideous human face surmounted by the head of a leopard.

Nyamwegi struck out blindly with his knife in the ensuing darkness, and simultaneously he was seized again from behind by rending talons that sank into his chest and

abdomen as the creature encircled him with hairy arms.
Again vivid lightning brought into high relief the tragic
scene. Nyamwegi could not see the creature that gripped him
from behind; but he saw three others menacing him in
front and on either side, and he abandoned hope as he recognized his assailants, from their leopard skins and masks,
as members of the feared secret order of Leopard Men.

Thus died Nyamwegi the Utengan.

2

The Hunter

THE dawn-light danced among the tree tops above the
grass-thatched huts of the village of Tumbai as the
chief's son, Orando arose from his crude pallet of straw
and stepped out into the village street to make an offering to
his *muzimo*, the spirit of the long dead ancestor for whom he
had been named, preparatory to setting out upon a day of
hunting. In his outstretched palm he held an offering of fine
meal as he stood like an ebony statue, his face upturned toward the heavens.

"My namesake, let us go to the hunt together." He
spoke as one might who addresses a familiar but highly re-
vered friend. "Bring the animals near to me and ward off
from me all danger. Give me meat today, oh, hunter!"

The trail that Orando followed as he set forth alone to hunt
was for a couple of miles the same that led to Kibbu village.
It was an old, familiar trail; but the storm of the preceding
night had wrought such havoc with it that in many places it
was as unrecognizable as it was impassable. Several times
fallen trees forced him to make detours into the heavy underbrush that often bordered the trail upon each side. It was
upon such an occasion that his attention was caught by the
sight of a human leg protruding from beneath the foliage of
a newly uprooted tree.

Orando halted in his tracks and drew back. There was a

movement of the foliage where the man lay. The warrior poised his light hunting spear, yet at the same time he was ready for instant flight. He had recognized the bronzed flesh as that of a white man, and Orando, the son of Lobongo, the chief, knew no white man as friend. Again the foliage moved, and the head of a diminutive monkey was thrust through the tangled verdure.

As its frightened eyes discovered the man the little creature voiced a scream of fright and disappeared beneath the foliage of the fallen tree, only to reappear again a moment later upon the opposite side where it climbed up into the branches of a jungle giant that had successfully withstood the onslaughts of the storm. Here, far above the ground, in fancied security, the small one perched upon a swaying limb and loosed the vials of its wrath upon Orando.

But the hunter accorded it no further attention. Today he was not hunting little monkeys, and for the moment his interest was focused upon the suggestion of tragedy contained in that single, bronzed leg. Creeping cautiously forward, Orrando stooped to look beneath the great mass of limbs and leaves that concealed the rest of the body from his view, for he must satisfy his curiosity.

He saw a giant white man, naked but for a loin cloth of leopard skin, pinned to the ground by one of the branches of the fallen tree. From the face turned toward him two grey eyes surveyed him; the man was not dead.

Orando had seen but few white men; and those that he had seen had worn strange, distinctive apparel. They had carried weapons that vomited smoke, and flame, and metal. This one was clothed as any native warrior might have been, nor was there visible any of those weapons that Orando hated and feared.

Nevertheless the stranger was white and, therefore, an enemy. It was possible that he might extricate himself from his predicament and, if he did, become a menace to the village of Tumbai. Naturally, therefore, there was but one thing for a warrior and the son of a chief to do. Orando fitted an arrow to his bow. The killing of this man meant no more to him than would have the killing of the little monkey.

"Come around to the other side," said the stranger; "your arrow cannot reach my heart from that position."

Orando dropped the point of his missile and surveyed the speaker in surprise, which was engendered, not so much by the nature of his command, as by the fact that he had spoken in the dialect of Orando's own people.

"You need not fear me," continued the man, noticing Orando's hesitation; "I am held fast by this branch and cannot harm you."

What sort of man was this? Had he no fear of death? Most men would have begged for their lives. Perhaps this one sought death.

"Are you badly injured?" demanded Orando.

"I think not. I feel no pain."

"Then why do you wish to die?"

"I do not wish to die."

"But you told me to come around and shoot you in the heart. Why did you say that if you do not wish to die?"

"I know that you are going to kill me. I asked you, to make sure that your first arrow enters my heart. Why should I suffer pain needlessly?"

"And you are not afraid to die?"

"I do not know what you mean."

"You do not know what fear is?"

"I know the word, but what has it to do with death? All things die. Were you to tell me that I must live forever, then I might feel fear."

"How is it that you speak the language of the Utengas?" demanded Orando.

The man shook his head. "I do not know."

"Who are you?" Orando's perplexity was gradually becoming tinged with awe.

"I do not know," replied the stranger.

"From what country do you come?"

Again the man shook his head. "I do not know."

"What will you do if I release you?"

"And do not kill me?" queried the white.

"No, not kill you."

The man shrugged. "What is there to do? I shall hunt for food because I am hungry. Then I shall find a place to lie up and sleep."

"You will not kill me?"

"Why should I? If you do not try to kill me I shall not try to kill you."

The warrior wormed his way through the tangled branches of the fallen tree to the side of the pinioned white man, where he found that a single branch resting across the latter's body prevented the prisoner from getting his arms, equipped with giant muscles, into any position where he might use them effectively for his release. It proved, however, a comparatively easy matter for Orando to raise the limb the few inches necessary to permit the stranger to worm his body from beneath it, and a moment later the two men faced one another beside the fallen tree while a little monkey chattered and grimaced from the safety of the foliage above them.

Orando felt some doubt as to the wisdom of his rash act. He could not satisfactorily explain what had prompted him to such humane treatment of a stranger, yet despite his doubts something seemed to assure him that he had acted wisely. However, he held his spear in readiness and watched the white giant before him with a cautious eye.

From beneath the tree that had held him prisoner the man recovered his weapons, a bow and spear. Over one shoulder hung a quiver of arrows; across the other was coiled a long, fiber rope. A knife swung in a sheath at his hip. His belongings recovered, he turned to Orando.

"Now, we hunt," agreed Orando.

"Where?"

"I know where the pigs feed in the morning and where they lie up in the heat of the day," said Orando.

As they spoke Orando had been appraising the stranger. He noted the clean-cut features, the magnificent physique. The flowing muscles that rolled beneath a skin sun-tanned almost to the hue of his own impressed him by their suggestion of agility and speed combined with great strength. A shock of black hair partially framed a face of rugged, masculine beauty from which two steady, grey eyes surveyed the world fearlessly. Over the left temple was a raw gash (legacy of the storm's fury) from which blood had flowed, and dried in the man's hair and upon his cheek. In moments of silence his brows were often drawn together in thought, and there was a puzzled expression in his eyes. At such times he impressed Orando as one who sought to recall something he had forgotten; but what it was, the man did not divulge.

Orando led the way along the trail that still ran in the direction of Kibbu village. Behind him came his strange companion upon feet so silent that the native occasionally cast a backward glance to assure himself that the white man had not deserted him. Close above them the little monkey swung through the trees, chattering and jabbering.

Presently Orando heard another voice directly behind him that sounded like another monkey speaking in lower tones than those of the little fellow above them. He turned his head to see where the other monkey, sounding so close, could be. To his astonishment he saw that the sounds issued from the throat of the man behind him. Orando laughed aloud. Never before had he seen a man who could mimic the chattering of monkeys so perfectly. Here, indeed, was an accomplished entertainer.

But Orando's hilarity was short-lived. It died when he saw the little monkey leap nimbly from an over-hanging branch to the shoulder of the white man and heard the two chattering to one another, obviously carrying on a conversation.

What sort of man was this, who knew no fear, who could speak the language of the monkeys, who did not know who he was, nor where he came from? This question, which he could not answer, suggested another equally unanswerable, the mere consideration of which induced within Orando qualms of uneasiness. *Was this creature a mortal man at all?*

This world into which Orando had been born was peopled by many creatures, not the least important and powerful of which were those that no man ever saw, but which exercised the greatest influence upon those one might see. There were demons so numerous that one might not count them all, and the spirits of the dead who more often than not were directed by demons whose purposes, always malign, they carried out. These demons and sometimes the spirits of the dead occasionally took possession of the body of a living creature, controlling its thoughts, its actions and its speech. Why, right in the river that flowed past the village of Tumbai dwelt a demon to which the villagers had made offerings of food for many years. It had assumed the likeness of a crocodile, but it had deceived no one; least of all the old witch-doctor who had recognized it immediately for what it was after the chief had threatened him with death when his charms had failed to frighten it away or his amulets to save villagers from its voracious jaws. It was easy, therefore, for Orando to harbor suspicions concerning the creature moving noiselessly at his heels.

A feeling of uneasiness pervaded the son of the chief. This was somewhat mitigated by the consciousness that he had treated the creature in a friendly way and, perhaps, earned its approbation. How fortunate it was that he had reconsidered his first intention of loosing an arrow into its body! That would have been fatal; not for the creature but for Orando. It was quite obvious now why the stranger had not feared death, knowing that, being a demon, it could not die. Slowly it was all becoming quite clear to the black hunter, but he did not know whether to be elated or terrified. To be the associate of a demon might be a distinction, but it also had its distressing aspects. One never knew what a demon might be contemplating, though it was reasonably certain to be nothing good.

Orando's further speculations along this line were rudely interrupted by a sight that met his horrified gaze at a turning of the trail. Before his eyes lay the dead and mutilated body of a warrior. The hunter required no second glance to recognize in the upturned face the features of his friend and comrade, Nyamwegi. But how had he come to his death?

The stranger came and stood at Orando's side, the little monkey perched upon his shoulder. He stooped and examined the body of Nyamwegi, turning the corpse over upon its face, revealing the cruel marks of steel claws.

"The Leopard Men," he remarked briefly and without emotion, as one might utter the most ordinary commonplace.

But Orando was bursting with emotion. Immediately when he had seen the body of his friend he had thought of the Leopard Men, though he had scarcely dared to acknowledge his own thought, so fraught with terror was the very suggestion. Deeply implanted in his mind was fear of this dread secret society, the weird cannibalistic rites which seemed doubly horrible because they could only be guessed at, no man outside their order ever having witnessed them and lived.

He saw the characteristic mutilation of the corpse, the parts cut away for the cannibalistic orgy, of which they would be the *pièce de résistance*. Orando saw and shuddered; but, though he shuddered, in his heart was more of rage than of fear. Nyamwegi had been his friend. From infancy they had grown to manhood together. Orando's soul cried out for vengeance against the fiends who had perpetrated this vile outrage, but what could one man do alone against many? The maze of footsteps in the soft earth about the corpse indicated that Nyamwegi had been overcome by numbers.

The stranger, leaning on his spear, had been silently watching the warrior, noting the signs of grief and rage reflected in the mobile features.

"You knew him?" he asked.

"He was my friend."

The stranger made no comment, but turned and followed a trail that ran toward the south. Orando hesitated. Perhaps the demon was leaving him. Well, in a way that would be a relief; but, after all, he had not been a bad demon, and certainly there was something about him that inspired confidence and a sense of security. Then, too, it was something to be able to fraternize with a demon and, perhaps, to show him off in the village. Orando followed.

"Where are you going?" he called after the retreating figure of the giant white.

"To punish those who killed your friend."

"But they are many," remonstrated Orando. "They will kill us."

"They are four," replied the stranger. "*I* kill."

"How do you know there are but four?" demanded the black.

The other pointed to the trail at his feet. "One is old and limps," he said; "one is tall and thin; the other two are young warriors. They step lightly, although one of them is a large man."

"You have seen them?"

"I have seen their spoor; that is enough."

Orando was impressed. Here, indeed, was a tracker of the first order; but perhaps he possessed something of a higher order than human skill. The thought thrilled Orando; but if it caused him a little fear, too, he no longer hesitated. He had cast his lot, and he would not turn back now.

"At least we can see where they go," he said. "We can follow them to their village, and afterward we can return to Tumbai, where my father, the chief, lives. He will send runners through the Watenga country; and the war drums will boom, summoning the Utenga warriors. Then will we go and make war upon the village of the Leopard Men, that Nyamwegi may be avenged in blood."

The stranger only grunted and trotted on. Sometimes Orando, who was rated a good tracker by his fellows, saw no spoor at all; but the white demon never paused, never hesitated. The warrior marvelled and his admiration grew; likewise his awe. He had leisure to think now, and the more he thought the more convinced he was that this was no mortal who guided him through the jungle upon the trail of the Leopard Men. If it were, indeed, a demon, then it was a most remarkable demon, for by no word or sign had it indicated any malign purpose. It was then, engendered by this line of reasoning, that a new and brilliant thought illuminated the mind of Orando like a bright light bursting suddenly through darkness. This creature, being nothing mortal, must be the protecting spirit of that departed ancestor for whom Orando had been named—his *muzimo!*

Instantly all fear left the warrior. Here was a friend and a protector. Here was the very *namesake* whose aid he had invoked before setting out upon the hunt, he whom he had propitiated with a handful of meal. Suddenly Orando regretted that the offering had not been larger. A handful of meal seemed quite inadequate to appease the hunger of the powerful creature trotting tirelessly ahead of him, but perhaps *muzimos* required less food than mortals. That seemed quite reasonable, since they were but spirits. Yet Orando distinctly recalled that before he had released the creature from beneath the tree it had stated that it wished to hunt for food as it was hungry. Oh, well, perhaps there were many things concerning *muzimos* that Orando did not know; so why trouble his head about details? It was enough that this must be his *muzimo*. He wondered if the little monkey perched upon his *muzimo's* shoulder was also a spirit. Perhaps it was Nyamwegi's ghost. Were not the two very friendly, as he and Nyamwegi had been throughout their lives? The thought appealed to Orando, and henceforth he thought of the little monkey as Nyamwegi. Now it occurred to him to test his theory concerning the white giant.

"Muzimo!" he called.

The stranger turned his head and looked about. "Why did you call '*muzimo*'?" he demanded.

"I was calling you, Muzimo," replied Orando.

"Is that what you call me?"

"Yes."

"What do you want?"

Now Orando was convinced that he had made no mistake. What a fortunate man he was! How his fellows would envy him!

"Why did you call to me?" insisted the other.

"Do you think we are close to the Leopard Men, Muzimo?" inquired Orando, for want of any better question to ask.

"We are gaining on them, but the wind is in the wrong direction. I do not like to track with the wind at my back, for then Usha can run ahead and tell those I am tracking that I am on their trail."

"What can we do about it?" demanded Orando. "The wind will not change for me, but perhaps you can make it blow in a different direction."

"No," replied the other, "but I can fool Usha, the wind. That I often do. When I am hunting up wind I can remain on the ground in safety, for then Usha can only carry tales to those behind me, for whom I care nothing; but when I hunt down wind I travel through the trees, and Usha carries my scent spoor above the head of my quarry. Or sometimes I move swiftly and circle the hunted one, and then Usha comes down to my nostrils and tells me where it is. Come!" The stranger swung lightly to the low-hanging branch of a great tree.

"Wait!" cried Orando. "I cannot travel through the trees."

"Go upon the ground, then. I will go ahead through the trees and find the Leopard Men."

Orando would have argued the wisdom of this plan; but the

white disappeared amidst the foliage, the little monkey cling-ing tightly to its perch upon his shoulder.

"That," thought Orando, "is the last that I shall see of my *muzimo*. When I tell this in the village they will not believe me. They will say that Orando is a great liar."

Plain before him now lay the trail of the Leopard Men. It would be easy to follow; but, again, what could one man hope to accomplish against four, other than his own death? Yet Orando did not think of turning back. Perhaps he could not, alone, wreak his vengeance upon the slayers of Nyam-wegi; but he could, at least, track them to their village, and later lead the warriors of Lobongo, the chief, his father, in battle against it.

The warrior moved tirelessly in a rhythmic trot that consumed the miles with stubborn certainty, relieving the monotony by reviewing the adventures of the morning. Thoughts of his *muzimo* occupied his mind almost to the ex-clusion of other subjects. Such an adventure was without parallel in the experience of Orando, and he enjoyed dwell-ing upon every phase of it. He recalled, almost with the pride of personal possession, the prowess of this other self of his from the spirit world. Its every mannerism and expression was photographed indelibly upon his memory; but that which impressed him most was an indefinable something in the steel-grey eyes, a haunting yearning that suggested a constant effort to recall an illusive memory.

What was his *muzimo* trying to recall? Perhaps it was the details of his earthly existence. Perchance he sought to con-jure once again the reactions of the flesh to worldy stimuli. Doubtless he regretted his spirit state and longed to live again—to live and fight and love.

With such thoughts as their accompaniment the miles re-treated beneath his pounding feet. With such thoughts his mind was occupied to the exclusion of matters which should have concerned him more. For instance, he did not note how fresh the spoor of his quarry had become. In puddles left by the rain of the previous night and roiled by the passage of feet the mud had not yet settled when Orando passed; in places the earth at the edges of footprints was still falling back into the depressions; but these things Orando failed to note, though he was accounted a good tracker. It is well that a man should keep his mind concentrated upon a single thing at a time unless he has a far more elastic mind than Orando. One may not dream too long in the savage jungle.

When Orando came suddenly into a small, natural clearing he failed to notice a slight movement of the surrounding jungle foliage. Had he, he would have gone more cautiously; and doubtless his jungle-craft would have suggested the truth, even though he could not have seen the four pairs of greedy, malevolent eyes that watched him from behind the concealing verdure; but when he reached the center of the clearing he saw all that he should have guessed before, as, with savage cries, four hideously caparisoned warriors leaped into the open and sprang toward him.

Never before had Orando, the son of Lobongo, seen one of the feared and hated members of the dread society of Leopard Men; but as his eyes fell upon these four there was no room for doubt as to their identity. And then they closed upon him.

3

Dead Men Who Spoke

As the girl fired, Golato voiced a cry of pain, wheeled and dashed from the tent, his left hand grasping his right arm above the elbow. Then Kali Bwana arose and dressed, strapping a cartridge belt, with its holster and gun, about her hips. There could be no more thought of sleep that night, for even though Golato might be *hors de combat* there were others to be feared almost as much as he.

She lighted a lantern and, seated in a camp-chair with her rifle across her knees, prepared to spend the remainder of the night in wakeful watching; but if she anticipated any further molestation she was agreeably disappointed. The night dragged its interminable length until outraged Nature could be no longer denied, and presently the girl dozed in her chair. When she awoke the new sun was an hour old. The storm

had passed leaving only mud and soggy canvas in its wake
to mark its passage across the camp. The girl stepped to the
flap of her tent and called to her *boy* to perpare her bath
and her breakfast. She saw the porters preparing the loads.
She saw Golato, his arm roughly bandaged and supported
in a crude sling. She saw her *boy* and called to him again,
this time peremptorily; but he ignored her summons and
went on with the roping of a pack. Then she crossed over
to him, her eyes flashing.

"You heard me call you, Imba," she said. "Why did
you not come and prepare my bath and my breakfast?"

The fellow, a middle-aged man of sullen demeanor,
scowled and hung his head. Golato, surly and glowering,
looked on. The other members of the safari had stopped
their work and were watching, and among them all there
was not a friendly eye.

"Answer me, Imba," commanded the girl. "Why do you
refuse to obey me?"

"Golato is headman," was the surly rejoinder. "He gives
orders. Imba obey Golato."

"Imba obeys me," snapped Kali Bwana. "Golato is no
longer headman." She drew her gun from its holster and let
the muzzle drop on Imba. "Get my bath ready. Last night it
was dark. I could not see well, so I only shot Golato in
the arm. This morning I can see to shoot straighter. Now
move!"

Imba cast an imploring glance in the direction of Golato,
but the ex-headman gave him no encouragement. Here was
a new Kali Bwana, bringing new conditions, to which Golato's slow mind had not yet adapted itself. Imba moved sheep-
ishly toward the tent of his mistress. The other natives
muttered in low tones among themselves.

Kali Bwana had found herself, but it was too late. The
seeds of discontent and mutiny were too deeply sown; they
had already germinated, and although she might wrest a
fleeting victory the end could bring only defeat. She had
the satisfaction, however, of seeing Imba prepare her bath
and, later, her breakfast; but while she was eating the latter
she saw her porters up-loading, preparatory to departure, although her own tent had not been struck, nor had she given
any orders for marching.

"What is the meaning of this?" she demanded, walking quickly to where the men were gathered. She did not address Golato, but another who had been his lieutenant and whom she had intended appointing headman in his place.

"We are going back," replied the man.

"You cannot go back and leave me alone," she insisted.

"You may come with us," said the native. "But you will have to look after yourself," he added.

"You shall not do anything of the sort," cried the girl, thoroughly exasperated. "You agreed to accompany me wherever I went. Put down your loads, and wait until you get marching orders from me."

As the men hesitated she drew her revolver. It was then that Golato interfered. He approached her with the askaris, their rifles ready. "Shut up, woman," he snarled, "and get back to your tent. We are going back to our own country. If you had been good to Golato this would not have happened; but you were not, and this is your punishment. If you try to stop us these men will kill you. You may come with us, but you will give no orders. Golato is master now."

"I shall not go with you, and if you desert me here you know what your punishment will be when I get back to railhead and report the matter to the commissioner."

"You will never get back," replied Golato sullenly. Then he turned to the waiting porters and gave the command to march.

It was with sinking heart that the girl saw the party file from camp and disappear in the forest. She might have followed, but pride had a great deal to do with crystallizing her decision not to. Likewise, her judgment assured her that she would be far from safe with this sullen, mutinous band at whose head was as great a menace to her personal safety as she might find in all Africa. Again, there was the pertinacity of purpose that had kept her forging ahead upon her hopeless mission long after mature judgment and convinced her of its futility. Perhaps it was no more than ordinary stubbornness; but whatever it was it held her to what she conceived to be her duty, even though it led to what she now knew must be almost certain death.

Wearily she turned back toward her tent and the single

load of provisions they had left behind for her sustenance. What was she to do? She could not go on, and she would not go back. There was but an single alternative. She must remain here, establishing a permanent camp as best she could, and await the remotely possible relief party that might come after long, long months.

She was confident that her safari could not return to civilization without her and not arouse comment and investigation; and when investigation was made some one at least among all those ignorant porters would divulge the truth. Then there would be a searching party organized unless Golato succeeded with his lying tongue in convincing them that she was already dead. There was a faint hope, however, and to that she would cling. If, perchance, she could cling to life also during the long wait she might be might be saved at the last.

Taking stock of the provisions that the men had left behind for her, she found that she had enough upon which to subsist for a month, provided that she exercised scrupulous economy in their use. If game proved plentiful and her hunting was successful, this time might be indefinitely prolonged. Starvation, however, was not the only menace that she apprehended nor the most dreaded. There were prowling carnivores against which she had little defense to offer. There was the possibility of discovery by unfriendly natives. There was always the danger (and this she dreaded most) of being stricken by one of the deadly jungle fevers.

She tried to put such thoughts from her mind, and to do so she occupied herself putting her camp in order, dragging everything perishable into her tent and, finally, commencing the construction of a crude *boma* as a protection against the prowlers of the night. The work was fatiguing, necessitating frequent rests, during which she wrote in her diary, to which she confided nothing of the fears that assailed her, fears that she dreaded admitting, even to herself. Instead, she confined herself to a narration of the events of the past few days since she had written. Thus she occupied her time as Fate marshalled the forces that were presently to drag her into a situation more horrible than any that she could possibly have conceived.

As the four, clothed in the leopard skins of their order,

closed upon Orando there flashed to the mind of the son of
the chief a vision of the mutilated corpse of his murdered
friend; and in that mental picture he saw a prophecy of his
own fate; but he did not flinch. He was a warrior, with a
duty to perform. These were the murderers of his comrade,
the enemies of his people. He would die, of that he was certain; but first he would avenge Nyamwegi. The enemy should
feel the weight of the wrath of a Utenga fighting-man.

The four Leopard Men were almost upon him as he
launched his spear. With a scream one of the foemen dropped,
pierced by the sharp tip of the Utenga's weapon. Fortunate
it was for Orando that the methods of the Leopard Men pre-
scribed the use of their improvised steel claws as weapons
in preference to spears or arrows, which they resorted to
only in extremities or when faced by superior numbers.
The flesh for their unholy rites must die beneath their
leopard claws, or it was useless for religious purposes. Maddened by fanaticism, they risked death to secure the coveted
trophies. To this Orando owed the slender chance he had to
overcome his antagonists. But at best the respite from death
could be but brief.

The remaining three pressed closer, preparing for the le-
thal charge in simulation of the carnivore they personified.
Silence enveloped the jungle, as though Nature awaited with
bated breath the consummation of this savage tragedy. Suddenly the quiet was shattered by the scream of a monkey
in a tree overhanging the clearing. The sound came from
behind Orando. He saw two opponents who were facing him
dart startled glances beyond him. He heard a scream that
forced his attention rearward in a brief glance, and what he
saw brought the sudden joy of an unexpected reprieve from
death. In the grasp of his *muzimo,* the third of the surviving
Leopard Men was struggling impotently against death.

Then Orando wheeled again to face his remaining enemies, while, from behind him, came savage growls that
stiffened the hairs upon his scalp. What new force had been
thus suddenly injected into the grim scene? He could not
guess, nor could he again risk even a brief backward glance.
His whole attention was now required by the hideous creatures sneaking toward him, their curved, steel talons opened,
claw-like, to seize him.

The action that is so long in the telling occupied but a few seconds of actual time. A shriek mingled with the growls that Orando had heard. The Leopard Men leaped swiftly toward him. A figure brushed past him from the rear and, with a savage growl, leaped upon the foremost Leopard Man. It was Orando's *muzimo*. The heart of the warrior missed a beat as he realized that those beast-like sounds had issued from the throat of his *namesake*. But if the fact perturbed Orando it utterly demoralized the fourth antagonist who had been advancing upon him, with the result that the fellow wheeled and bolted for the jungle, leaving the sole survivor of his companions to his fate.

Orando was free now to come to the aid of his *muzimo*, who was engaged with the larger of the two younger Leopard Men; but he quickly realized that his *muzimo* required no aid. In a grip of steel he held the two clawed hands, while his free hand grasped the throat of his antagonist. Slowly but as inexorably as Fate he was choking the life from the struggling man. Gradually his victim's efforts grew weaker, until suddenly, with a convulsive shudder, the body went limp. Then he cast it aside. For a moment he stood gazing at it, a puzzled expression upon his face; and then, apparently mechanically, he advanced slowly to its side and placed a foot upon it. The reaction was instantaneous and remarkable. Doubt and hesitation were suddenly swept from the noble features of the giant to be replaced by an expression of savage exultation as he lifted his face to the heavens and gave voice to a cry so awesome that Orando felt his knees tremble beneath him.

The Utenga had heard that cry before, far in the depths of the forest, and knew it for what it was; the victory cry of the bull ape. But why was his *muzimo* voicing the cry of a beast? Here was something that puzzled Orando quite as much as had the materialization of this ancestral spirit. There had never been any doubt in his mind as to the existence of *muzimos*. Everyone possessed a *muzimo;* but there were certain attributes that all men attributed to *muzimos,* and all these were human attributes. Never in his life had Orando heard it even vaguely hinted that *muzimos* growled like Simba, the lion, or screamed as the bull apes scream when they have made a kill. He was troubled and puzzled. Could it be that his *muzimo* was also the *muzimo* of some dead lion and departed ape? And if such were the case might it not be possible that, when actuated by the spirit of the lion or the ape, instead of by that of Orando's ancestor, he would become a menace instead of a blessing?

Suspiciously, now, Orando watched his companion, noting with relief the transition of the savage facial expression to that of quiet dignity that normally marked his mien. He saw the little monkey that had fled to the trees during the battle return to the shoulder of the *muzimo,* and considering this an accurate gauge of the latter's temper he approached, though with some trepidation.

"Muzimo," he ventured timidly, "you came in time and saved the life of Orando. It is yours."

The white was silent. He seemed to be considering this statement. The strange, half bewildered expression returned to his eyes.

"Now I remember," he said presently. "You saved my life. That was a long time ago."

"It was this morning, Muzimo."

The white man shook his head and passed a palm across his brow.

"This morning," he repeated thoughtfully. "Yes, and we were going to hunt. I am hungry. Let us hunt."

"Shall we not follow the one who escaped?" demanded Orando. "We were going to track the Leopard Men to their village, that my father, the chief, might lead the Utengas against it."

"First let us speak with the dead men," said Muzimo. "We shall see what they have to tell us."

"You can speak with the dead?" Orando's voice trembled at the suggestion.

"The dead do not speak with words," explained Muzimo; "but nevertheless they often have stories to tell. We shall see. This one," he continued, after a brief inspection of the corpse of the man he had killed last, "is the larger of the two young men. There lies the tall thin man, and yonder, with your spear through his heart, is he who limped, an old man with a crippled leg. These three, then, have told us that he who escaped is the smaller of the two young men."

Now, more carefully, he examined each of the corpses, noting their weapons and their ornaments, dumping the contents of their pouches upon the ground. These he scanned carefully, paying particular attention to the amulets, of the dead men. In a large package carried by the crippled old man, he found parts of a human body.

"There is no doubt now but that these were the killers of Nyamwegi," said Orando; "for these are the same parts that were removed from his body."

"There was never any doubt," asserted Muzimo confidently. "The dead men did not have to tell me that."

"What have they told you, Muzimo?"

"Their filed teeth have told me that they are eaters of men; their amulets and the contents of their pouches have told me that their village lies upon the banks of a large river. They are fishermen; and they fear Gimla, the crocodile, more than they fear aught else. The hooks in their pouches tell me the one their amulets the other. From their ornaments and weapons, by the cicatrices upon their foreheads and chins I know their tribe and the country it inhabits. I do not need to follow the young warrior; his friends have told me where he is going. Now we may hunt. Later we can go to the village of the Leopard Men."

"Even as I prayed today before setting out from the village, you have protected me from danger," observed Orando, "and now, if you bring the animals near to me and give me meat, all of my prayer will have been fulfilled."

"The animals go where they will," responded Muzimo. "I cannot lead them to you, but I can lead you to them; and when you are near, then, perhaps, I can frighten them toward you. Come."

He turned backward along the trail down which they had followed the Leopard Men and fell into an easy trot, while Orando followed, his eyes upon the broad shoulders of his *muzimo* and the spirit of Nyamwegi, perched upon one of them. Thus they continued silently for a half hour, when Muzimo halted.

"Move forward slowly and cautiously," he directed. "The scent spoor of Wappi, the antelope, has grown strong in my nostrils. I go ahead through the trees to get upon the other side of him. When he catches my scent he will move away from me toward you. Be ready."

Scarcely had Muzimo ceased speaking before he disappeared amidst the overhanging foliage of the forest, leaving Orando filled with wonder and admiration, with which was combined overweening pride in his possession of a *muzimo* such as no other man might boast. He hoped that the hunting would be quickly concluded that he might return to the village of Tumbai and bask in the admiration and envy of his fellows as he nonchalantly paraded his new and wondrous acquisition before their eyes. It was something, of course, to be a chief's son, just as it was something to be a chief or a witch-doctor; but to possess a *muzimo* that one might see and talk to and hunt with—ah, that was glory transcending any that might befall mortal man.

Suddenly Orando's gloating thoughts were interrupted by a slight sound of something approaching along the trail from the direction in which he was moving. Just the suggestion of a sound it was, but to the ears of the jungle hunter it was sufficient. You or I could not have heard it; nor, hearing it, could we have interpreted it; but to Orando it bore a message as clear to his ears as is the message of a printed page to our eyes. It told him that a hoofed animal was approaching him, walking quickly, though not yet in full flight. A turn in the trail just ahead of him concealed him from the view of the approaching animal. Orando grasped his spear more firmly, and stepped behind the bole of a small tree that partially hid him from the sight of any creature coming toward him. There he stood, motionless as a bronze statue, knowing that motion and scent are the two most potent stimuli to fear in the lower orders. What wind there was moved from the unseen animal toward the man, precluding the possibility of his scent reaching the nostrils of the hunted; and as long as Orando did not move, the animal, he knew, would come fearlessly until it was close enough to catch his scent, which would be well within spear range.

A moment later there came into view one of those rarest of African animals, an okapi. Orando had never before seen one of them, for they ranged much farther to the west than the Watenga country. He noted the giraffe-like markings on the hind quarters and forelegs; but the short neck deceived him, and he still thought that it was an antelope. He was all excitement now, for here was real meat and plenty of it, the animal being larger than an ordinary cow. The blood raced through the hunter's veins, but outwardly he was calm. There must be no bungling now; every movement must be perfectly timed—a step out into the trail and, simultaneously, the casting of the spear, the two motions blending into each other as though there was but one.

At that instant the okapi wheeled to flee. Orando had not moved, there had been no disturbing sound audible to the ears of the man; yet something had frightened the quarry just a fraction of a second too soon. Orando was disgusted. He leaped into the trail to cast his spear, in the futile hope that it might yet bring down his prey; and as he raised his arm he witnessed a scene that left him gaping in astonishment.

From the trees above the okapi, a creature launched itself onto the back of the terrified animal. It was Muzimo. From his throat rumbled a low growl. Orando stood spellbound. He saw the okapi stumble and falter beneath the weight of the savage man-beast. Before it could recover itself a hand shot out and grasped it by the muzzle. Then steel thews wrenched the head suddenly about, so that the vertebrae of the neck snapped. An instant later a keen knife had severed the jugular, and as the blood gushed from the carcass Orando heard again the victory cry of the bull-ape. Faintly, from afar, came the answering challenge of a lion.

"Let us eat," said Muzimo, as he carved generous portions from the quivering carcass of his kill.

"Yes, let us eat," agreed Orando.

Muzimo grunted as he tossed a piece of the meat to the native. Then he squatted on his haunches and tore at his portion with his strong, white teeth. Cooking fires were for the effete, not for this savage jungle god whose *mores* harked back through the ages to the days before men had mastered the art of making fire.

Orando hesitated. He perferred his meat cooked, but he dreaded losing face in the presence of his *muzimo*. He deliberated for but a second; then he approached Muzimo with the intention of squatting down beside him to eat. The forest god looked up, his teeth buried in the flesh from which he was tearing a piece. A sudden, savage light blazed in his eyes. A low growl rumbled warningly in his throat. Orando had seen lions disturbed at their kills. The analogy was perfect. The warrior withdrew and squatted at a distance. Thus the two finished their meal in a silence broken only by the occasional low growls of the white.

4

Sobito, the Witch-Doctor

TWO white men sat before a much patched, weatherworn tent. They sat upon the ground, for they had no chairs. Their clothing was, if possible, more patched and weatherworn than their tent. Five natives squatted about a cook-fire at a little distance from them. Another native was preparing food for the white men at a small fire near the tent.

"I'm sure fed up on this," remarked the older man.

"Then why don't you beat it?" demanded the other, a young man of twenty-one or twenty-two.

His companion shrugged. "Where? I'd be just another dirty bum, back in the States. Here, I at least have the satisfaction of servants, even though I know damn well they don't respect me. It gives me a certain sense of *class* to be waited upon. There, I'd have to wait on somebody else. But you— I can't see why you want to hang around this lousy God-forsaken country, fighting bugs and fever. You're young. You've got your whole life ahead of you and the whole world to carve it out of any way you want."

"Hell!" exclaimed the younger man. "You talk as though you were a hundred. You aren't thirty yet. You told me your age, you know, right after we threw in together."

"Thirty's old," observed the other. "A guy's got to get a start long before thirty. Why, I know fellows who made theirs and retired by the time they were thirty. Take my dad for instance—" He went silent then, quite suddenly. The other urged no confidences.

"I guess we'd be a *couple* of bums back there," he remarked laughing.

"You wouldn't be a bum anywhere, Kid," remonstrated his companion. He broke into sudden laughter.

"What you laughing about?"

"I was thinking about the time we met; it's just about a year now. You tried to make me think you were a tough guy from the slums. You were a pretty good actor—while you were thinking about it."

The Kid grinned. "It was a hell of a strain on my histrionic abilities," he admitted; "but, say, Old Timer, you didn't fool anybody much, yourself. To listen to you talk one would have imagined that you were born in the jungle and brought up by apes, but I tumbled to you in a hurry. I said to myself, 'Kid, it's either Yale or Princeton; more likely Yale.'"

"But you didn't ask any questions. That's what I liked about you."

"And you didn't ask any. Perhaps that's why we've gotten along together so well. People who ask questions should be taken gently, but firmly, by the hand, led out behind the barn and shot. It would be a better world to live in."

"Oke, Kid; but still it's rather odd, at that, that two fellows should pal together for a year, as we have, and not know the first damn thing about one another—as though neither trusted the other."

"It isn't that with me," said the Kid; "but there are some things that a fellow just *can't* talk about—to any one."

"I know," agreed Old Timer. "The thing each of us can't talk about probably explains why he is here. It was a woman with me; that's why I hate 'em."

"Hooey!" scoffed the younger man. "I'd bet you fall for the first skirt you see—if I had anything to bet."

"We won't have anything to eat or any one to cook it for us if we don't have a little luck pronto," observed the other. "It commences to look as though all the elephants in Africa had beat it for parts unknown."

"Old Bobolo swore we'd find 'em here, but I think old Bobolo is a liar."

"I have suspected that for some time," admitted Old Timer.

The Kid rolled a cigarette. "All he wanted was to get rid of us, or, to state the matter more accurately, to get rid of you."

"Why me?"

"He didn't like the goo-goo eyes his lovely daughter was making at you. You've sure got a way with the women, Old Timer."

"It's because I haven't that I'm here," the older man assured him.

"Says you."

"Kid, I think *you* are the one who is girl-crazy. You can't get your mind off the subject. Forget 'em for a while, and let's get down to business. I tell you we've got to do something and do it damn sudden. If these loyal retainers of ours don't see a little ivory around the diggings pretty soon they'll quit us. They know as well as we do that it's a case of no ivory, no pay."

"Well, what are we going to do about it; manufacture elephants?"

"Go out and find 'em. Thar's elephants in them thar hills, men; but they aren't going to come trotting into camp to be shot. The natives won't help us; so we've got to get out and scout for them ourselves. We'll each take a couple of men and a few days' rations; then we'll head in different directions, and if one of us doesn't find elephant tracks I'm a zebra."

"How much longer do you suppose we'll be able to work this racket without getting caught?" demanded The Kid.

"I've been working it for two years, and I haven't been nabbed yet," replied Old Timer; "and, believe me, I don't want to be nabbed. Have you ever seen their lousy jail?"

"They wouldn't put white men in that, would they?" The Kid looked worried.

"They might. Ivory poachin' makes 'em sorer than Billy Hell."

"I don't blame 'em," said The Kid. "It's a lousy racket."

"Don't I know it?" Old Timer spat vehemently. "But a man's got to eat, hasn't he? If I knew a better way to eat I wouldn't be an ivory poacher. Don't think for a minute that I'm stuck on the job or proud of myself. I'm not. I just try not to think of the ethics of the thing, just like I try to forget that I was ever decent. I'm a bum, I tell you, a dirty, low down bum; but even bums cling to life—though God only knows why. I've never dodged the chance of kicking off, but somehow I always manage to wiggle through. If I'd been any good on earth; or if any one had cared whether I croaked or not, I'd have been dead long ago. It seems as though the Devil watches over things like me and protects them, so that they can suffer as long as possible in this life before he forks them into eternal hell-fire and brimstone in the next."

"Don't brag," advised The Kid. "I'm just as big a bum as you. Likewise, I have to eat. Let's forget ethics and get busy."

"We'll start tomorrow," agreed Old Timer.

*   *   *   *   *   *   *

Muzimo stood silent with folded arms, the center of a chattering horde of natives in the village of Tumbai. Upon his shoulders squatted The Spirit of Nyamwegi. He, too, chattered. It was fortunate, perhaps, that the villagers of Tumbai could not understand what The Spirit of Nyamwegi said. He was hurling the vilest of jungle invective at them, nor was there in all the jungle another such master of diatribe. Also, from the safety of Muzimo's shoulder, he challenged them to battle, telling them what he would do to them if he ever got hold of them. He challenged them single and *en masse*. It made no difference to The Spirit of Nyamwegi how they came, just so they came.

If the villagers were not impressed by The Spirit of Nyamwegi, the same is not true of the effect that the presence of Muzimo had upon them after they had heard Orando's story, even after the first telling. By the seventh or eighth telling their awe was prodigious. It kept them at a safe distance from this mysterious creature of another world.

There was one skeptic, however. It was the village witch-doctor, who doubtless felt that it was not good business to admit too much credence in a miracle not of his own making. Whatever he felt, and it is quite possible that he was as much in awe as the others, he hid it under a mask of indifference, for he must always impress the laity with his own importance.

The attention bestowed upon this stranger irked him; it also pushed him entirely out of the limelight. This nettled him

greatly. Therefore, to call attention to himself, as well as to
reëstablish his importance, he strode boldly up to Muzimo.
Whereupon The Spirit of Nyamwegi screamed shrilly and took
refuge behind the back of his patron. The attention of the
villagers was now attracted to the witch-doctor, which was
precisely what he desired. The chattering ceased. All eyes
were on the two. This was the moment the witch-doctor had
awaited. He puffed himself to his full height and girth. He
swaggered before the spirit of Orando's ancestor. Then he
addressed him in a loud tone.

"You say that you are the *muzimo* of Orando, the son of
Lobongo; but how do we know that your words are true
words? You say that the little monkey is the ghost of
Nyamwegi. How do we know that, either?"

"Who are you, old man, who asks me these questions?"
demanded Muzimo.

"I am Sobito, the witch-doctor."

"You say that you are Sobito, the witch-doctor; but how
do I know that your words are true words?"

"Every one knows that I am Sobito, the witch-doctor."
The old man was becoming excited. He discovered that he
had been suddenly put upon the defensive, which was not at
all what he had intended. "Ask any one. They all know me."

"Very well, then," said Muzimo; "ask Orando who I
am. He, alone, knows me. I have not said that I am his
muzimo. I have not said that the little monkey is the ghost
of Nyamwegi. I have not said who I am. I have not said
anything. It does not make any difference to me who you
think I am; but if it makes a difference to you, ask Orando," whereupon he turned about and walked away, leaving Sobito to feel that he had been made to appear ridiculous
in the eyes of his clansmen.

Fanatical, egotistical, and unscrupulous, the old witch-doctor
was a power in the village of Tumbai. For years he had exercised his influence, sometimes for good and sometimes for
evil, upon the villagers. Even Lobongo, the chief, was not as
powerful as Sobito, who played upon the superstitions and
fears of his ignorant followers until they dared not disobey
his slightest wish.

Tradition and affection bound them to Lobongo, their hereditary chief; fear held them in the power of Sobito, whom

they hated. Inwardly they were pleased that Orando's *muzimo* had flaunted him; but when the witch-doctor came among them and spoke disparagingly of the *muzimo* they only listened in sullen silence, daring not to express their belief in him.

Later, the warriors gathered before the hut of Lobono to listen to the formal telling of the story of Orando. It was immaterial that they had heard it several times already. It must be told again in elaborate detail before a council of the chief and his warriors; and so once more Orando retold the oft-told tale, nor did it lose anything in the telling. More and more courageous became the deeds of Orando, more and more miraculous those of Muzimo; and when he closed his oration it was with an appeal to the chief and his warriors to gather the Utengas from all the villages of the tribe and go forth to avenge Nyamwegi. Muzimo, he told them, would lead them to the village of the Leopard Men.

There were shouts of approval from the younger men, but the majority of the older men sat in silence. It is always thus; the younger men for war, the older for peace. Lobongo was an old man. He was proud that his son should be warlike. That was the reaction of the father, but the reaction of age was all against war. So he, too, remained silent. Not so, Sobito. To his personal grievance against Muzimo were added other considerations that inclined him against this contemplated foray; at least one of which (and the most potent) was a secret he might not divulge with impunity. Scowling forbiddingly he leaped to his feet.

"Who makes this foolish talk of war?" he demanded. "Young men. What do young men know of war? They think only of victory. They forget defeat. They forget that if they make war upon a village the warriors of that village will come some day and make war upon us. What is to be gained by making war upon the Leopard Men? Who knows where their village lies? It must be very far away. Why should our warriors go far from their own country to make war upon the Leopard Men? Because Nyamwegi has been killed? Nyamwegi has already been avenged. This is foolish talk, this war-talk. Who started it? Perhaps it is a stranger among us who wishes to make trouble for us." He looked at Muzimo. "Who knows why? Perhaps the Leopard Men have sent

one of their own people to lure us into making war upon
them. Then all our warriors will be ambushed and killed.
That is what will happen. Make no more foolish talk about
war."

As Sobito concluded his harangue and again squatted upon
his heels Orando arose. He was disturbed by what the old
witch-doctor had said; and he was angry, too; angry because
Sobito had impugned the integrity of his *muzimo*. But his
anger was leashed by his fear of the powerful old man; for
who dares openly oppose one in league with the forces of
darkness, one whose enmity can spell disaster and death? Yet
Orando was a brave warrior and a loyal friend, as befitted
one in whose views flowed the blood of hereditary chieftainship; and so he could not permit the innuendoes of Sobito
to go entirely unchallenged.

"Sobito has spoken against war," he began. Old men always speak against war, which is right if one is an old man.
Orando is a young man yet he, too, would speak against war
if it were only the foolish talk of young men who wished to
appear brave in the eyes of women; but now there is a reason
for war. Nyamwegi has been killed. He was a brave warrior.
He was a good friend. Because we have killed three of those
who killed Nyamwegi we cannot say that he is avenged. We
must go and make war upon the chief who sent these murderers into the Watenga country, or he will think that the
Utengas are all old women. He will think that whenever his
people wish to eat the flesh of man they have only to come
to the Watenga country to get it.

"Sobito has said that perhaps the Leopard Men sent a
stranger among us to lure us into ambush. There is only
one stranger among us—Muzimo. But Muzimo cannot be a
friend of the Leopard Men. With his own eyes Orando saw
him kill two of the Leopard Men; he saw the fourth run
away very fast when his eyes discovered the might of Muzimo. Had Muzimo been his friend he would not have run
away.

"I am Orando, the son of Lobongo. Some day I shall be
chief. I would not lead the warriors of Lobongo into a
foolish war. I am going to the village of the Leopard Men
and make war upon them, that they may know that not all
the Utenga warriors are old women. Muzimo is going with

me. Perhaps there are a few brave men who will accompany us. I have spoken."

Several of the younger warriors leaped from their haunches and stamped their feet in approval. They raised their voices in the war-cry of their clan and brandished their spears. One of them danced in a circle, leaping high and jabbing with his spear.

"Thus will I kill the Leopard Men!" he cried.

Another leaped about, slashing with his knife. "I cut the heart from the chief of the Leopard Men!" He pretended to tear at something with his teeth, while he held it tightly in his hands. "I eat the heart of the chief of the Leopard Men!"

"War! War!" cried others, until there were a dozen howling savages dancing in the sunlight, their sleek hides glistening with sweat, their features contorted by hideous grimaces.

The Lobongo arose. His deep voice boomed above the howling of the dancers as he commanded them to silence. One by one they ceased their howling, but they gathered together in a little knot behind Orando.

"A few of the young men have spoken for war," he announced, "but we do not make war lightly because a few young men wish to fight. There are times for war and times for peace. We must find out if this is the time for war; otherwise we shall find only defeat and death at the end of the war-trail. Before undertaking war we must consult the ghosts of our dead chiefs."

"They are waiting to speak to us," cried Sobito. "Let there be silence while I speak with the spirits of the chiefs who are gone."

As he spoke there was the gradual beginning of a movement among the tribesmen that presently formed a circle in the center of which squatted the witch-doctor. From a pouch he withdrew a number of articles which he spread upon the ground before him. Then he called for some dry twigs and fresh leaves, and when these were brought he built a tiny fire. With the fresh leaves he partially smothered it, so that it threw off a quantity of smoke. Stooping, half doubled, the witch-doctor moved cautiously around the fire, describing a small circle, his eyes constantly fixed upon the thin column of smoke spiraling upward in the quiet air of the drowsy afternoon. In one hand Sobito held a small pouch made of the skin of a rodent, in the other the tail of a hyaena, the root bound with copper wire to form a handle.

Gradually the old man increased his pace until at last, he was circling the fire rapidly in prodigious leaps and bounds; but always his eyes remained fixed upon the spiraling smoke column. As he danced he intoned a weird jargon, a combination of meaningless syllables interspersed with an occasional shrill scream that brought terror to the eyes of his spell-bound audience.

Suddenly he halted, and stooping low tossed some powder from his pouch upon the fire; then with the root of the hyaena tail he drew a rude geometric figure in the dust before the blaze. Stiffening, he closed his eyes and appeared to be listening intently, his face turned partially upward.

In awestruck silence the warriors leaned forward, waiting. It was a tense moment and quite effective. Sobito prolonged it to the utmost. At last he opened his eyes and let them move solemnly about the circle of expectant faces, waiting again before he spoke.

"There are many ghosts about us," he announced. "They all speak against war. Those who go to battle with the Leopard Men will die. None will return. The ghosts are angry with Orando. The true *muzimo* of Orando spoke to me; it is very angry with Orando. Let Orando beware. That is all; the young men will not go to war against the Leopard Men."

The warriors gathered behind Orando looked questioningly at him and at Muzimo. Doubt was written plainly upon every face. Gradually they began to move, drifting imperceptibly away from Orando. Then the son of the chief looked at Muzimo questioningly. "If Sobito has spoken true words," he said, "you are not my *muzimo*." The words seemed a challenge.

"What does Sobito know about it?" demanded Muzimo. "I could build a fire and wave the tail of Dango. I could make marks in the dirt and throw powders on the fire. Then I could tell you whatever I wanted to tell you, just as Sobito has told you what he wanted you to believe; but such things prove nothing. The only way you can know if a war against the Leopard Men will succeed is to send warriors to fight them. Sobito knows nothing about it."

The witch-doctor trembled from anger. Never before had a creature dared voice a doubt as to his powers. So abjectly had the members of his clan acknowledged his infallibility that he had almost come to believe in it himself. He shook a withered finger at Muzimo.

"You speak with a lying tongue," he cried. "You have angered my fetish. Nothing can save you. You are lost. You will die." He paused as a new idea was born in his cunning brain. "Unless," he added, "you go away, and do not come back."

Having no idea as to his true identity, Muzimo had had to accept Orando's word that he was the ancestral spirit of the chief's son; and having heard himself described as such innumerable times he had come to accept it as fact. He felt no fear of Sobito, the man, and when Sobito, the witch-doctor, threatened him he recalled that he was a *muzimo* and, as such, immortal. How, therefore, he reasoned, could the fetish of Sobito kill him? Nothing could kill a spirit.

"I shall not go away," he announced. "I am not afraid of Sobito."

The villagers were aghast. Never had they heard a witch-doctor flouted and defied as Muzimo had flouted and defied Sobito. They expected to see the rash creature destroyed before their eyes, but nothing happened. They looked at Sobito, questioningly, and that wily old fraud, sensing the critical turn of the event and fearing for his prestige, overcame his physical fear of the strange, white giant in the hope of regaining his dignity by a single bold stroke.

Brandishing his hyaena tail, he leaped toward Muzimo. "Die!" he screamed. "Nothing can save you now. Before the moon has risen the third time you will be dead. My fetish has spoken!" He waved the hyaena tail in the face of Muzimo.

The white man stood with folded arms, a sneer upon his lips. "I am Muzimo," he said; "I am the spirit of the ancestor of Orando. Sobito is only a man; his fetish is only the tail of Dango." As he ceased speaking his hand shot out and snatched the fetish from the grasp of the witch-doctor. "Thus does Muzimo with the fetish of Sobito!" he cried, tossing the tail into the fire to the consternation of the astonished villagers.

Seized by the unreasoning rage of fanaticism Sobito threw caution to the winds and leaped for Muzimo, a naked blade in his upraised hand. There was the froth of madness upon his bared lips. His yellow fangs gleamed in a hideous snarl. He was the personification of hatred and maniacal fury. But swift and vicious as was his attack it did not find Muzimo unprepared. A bronzed hand seized the wrist of the witch-doctor in a grip of steel; another tore the knife from his grasp. Then Muzimo picked him up and held him high above his head as though Sobito were some incorporeal thing without substance or weight.

Terror was writ large upon the countenances of the astounded onlookers; an idol was in the clutches of an iconoclast. The situation had passed beyond the scope of their simple minds, leaving them dazed. Perhaps it was well for Muzimo that Sobito was far from being a beloved idol.

Muzimo looked at Orando. "Shall I kill him?" he asked, almost casually.

Orando was as shocked and terrified as his fellows. A lifetime of unquestioning belief in the supernatural powers of witch-doctors could not be overcome in an instant. Yet there was another force working upon the son of the chief. He was only human. Muzimo was his *muzimo,* and being very human he could not but feel a certain justifiable pride in the fearlessness and prowess of this splendid enigma whom he had enthusiastically accepted as the spirit of his dead ancestor. However, witch-doctors were witch-doctors. Their powers were well known to all men. There was, therefore, no wisdom in tempting fate too far.

Orando ran forward. "No!" he cried. "Do not kill him."

Upon the branch of a tree a little monkey danced, screaming and scolding. "Kill him!" he shrieked. "Kill him!" He was a very blood-thirsty little monkey, was The Spirit of Nyamwegi. Muzimo tossed Sobito to the ground in an ignominious heap.

"He is no good," he announced. "No witch-doctor is any good. His fetish was not good. If it had been, why did it not protect Sobito? Sobito did not know what he was talking about. If there are any brave warriors among the Utengas they will come with Orando and Muzimo and make war on the Leopard Men."

A low cry, growing in volume, rose among the younger

warriors; and in the momentary confusion Sobito crawled to his feet and sneaked away toward his hut. When he was safely out of reach of Muzimo he halted and faced about. "I go," he called back, "to make powerful medicine. To-night the white man who calls himself Muzimo dies."

The white giant took a few steps in the direction of Sobito, and the witch-doctor turned and fled. The young men, seeing the waning of Sobito's power, talked loudly now of war. The older men talked no more of peace. One and all, they feared and hated Sobito. They were relieved to see his power broken. Tomorrow they might be afraid again, but today they were free from the domination of a witch-doctor for the first time in their lives.

Lobongo, the chief, would not sanction war; but, influenced by the demands of Orando and other young men, he at last grudgingly gave his approval to the formation of a small raiding party. Immediately runners were dispatched to other villages to seek recruits, and preparations were begun for a dance to be held that night.

Because of Lobongo's refusal to make general war against the Leopard Men there was no booming of war-drums; but news travels fast in the jungle; and night had scarcely closed down upon the village of Tumbai before warriors from the nearer villages commenced coming in to Tumbai by ones and twos to join the twenty volunteers from Loblongo's village, who swaggered and strutted before the admiring eyes of the dusky belles preparing the food and native beer that would form an important part of the night's festivities.

From Kibbu came ten young warriors, among them the brother of the girl Nyamwegi had been courting and one Lupingu, from whom the murdered warrior had stolen her heart. That Lupingu should volunteer to risk his life for the purpose of avenging Nyamwegi passed unnoticed, since already thoughts of vengeance had been submerged by lust for glory and poor Nyamwegi practically forgotten by all but Orando.

There was much talk of war and of brave deeds that would be accomplished; but the discomfiture of Sobito, being still fresh in every mind, also had an important part in the conversations. The village gossips found it a choice morsel with which to regale the warriors from other villages, with the result that Muzimo became an outstanding figure that reflected more glory upon the village of Tumbai than ever Sobito had. The visiting warriors regarded him with awe and some misgivings. They were accustomed to spirits that no one ever saw; the air was full of them. It was quite another matter to behold one standing in their midst.

Lupingu, especially, was perturbed. Recently he had purchased a love charm from Sobito. He was wondering now if he had thrown away, uselessly, the little treasure he had paid for it. He decided to seek out the witch-doctor and make inquiries; perhaps there was not so much truth in what he had heard. There was also another reason why he wished to consult Sobito, a reason of far greater importance than a love charm.

When he could do so unnoticed, Lupingu withdrew from the crowd milling in the village street and sneaked away to Sobito's hut. Here he found the old witch-doctor squatting upon the floor surrounded by charms and fetishes. A small fire burning beneath a pot fitfully lighted his sinister features, which were contorted by so hideous a scowl that Lupingu almost turned and fled before the old man looked up and recognized him.

For a long time Lupingu sat in the hut of the witch-doctor. They spoke in whispers, their heads close together. When Lupingu left he carried with him an amulet of such prodigious potency that no enemy could inflict injury upon him, and in his head he carried a plan that caused him both elation and terror.

5

"Unspeakable Boor!"

L ONG days of loneliness. Long nights of terror. Hopelessness and vain regrets so keen that they pained as might physical hurts. Only a brave heart had kept the girl from going mad since her men had deserted her. That seemed an eternity ago; days were ages.

Today she had hunted. A small boar had fallen to her rifle. At the sound of the shot, coming faintly to his ears, a white man had halted, scowling. His three companions jabbered excitedly.

With difficulty the girl had removed the viscera of the boar, thus reducing its weight sufficiently so that she could drag it to her camp; but it had been an ordeal that had taxed her strength and endurance to their limits. The meat was too precious, however, to be wasted; and she had struggled for hours, stopping often to rest, until at last, exhausted, she had sunk beside her prize before the entrance to her tent.

It was not encouraging to consider the vast amount of labor that still confronted her before the meat would be safe for future use. There was the butchering. The mere thought of it appalled her. She had never seen an animal butchered until after she had set out upon this disastrous safari. In all her life she had never even so much as cut a piece of raw meat. Her preparation, therefore, was most inadequate; but necessity overcomes obstacles, as it mothers inventions. She knew that the boar must be butchered, and the flesh cut into strips and that these strips must be smoked. Even then they would not keep long, but she knew no better way.

With her limited knowledge of practical matters, with the means at hand, she must put up the best fight for life of which she was capable. She was weak and inexperienced and afraid; but none the less it was a courageous heart that beat beneath her once chic but now soiled and disreputable flannel shirt. She was without hope, yet she would not give up.

Wearily, she had commenced to skin the boar, when a movement at the edge of the clearing in which her camp had been pitched attracted her attention. As she looked up she saw four men standing silently, regarding her. One was a white man. The other three were natives. As she sprang to her feet hope welled so strongly within her that she reeled slightly with dizziness; but instantly she regained control of herself and surveyed the four, who were now advancing, the white man in the lead, then, when closer scrutiny was possible, hope waned. Never in her life had she seen so disreputable appearing a white man. His filthy clothing was a motley of rags and patches; his face was unshaven; his hat was a nondescript wreck that might only be distinguished as a hat by the fact that it surmounted his head; his face was stern and forbidding. His eyes wandered suspiciously about her camp; and when he halted a few paces from her, scowling, there was no greeting on his lips.

"Who are you?" he demanded. "What are you doing here?"

His tone and words antagonized her. Never before had any white man addressed her in so cavalier a manner. In a proud and spirited girl the reaction was inevitable. Her chin went up; she eyed him coldly; the suggestion of a supercilious sneer curved her short upper lip; her eyes evaluated him disdainfully from his run-down boots to the battered thing that covered his dishevelled hair. Had his manner and address been different she might have been afraid of him, but now for the moment at least she was too angry to be afraid.

"I cannot conceive that either matter concerns you," she said, and turned her back on him.

The scowl deepened on the man's face, and angry words leaped to his tongue; but he controlled himself, regarding her silently. Had he not already seen her face he would have guessed from the lines of her haughty little back that she was young. Having seen her face he knew that she was beautiful. She was dirty, hot, perspiring, and covered with blood; but she was still beautiful. How beautiful she must be when properly garbed and groomed he dared not even imagine. He had noticed her blue-grey eyes and long lashes; they alone would have made any face beautiful. Now he was appraising her hair, confined in a loose knot at the nape of her neck; it had that peculiar quality of blondness that is described, today, as platinum.

It had been two years since Old Timer had seen a white woman. Perhaps if this one had been old and scrawny, or had buckteeth and a squint, he might have regarded her with less disapprobation and addressed her more courteously. But the moment that his eyes had beheld her, her beauty had recalled all the anguish and misery that another beautiful girl had caused him, arousing within him the hatred of women that he had nursed and cherished for two long years.

He stood in silence for a moment; and he was glad that he had; for it permitted him to quell the angry, bitter words that he might otherwise have spoken. It was not that he liked women any better, but that he realized and admired the courageousness of her reply.

"It may not be any of my business," he said presently, "but perhaps I shall have to make it so. It is rather unusual to see a white woman alone in this country. You *are* alone?" There was a faint note of concern in the tone of his question.

"I *was* quite alone," she snapped, "and I should prefer being so again."

"You mean that you are without porters or white companions?"

"Quite."

As her back was toward him she did not see the expression of relief that crossed his face at her admission. Had she, she might have felt greater concern for her safety, though his relief had no bearing upon her welfare; his anxiety as to the presence of white men was simply that of the elephant poacher.

"And you have no means of transportation?" he queried.

"None."

"You certainly did not come this far into the interior alone. What became of the other members of your party?"

"They deserted me."

"But your white companions—what of them?"

"I had none." She had faced him by now, but her attitude was still unfriendly.

"You came into the interior without any white men?" There was skepticism in his tone.

"I did."

"When did your men desert you?"

"Three days ago."

"What do you intend doing? You can't stay here alone, and I don't see how you can expect to go on without porters."

"I have stayed here three days alone; I can continue to do so until——"

"Until what?"

"I don't know."

"Look here," he demanded; "what in the world are you doing here, anyway?"

A sudden hope seemed to flash to her brain. "I am looking for a man," she said. "Perhaps you have heard of him; perhaps you know where he is." Her voice was vibrant with eagerness.

"What's his name?" asked Old Timer.

"Jerry Jerome." She looked up into his face hopefully.

He shook his head. "Never heard of him."

The hope in her eyes died out, suffused by the faintest suggestion of tears. Old Timer saw the moisture in her eyes, and it annoyed him. Why did women always have to cry? He steeled his heart against the weakness that was sympathy and spoke brusquely. "What do you think you're going to do with that meat?" he demanded.

Her eyes widened in surprise. There were no tears in them now, but a glint of anger. "You are impossible. I wish you would get out of my camp and leave me alone."

"I shall do nothing of the kind," he replied. Then he spoke rapidly to his three followers in their native dialect, whereupon the three advanced and took possession of the carcass of the boar.

The girl looked on in angry surprise. She recalled the heart-breaking labor of dragging the carcass to camp. Now it was being taken from her. The thought enraged her. She drew her revolver from its holster. "Tell them to leave that alone," she cried, "or I'll shoot them. It's mine."

"They're only going to butcher it for you," explained Old Timer. "That's what you wanted, isn't it? Or were you going to frame it?"

His sarcasm nettled her, but she realized that she had misunderstood their purpose. "Why didn't you say so?" she demanded. "I was going to smoke it. I may not always be able to get food easily."

"You won't have to," he told her; "we'll look after that."

"What do you mean?"

"I mean that as soon as I'm through here you're going back to my camp with me. It ain't my fault that you're here; and you're a damn useless nuisance, like all other women; but I couldn't leave a white rat here alone in the jungle, much less a white woman."

"What if I don't care to go with you?" she inquired haughtily.

"I don't give a damn what you think about it," he snapped; "you're going with me. If you had any brains you'd be grateful. It's too much to expect you to have a heart. You're like all the rest—selfish, inconsiderate, ungrateful."

"Anything else?" she inquired.

"Yes. Cold, calculating hard."

"You do not think much of women, do you?"

"You are quite discerning."

"And just what do you propose doing with me when we get to your camp?" she asked.

"If we can scrape up a new safari for you I'll get you out of Africa as quickly as I can," he replied.

"But I do not wish to get out of Africa. You have no right to dictate to me. I came here for a purpose, and I shall not leave until that purpose is fulfilled."

"If you came here to find that Jerome fellow it is my duty to a fellow man to chase you out before you can find him."

Her level gaze rested upon him for several moments before she replied. She had never before seen a man like this. Such candor was unnatural. She decided that he was mentally unbalanced; and having heard that the insane should be humored, lest they become violent, she determined to alter her attitude toward him.

"Perhaps you are right," she admitted. "I will go with you."

"That's better," he commented. "Now that that's settled let's have everything else clear. We're starting back to my camp as soon as I get through with my business here. That may be tomorrow or next day. You're coming along. One of my boys will look after you—cooking and all that sort of stuff. But I don't want to be bothered with any women. You leave me alone, and I'll leave you alone. I don't even want to talk to you."

"That will be mutually agreeable," she assured him, not without some asperity. Since she was a woman and had been for as long as she could recall the object of masculine adulation, such a speech, even from the lips of a disreputable ragamuffin whose sanity she questioned, could not but induce a certain pique.

"One more thing," he added. "My camp is in Chief Bobo-

lo's country. If anything happens to me have my boys take
you back there to my camp. My partner will look after you.
Just tell him that I promised to get you back to the coast."
He left her then and busied himself with the simple preparation of his modest camp, calling one of the men from the
butchering to pitch his small tent and prepare his evening
meal, for it was late in the afternoon. Another of the boys
was detailed to serve the girl.

From her tent that evening she could see him sprawled before a fire, smoking his pipe. From a distance she gazed
at him contemptuously, convinced that he was the most
disagreeable person she had ever encountered, yet forced
to admit that his presence gave her a feeling of security
she had not enjoyed since she had entered Africa. She concluded that even a crazy white man was better than none.
But was he crazy? He seemed quite normal and sane in all
respects other than his churlish attitude toward her. Perhaps
he was just an ill-bred boor with some fancied grievance
against women. Be that as it might he was an enigma, and
unsolved enigmas have a way of occupying one's thoughts.
So, notwithstanding her contempt for him, he filled her reveries quite to the exclusion of all else until sleep claimed her.

Doubtless she would have been surprised to know that
similarly the man's mind was occupied with thoughts of her,
thoughts that hung on with bulldog tenacity despite his every
effort to shake them loose. In the smoke of his pipe he saw
her, unquestionably beautiful beyond comparison. He saw
the long lashes shading the depths of her blue-grey eyes;
her lips, curved deliciously; the alluring sheen of her wavy
blond hair; the perfection of her girlish figure.

"Damn!" muttered Old Timer. "Why in hell did I have to
run into *her?*"

The following morning he left camp early, taking two of the
boys with him; leaving the third, armed with an old rifle, to
protect the girl and attend to her wants. She was already up
when he departed, but he did not look in her direction as he
strode out of camp, though she furtively watched him go,
feeding her contempt on a final disparaging appraisement of
his rags and tatters.

"Unspeakable boor!" she whispered venomously as a par-
tial outlet for her pent up hatred of the man.

Old Timer had a long, hard day. No sign of elephant rewarded his search, nor did he contact a single native from whom he might obtain information as to the whereabouts of the great herd that rumor and hope had located in this vicinity.

Not only was the day one of physical hardship, but it had been mentally trying as well. He had been disappointed in not locating the ivory they needed so sorely, but this had been the least of his mental perturbation. He had been haunted by thoughts of the girl. All day he had tried to rid his mind of recollection of that lovely face and the contours of her perfect body, but they persisted in haunting him. At first they had aroused other memories, painful memories of another girl. But gradually the vision of that other girl had faded until only the blue-grey eyes and blond hair of the girl in the lonely camp persisted in his thoughts.

When he turned back toward camp at the end of his fruitless search for elephant signs a new determination filled him with disquieting thoughts and spurred him rapidly upon the back-trail. It had been two years since he had seen a white woman, and then Fate had thrown this lovely creature across his path. What had women ever done for him? "Made a bum of me," he soliloquized; "ruined my life. This girl would have been lost but for me. She owes me something. All women owe me something for what one woman did to me. This girl is going to pay the debt.

"God, but she's beautiful! And she belongs to me. I found her, and I am going to keep her until I am tired of her. Then I'll throw her over the way I was thrown over. See how the woman will like it! Gad, what lips! Tonight they will be mine. She'll be all mine, and I'll make her like it. It's only fair. I've got something coming to me in this world. I'm entitled to a little happiness; and, by God, I'm owing to have it."

The great sun hung low in the west as the man came in sight of the clearing. The tent of the girl was the first thing that greeted his eyes. The soiled canvas suggested an intimacy that was provocative; it had sheltered and protected her; it had shared the most intimate secrets of her alluring charm. Like all inanimate objects that have been closely associated with an individual the tent reflected something of the per-

sonality of the girl. The mere sight of it stirred the man
deeply. His passions, aroused by hours of anticipation, surged
through his head like wine. He quickened his pace in his
eagerness to take the girl in his arms.

Then he saw an object lying just beyond her tent that
turned him cold with apprehension. Springing forward at a
run, closely followed by his two retainers, he came to a halt
beside the grisly thing that had attracted his horrified attention and turned the hot wave of his desire to cold dread. It
was the dead and horribly mutilated body of the native he
had left to guard the girl. Cruel talons had lacerated the flesh
with deep wounds that might have been inflicted by one of the
great carnivores, but the further mutilation of the corpse
had been the work of man.

Stooping over the body of their fellow the two Negroes
muttered angrily in their native tongue; then one of them
turned to Old Timer. "The Leopard Men, Bwana," he said.

Fearfully, the white man approached the tent of the girl,
dreading what he might find there, dreading even more that
he might find nothing. As he threw aside the flap and looked
in, his worst fears were realized; the girl was not there. His
first impulse was to call aloud to her as though she might
be somewhere near in the forest; but as he turned to do so
he suddenly realized that he did not know her name, and in
the brief pause that this realization gave him the futility of the
act was borne in upon him. If she still lived she was far
away by now in the clutches of the fiends who had slain
her protector.

A sudden wave of rage overwhelmed the white man, his
hot desire for the girl transmuted to almost maniacal anger
toward her abductors. He forgot that he himself would
have wronged her. Perhaps he thought only of his own frustrated hopes; but he believed that he was thinking only of the
girl's helplessness, of the hideousness of her situation. Ideas
of rescue and vengeance filled his whole being, banishing the
fatigue of the long, arduous day.

It was already late in the afternoon, but he determined
upon immediate pursuit. Following his orders the two
hastily buried their dead comrade, made up two packs with
such provisions and camp necessities as the marauders had

not filched, and with the sun but an hour high followed their mad master upon the fresh trail of the Leopard Men.

6

The Traitor

THE warriors of Watenga had not responded with great enthusiasm to the call to arms borne by the messengers of Orando. There were wars, and wars. One directed against the feared secret order of the Leopard Men did not appear to be highly popular. There were excellent reasons for this. In the first place the very name of Leopard Man was sufficient to arouse terror in the breast of the bravest, the gruesome methods of the Leopard Men being what they were. There was also the well known fact that, being a secert order recruited among unrelated clans, some of one's own friends might be members, in which event an active enemy of the order could easily be marked for death. And such a death!

It is little wonder, then, that from thousands of potential crusaders Orando discovered but a scant hundred awaiting the call to arms the morning following the celebration and war dance at Tumbai. Even among the hundred there were several whose martial spirit had suffered eclipse over night Perhaps this was largely due to the after effects of an over-dose of native beer. It is not pleasant to set out for war with a headache.

Orando was moving about among the warriors squatting near the numerous cooking fires. There was not much talk this morning and less laughter; the boasting of yestereve was stilled. Today war seemed a serious business; yet, their bellies once filled with warm food, they would go forth presently with loud yells, with laughter, and with song.

Orando made inquiries. "Where is Muzimo?" he asked, but no one had seen Muzimo. He and The Spirit of Nyamwegi had disappeared. This seemed an ill omen. Some one suggested that possibly Sobito had been right; Muzimo might be in

league with the Leopard Men. This aroused inquiry as to the
whereabouts of Sobito. No one had seen him either; which
was strange, since Sobito was an early riser and not one to
be missing when the cook-pots were a-boil. An old man went
to his hut and questioned one of the witch-doctor's wives.
Sobito was gone! When this fact was reported conversation
waxed. The enmity between Muzimo and Sobito was recalled,
as was the latter's threat that Muzimo would die before morning. There were those who suggested that perhaps it was
Sobito who was dead, while others recalled the fact that
there was nothing unusual in his disappearance. He had disappeared before. In fact, it was nothing unusual for him to
absent himself mysteriously from the village for days at a
time. Upon his return after such absences he had darkly
hinted that he had been sitting in council with the spirits and
demons of another world, from whom he derived his supernatural powers.

Lupingu of Kibbu thought that they should not set out upon
the war trail in the face of such dire omens. He went
quietly among the warriors seeking adherents to his suggestion that they disband and return to their own villages, but
Orando shamed them out of desertion. The old men and the
women would laugh at them, he told them. They had made
too much talk about war; they had boasted too much. They
would lose face forever if they failed to go through with it
now.

"But who will guide us to the village of the Leopard Men
now that your *muzimo* has deserted you?" demanded Lupingu.

"I do not believe that he has deserted me," maintained
Orando stoutly. "Doubtless he, too, has gone to take council
with the spirits. He will return and lead us."

As though in answer to his statement, which was also a
prayer, a giant figure dropped lightly from the branches of a
nearby tree and strode toward him. It was Muzimo. Across
one of his broad shoulders rested the carcass of a buck. On
top of the buck sat The Spirit of Nyamwegi, screaming shrilly
to attract attention to his prowess. "We are mighty hunters,"
he cried. "See what we have killed." No one but Muzimo
understood him, but that made no difference to The Spirit
of Nyamwegi because he did not know that they could not

understand him. He thought that he was making a fine impression, and he was quite proud of himself.

"Where have you been, Muzimo?" asked Orando. "Some said that Sobito had slain you."

Muzimo shrugged. "Words do not kill. Sobito is full of words."

"Have you killed Sobito?" demanded an old man.

"I have not seen Sobito since before Kudu, the sun, went to his lair last night," replied Muzimo.

"He is gone from the village," explained Orando. "It was thought that maybe——"

"I went to hunt. Your food is no good; you spoil it with fire." He squatted down at the bole of a tree and cut meat from his kill, which he ate, growling. The warriors looked on terrified, giving him a wide berth.

When he had finished his meal he arose and stretched his great frame, and the action reminded them of Simba, the lion. "Muzimo is ready," he announced. "If the Utengas are ready let us go."

Orando gathered his warriors. He selected his captains and gave the necessary orders for the conduct of the march. This all required time, as no point could be decided without a general argument in which all participated whether the matter concerned them or not.

Muzimo stood silently aside. He was wondering about these people. He was wondering about himself. Physically he and they were much alike; yet in addition to the difference in coloration there were other differences, those he could see and those he could not see but sensed. The Spirit of Nyamwegi was like them and like him, too; yet here again was a vast difference. Muzimo knit his brows in perplexity. Vaguely, he almost recalled a fleeting memory that seemed the key to the riddle; but it eluded him. He felt dimly that he had had a past, but he could not recall it. He recalled only the things that he had seen and the experiences that had come to him since Orando had freed him from the great tree that had fallen on him; yet he appreciated the fact that when he had seen each seemingly new thing he had instantly recognized it for what it was—man, the okapi, the buck, each and every animal and bird that had come within the range of his vision or his sensitive ears or nostrils. Nor had he been at a loss to meet each new emergency of life as it confronted him.

He had thought much upon this subject (so much that at times the effort of sustained thought tired him), and he had come to the conclusion that somewhere, sometime he must have experienced many things. He had questioned Orando casually as to the young man's past, and learned that he could recall events in clear detail as far back as his early childhood. Muzimo could recall but a couple of yesterdays. Finally he came to the conclusion that his mental state must be the natural state of spirits, and because it was so different from that of man he found in it almost irrefutable proof of his spirithood. With a feeling of detachment he viewed the antics of man, viewed them contemptuously. With folded arms he stood apart in silence, apparently as oblivious to the noisy bickerings as to the chattering and scolding of The Spirit of Nyamwegi perched upon his shoulder.

But at last the noisy horde was herded into something approximating order; and, followed by laughing, screaming women and children, started upon its march toward high adventure. Not, however, until the latter turned back did the men settle down to serious marching, though Lupingu's croakings of eventual disaster had never permitted them to forget the seriousness of their undertaking.

For three days they marched, led by Orando and guided by Muzimo. The spirits of the warriors were high as they approached their goal. Lupingu had been silenced by ridicule. All seemed well. Muzimo had told them that the village of the Leopard Men lay near at hand and that upon the following morning he would go ahead alone and reconnoiter.

With the dawning of the fourth day all were eager, for Orando had never ceased to incite them to anger against the murderers of Nyamwegi. Constantly he had impressed them with the fact that The Spirit of Nyamwegi was with them to watch over and protect them, that his own *muzimo* was there to insure them victory.

It was while they were squatting about their breakfast fires that some one discovered that Lupingu was missing. A careful search of the camp failed to locate him; and it was at once assumed that, nearing the enemy, he had deserted through fear. Loud was the condemnation, bitter the scorn that this cowardly defection aroused. It was still the topic of angry discussion as Muzimo and The Spirit of Nyamwegi slipped silently away through the trees toward the village of the Leopard Men.

* * * * * * *

A fiber rope about her neck, the girl was being half led, half dragged through the jungle. A powerful young native walking ahead of her held the free end of the rope; ahead of him an old man led the way; behind her was a second young man. All three were strangely garbed in leopard skins. The heads of leopards, cunningly mounted, fitted snugly over their woolly pates. Curved steel talons were fitted to their fingers. Their teeth were filed, their faces hideously painted. Of the three, the old man was the most terrifying. He was the leader. The other cringed servilely when he gave commands.

The girl could understand little that they said. She had no idea as to the fate that was destined for her. As yet they had not injured her, but she could anticipate nothing other than a horrible termination of this hideous adventure. The young man who led her was occasionally rough when she stumbled or faltered, but he had not been actually brutal. Their appearance, however, was sufficient to arouse the direst forebodings in her mind; and she had always the recollection of the horrid butchery of the faithful Negro who had been left to guard her.

Thoughts of him reminded her of the white man who had left him to protect her. She had feared and mistrusted him; she had wanted to be rid of him. Now she wished that she were back in his camp. She did not admire him any more than she had. It was merely that she considered him the lesser of two evils. As she recalled him she thought of him only as an ill-mannered boor, as quite the most disagreeable person she had ever seen. Yet there was that about him which aroused her curiosity. His English suggested anything other than illiteracy. His clothes and his attitude toward her placed him upon the lowest rung of the social scale. He occupied her thoughts to a considerable extent, but he still remained an inexplicable enigma.

For two days her captors followed obscure trails. They passed no villages, saw no other human beings than themselves. Then, toward the close of the second day they came suddenly upon a large, palisaded village beside a river. The heavy gates that barred the entrance were closed, although the sun had not yet set; but when they had approached closely enough to be recognized they were admitted following a short parlay between the old man and the keepers of the gate.

The stronghold of the Leopard Men was the village of Gato Mgungu, chief of a once powerful tribe that had dwindled in numbers until now it boasted but this single village. But Gato Mgungu was also chief of the Leopard Men, a position which carried with it a sinister power far above that of many a chief whose villages were more numerous and whose tribes were numerically far stronger. This was true largely because of the fact that the secret order whose affairs he administered was recruited from unrelated clans and villages; and, because of the allegiance enforced by its strict and merciless code, Gato Mgungu demanded the first loyalty of its members, even above their loyalty to their own tribes or families. Thus, in nearly every village within a radius of a hundred miles Gato Mgungu had followers who kept him informed as to the plans of other chiefs, followers who must even slay their own kin if the chief of the Leopard Men so decreed.

In the village of Gato Mgungu alone were all the inhabitants members of the secret order; in the other villages his adherents were unknown, or, at most, only suspected of membership in the feared and hated order. To be positively identified as a Leopard Man, in most villages, would have been to meet, sudden, mysterious death; for so loathed were they a son would kill his own father if he knew that he was a member of the sect, and so feared that no man dared destroy one except in secret lest the wrath and terrible vengeance of the order fall upon him.

In secret places, deep hidden in impenetrable jungle, the Leopard Men of outlying districts performed the abhorrent rites of the order except upon those occasions when they gathered at the village of Gato Mgungu, near which was located their temple. Such was the reason for the gathering that now filled the village with warriors and for the relatively small number of women and children that the girl noticed as she was dragged through the gateway into the main street.

Here the women, degraded, hideous, filed-toothed harpies,

would have set upon her and torn her to pieces but for the interference of her captors, who laid about them with the hafts of their spears, driving the creatures off until the old man could make himself heard. He spoke angrily with a voice of authority; and immediately the women withdrew, though they cast angry, venemous glances at the captive that boded no good for her should she fall into their hands.

Guarding her closely, her three captors led her through a horde of milling warriors to a large hut before which was seated an old, wrinkled Negro, with a huge belly. This was Gato Mgungu, chief of the Leopard Men. As the four approached he looked up, and at sight of the white girl a sudden interest momentarily lighted his blood-shot eyes that ordinarily gazed dully from between red and swollen lids. Then he recognized the old man and addressed him.

"You have brought me a present, Lulimi?" he demanded.

"Lulimi has brought a present," replied the old man, "but not for Gato Mgungu alone."

"What do you mean?" The chief scowled now.

"I have brought a present for the whole clan and for the Leopard God."

"Gato Mgungu does not share his slaves with others," the chief growled.

"I have brought no slave," snapped Lulimi. It was evident that he did not greatly fear Gato Mgungu. And why should he, who was high in the priesthood of the Leopard Clan?

"Then why have you brought this white woman to my village?"

By now there was a dense half-circle of interested auditors craning their necks to view the prisoner and straining their ears to catch all that was passing between these two great men of their little world. For this audience Lulimi was grateful, for he was never so happy as when he held the center of the stage, surrounded by credulous and ignorant listeners. Lulimi was a priest.

"Three nights ago we lay in the forest far from the village of Gato Mgungu, far from the temple of the Leopard God." Already he could see his auditors pricking up their ears. "It was a dark night. The lion was abroad, and the leopard. We kept a large fire burning to frighten them away. It was my turn to watch. The others slept. Suddenly I saw two green eyes shining just beyond the fire. They blazed like living coals. They came closer, and I was afraid; but I could not move. I could not call out. My tongue stuck to the roof of my mouth. My jaws would not open. Closer and closer they came, those terrible eyes, until, just beyond the fire, I saw a great leopard, the largest leopard that I have ever seen. I thought that the end of my days had come and that I was about to die.

"I waited for him to spring upon me, but he did not spring. Instead he opened his mouth and spoke to me." Gasps of astonishment greeted this statement while Lulimi paused for effect.

"What did he say to you?" demanded Gato Mgungu.

"He said, 'I am the brother of the Leopard God. He sent me to find Lulimi, because he trusts Lulimi. Lulimi is a great man. He is very brave and wise. There is no one knows as much as Lulimi.'"

Gato Mgungu looked bored. "Did the Leopard God send his brother three marches to tell you that?"

"He told me other things, many things. Some of them I can repeat, but others I may never speak of. Only the Leopard God, and his brother, and Lulimi know these things."

"What has all this to do with the white woman?" demanded Gato Mgungu.

"I am getting to that," replied Lulimi sourly. He did not relish these interruptions. "Then, when the brother of the Leopard God had asked after my health, he told me that I was to go to a certain place the next day and that there I should find a white woman. She would be alone in the jungle with one man. He commanded me to kill the black man and bring the woman to his temple to be high priestess of the Leopard Clan. This Lulimi will do. Tonight Lulimi takes the while high priestess to the great temple. I have spoken."

For a moment there was awed silence. Gato Mgungu did not seem pleased; but Lulimi was a powerful priest to whom the rank and file looked up, and he had greatly increased his prestige by this weird tale. Gato Mgungu was sufficiently a judge of men to know that. Furthermore, he was an astute old politician with an eye to the future. He knew that Imigeg, the high priest, was a very old man who could not live much longer and that Lulimi, who had been laying his plans to that end for years, would doubtless succeed him.

Now a high priest friendly to Gato Mgungu could do much to increase the power and prestige of the chief and, incidentally, his revenues; while one who was inimical might threaten his ascendancy. Therefore, reading thus plainly the handwriting on the wall, Gato Mgungu seized this opportunity to lay the foundations of future friendship and understanding between them though he knew that Lulimi was an old fraud and his story doubtless a canard.

Many of the warriors, having sensed in the chief's former attitude a certain antagonism to Lulimi, were evidently waiting a cue from their leader. As Gato Mgungu jumped, so would the majority of the fighting men; but when the day came that a successor to Imigeg must be chosen it would be the priests who would make the selection, and Gato Mgungu knew that Lulimi had a long memory.

All eyes were upon the chief as he cleared his royal throat. "We have heard the story of Lulimi," he said. "We all know Lulimi. In his own village he is a great witch-doctor. In the temple of the Leopard God there is no greater priest after Imigeg. It is not strange that the brother of the Leopard God should speak to Lulimi. Gato Mgungu is only a fighting man. He does not talk with gods and demons. This is not a matter for warriors. It is a matter for priests. All that Lulimi has said we believe, but let us take the white woman to the temple. The Leopard God and Imigeg will know whether the jungle leopard spoke true words to Lulimi or not. Has not my tongue spoken wise words, Lulimi?"

"The tongue of Gato Mgungu, the chief, always speaks wise words," replied the priest, who was inwardly delighted that the chief's attitude had not been, as he had feared, antagonistic. And thus the girl's fate was decided by the greed of corrupt politicians, temporal and ecclesiastical, suggesting that the benighted of central Africa are in some respects quite as civilized as we.

As preparations were being made to conduct the girl to the temple, a lone warrior, sweat-streaked and breathless, approached the gates of the village. Here he was halted, but when he had given the secret sign of the Leopard Clan he was admitted. There was much excited jabbering at the gateway; but to all questions the newcomer insisted that he must speak to Gato Mgungu immediately upon a matter of urgent importance, and presently he was brought before the chief.

Again he gave the secret sign of the Leopard Clan as he faced Gato Mgungu.

"What message do you bring?" demanded the chief.

"A few hours' march from here a hundred Utenga warriors led by Orando, the son of Lobongo, the chief, are waiting to attack your village. They come to avenge Nyamwegi of Kibbu, who was killed by members of the clan. If you send warriors at once to hide beside the trail they can ambush the Utengas and kill them all."

"Where lies their camp?"

The messenger described the location minutely; and when he had finished, Gato Mgungu ordered a sub-chief to gather three hundred warriors and march against the invaders; then he turned to the messenger. "We shall feast tonight upon our enemies," he growled, "and you shall sit beside Gato Mgungu and have the choicest morsels."

"I may not remain," replied the messenger. "I must return from whence I came lest I be suspected of carrying word to you."

"Who are you?" demanded Gato Mgungu.

"I am Lupingu of Kibbu, in the Watenga country," replied the messenger.

7

The Captive

KNOWING nothing of the meaning of what was transpiring around her, the girl sensed in the excitement and activity following the coming of the messenger something of the cause that underlay them. She saw fighting men hurriedly arming themselves; she saw them depart from the village. In her heart was a hope that perhaps the enemy they went to meet might be a succoring party in search of her. Reason argued to the contrary; but hope catches at straws, unreasoning.

When the war party had departed, attention was again focused upon the girl. Lulimi waxed important. He ordered people about right and left. Twenty men armed with spears and shields and carrying paddles formed about her as an excort. Led by Lulimi, they marched through the gateway of the village down to the river. Here they placed her in a large canoe which they launched in silence, knowing that enemies were not far distant. There was no singing or shouting as there would have been upon a similar occasion under ordinary circumstances. In silence they dipped their paddles into the swift stream; silently they sped with the current down the broad river, keeping close to the river bank upon the same side as that upon which they had launched the craft by the village of Gato Mgungu.

Poor little Kali Bwana! They had taken the rope from about her neck; they treated her now with a certain respect, tinged with awe, for was she not to be the high priestess of the Leopard God? But of that she knew nothing. She could only wonder, as numb with hopelessness she watched the green verdure of the river bank move swiftly past. Where were they taking her? To what horrid fate? She noted the silence and the haste of her escort; she recalled the excitement following the coming of the messenger to the village and the hasty exodus of the war party.

All these facts combined to suggest that her captors were hurrying her away from a rescuing party. But who could have organized such an expedition? Who knew of her plight? Only the bitter man of rags and patches. But what could he do to effect her rescue, even if he cared to do so? It had been evident to her that he was a poor and worthless vagabond. His force consisted now of but two natives. His camp, he had told her, was several marches from where he had found her. He could not possibly have obtained reinforcements from that source in the time that had elapsed since her capture, even if they existed, which she doubted. She could not imagine that such a sorry specimen of poverty commanded any resources whatever. Thus she was compelled to abandon hope of succor from this source; yet hope did not die. In the last extremity one may always expect a miracle.

For a mile or two the canoe sped down the river, the paddles rising and falling with clock-like regularity and almost in silence; then suddenly the speed of the craft was checked, and its nose turned toward the bank. Ahead of them the girl saw the mouth of a small affluent of the main river, and presently the canoe slid into its sluggish waters.

Great trees arched above the narrow, winding stream; dense underbrush choked the ground between their boles; matted vines and creepers clung to their mossy branches, or hung motionless in the breathless air, trailing almost to the surface of the water; gorgeous blooms shot the green with vivid color. It was a scene of beauty, yet there hung about it an air of mystery and death like a noxious miasma. It reminded the girl of the face of a lovely woman behind whose mask of beauty hid a vicious soul. The silence, the scent of rotting things in the heavy air oppressed her.

Just ahead a great, slimy body slid from a rotting log into the slow moving waters. It was a crocodile. As the canoe glided silently through the semi-darkness the girl saw that the river was fairly alive with these hideous reptiles whose presence served but to add to the depression that already weighed so heavily upon her.

She sought to arouse her drooping spirits by recalling the faint hope of rescue that she had entertained and clung to ever since she had been so hurriedly removed from the village. Fortunately for her peace of mind she did not know her destination, nor that the only avenue to it lay along this crocodile-infested stream. No other path led through the matted jungle to the cleverly hidden temple of the Leopard God. No other avenue than this fetid river gave ingress to it, and this was known to no human being who was not a Leopard Man.

The canoe had proceeded up the stream for a couple of miles when the girl saw upon the right bank just ahead of them a large, grass-thatched building. Unaccustomed as she had been during the past few months to seeing any structure larger than the ordinary native huts, the size of this building filled her with astonishment. It was quite two hundred long and fifty wide, nor less than fifty feet in height. It lay parallel to the river, its main entrance being in the end they were approaching. A wide verandah extended across the front of the building and along the side facing the river. The entire structure was elevated on piles to a height of about ten feet above the ground. She did not know it, but this was the temple of the Leopard God, whose high priestess she was destined to be.

As the canoe drew closer to the building a number of men emerged from its interior. Lulimi rose from the bottom of the craft where he had been squatting and shouted a few words to the men on the temple porch. They were the secret passwords of the order, to which one of the guardians of the temple replied, whereupon the canoe drew in to the shore.

A few curious priests surrounded Lulimi and the girl as the old man escorted her up the temple steps to the great entrance flanked by grotesquely carved images and into the half-light of the interior. Here she found herself in an enormous room open to the rafters far above her head. Hideous masks hung upon the supporting columns with shields, and spears, and knives, and human skulls. Idols, crudely carved, stood about the floor. Many of these represented a human body with the head of an animal, though so rude was the craftsmanship that the girl could not be certain what animal they were intended to represent. It might be a leopard, she thought.

At the far end of the room, which they were approaching, she discerned a raised dais. It was, in reality, a large platform paved with clay. Upon it, elevated a couple of feet, was a smaller dais about five feet wide and twice as long, which was covered with the skins of animals. A heavy post supporting a human skull was set in the center of the long dimension of the smaller dais close to its rear edge. These details she noted only casually at the time. She was to have reason to remember them vividly later.

As Lulimi led her toward the dais a very old man emerged from an opening in the wall at its back and came toward them. He had a particularly repellant visage, the ugliness of which was accentuated by the glowering scowl with which he regarded her.

As his old eyes fell upon Lulimi they were lighted dimly by a feeble ray of recognition. "It is you?" he mumbled.

"But why do you bring this white woman? Who is she? A sacrifice?"

"Listen, Imigeg," whispered Lulimi, "and think well. Remember your prophecy."

"What prophecy?" demanded the high priest querulously. He was very old; and his memory sometimes played him tricks, though he did not like to admit it.

"Long ago you said that some day a white priestess would sit with you and the Leopard God, here on the great throne of the temple. Now your prophecy shall be fulfilled. Here is the white priestess, brought by Lulimi, just as you prophesied."

Now Imigeg did not recall having made any such prophecy, for the very excellent reason that he never had done so; but Lulimi was a wily old person who knew Imigeg better than Imigeg knew himself. He knew that the old high priest was rapidly losing his memory; and he knew, too, that he was very sensitive on the subject, so sensitive that he would not dare deny having made such a prophecy as Lulimi imputed to him.

For reasons of his own Lulimi desired a white priestess. Just how it might redound to his benefit is not entirely clear, but the mental processes of priests are often beyond the ken of lay minds. Perhaps his reasons might have been obvious to a Hollywood publicity agent; but however that may be, the method he had adopted to insure the acceptance of his priestess was entirely successful.

Imigeg swallowed the bait, hook, line, and sinker. He swelled with importance. "Imigeg talks with the demons and the spirits," he said; "they tell him everything. When we have human flesh for the Leopard God and his priests, the white woman shall be made high priestess of the order."

"That should be soon then," announced Lulimi.

"How do you know that?" demanded Imigeg.

"My *muzimo* came to me and told me that the warriors now in the village of Gato Mgungu would march forth today, returning with food enough for all."

"Good," exclaimed Imigeg quickly; "it is just as I prophesied yesterday to the lesser priests."

"Tonight then," said Lulimi. "Now you will want to have the white woman prepared."

At the suggestion Imigeg clapped his hands, whereupon several of the lesser priests advanced. "Take the woman," he instructed one of them "to the quarters of the priest-esses. She is to be high priestess of the order. Tell them this and that they shall prepare her. Tell them, also, that Imigeg holds them responsible for her safety."

The lesser priest led the girl through the opening at the rear of the dais, where she discovered herself in a corridor flanked on either side by rooms. To the door of one of these the man conducted her and, pushing her ahead, en-tered. It was a large room in which were a dozen women, naked but for tiny G strings. Nearly all of them were young; but there was one toothless old hag, and it was she whom the man addressed.

The angry and resentful movement of the women toward the white girl at the instant that she entered the room was halted at the first words of her escort. "This is the new high priestess of the Leopard God," he announced. "Imigeg sends orders that you are to prepare her for the rites to be held tonight. If any harm befalls her you will be held ac-countable, and you all know the anger of Imigeg."

"Leave her with me," mumbled the old woman. "I have served in the temple through many rains, but I have not filled the belly of the Leopard God yet."

"You are too old and tough," snarled one of the younger women.

"You are not," snapped the old hag. "All the more rea-son that you should be careful not to make Imigeg angry, or Mumga, either. Go," she directed the priest. "The white woman will be safe with old Mumga."

As the man left the room the women gathered about the girl. Hatred distorted their features. The younger women tore at her clothing. They pushed and pulled her about, all the while jabbering excitedly; but they did not injure her aside from a few scratches from claw-like nails.

The reason for bringing her here at all was unknown to Kali Bwana; the intentions of the women were, similarly, a mystery. Their demeanor boded her no good, and she be-lieved that eventually they would kill her. Their degraded faces, their sharp-filed, yellow fangs, their angry voices and glances left no doubt in her mind as to the seriousness of her

situation or the desires of the harpies. That a power which
they feared restrained them she did not know. She saw only
the menace of their attitude toward her and their rough and
brutal handling of her.

One by one they stripped her garments from her until she
stood even more naked than they, and then she was accorded a respite as they fell to fighting among themselves
for her clothing. For the first time she had an opportunity
to note her surroundings. She saw that the room was the
common sleeping and eating apartment of the women. Straw
mats were stretched across one of its sides. There was a clay
hearth at one end directly below a hole in the roof, through
which some of the smoke from a still smoldering fire was
finding its way into the open air, though most of it hung
among the rafters of the high ceiling, from whence it settled
down to fill the apartment with acrid fumes. A few cooking
pots stood on or beside the hearth. There were earthen jars
and wooden boxes, fiber baskets and pouches of skin strewn
upon the floor along the walls, many near the sleeping mats.
From pegs stuck in the walls depended an array of ornaments
and finery: strings of beads, necklaces of human teeth and of
the teeth of leopards, bracelets of copper and iron and
anklets of the same metals, feather head-dresses and breast-
plates of metal and of hide, and innumerable garments
fashioned from the black-spotted, yellow skins of leopards.
Everything in the apartment bespoke primtive savagery in
keeping with its wild and savage inmates.

When the final battle for the last vestige of her apparel
had terminated, the women again turned their attention to
the girl. Old Mumga addressed her at considerable length,
but Kali Bwana only shook her head to indicate that she
could understand nothing that was said to her. Then at a
word from the old woman they laid hold of her again, none
too gently. She was thrown upon one of the filthy sleeping
mats, an earthen jar was dragged to the side of the mat,
and two young women proceeded to anoint her with a vile
smelling oil, the base of which might have been rancid but-
ter. This was rubbed in by rough hands until her flesh was
almost raw; then a greenish liquid, which smelled of bay
leaves and stung like fire, was poured over her; and again she
was rubbed until the liquid had evaporated.

When this ordeal had been concluded, leaving her weak and sick from its effects, she was clothed. Much discussion accompanied this ceremony, and several times women were sent to consult Imigeg and to fetch apparel from other parts of the temple. Finally they seemed satisfied with their handiwork, and Kali Bwana, who had worn some of the most ridiculous creations of the most famous *couturiers* of Paris, stood clothed as she had never been clothed before.

First they had adjusted about her slim, fair waist a loin cloth made from the skins of unborn leopard cubs; and then, over one shoulder, had been draped a gorgeous hide of vivid yellow, spotted with glossy black. This garment hung in graceful folds almost to her knee on one side, being shorter on the other. A rope of leopard tails gathered it loosely about her hips. About her throat was a necklace of human teeth; upon her wrists and arms were heavy bracelets, at least two of which she recognized as a gold. In similar fashion were her ankles adorned, and then more necklaces were hung about her neck. Her head-dress consisted of a diadem of leopard skin supporting a variety of plumes and feathers which entirely encircled her head. But the finishing touch brought a chill of horror to her; long, curved talons of gold were affixed to her fingers and thumbs, recalling the cruel death of the native who had striven so bravely and so futilely to protect her.

Thus was Kali Bwana prepared for the hideous rites of the Leopard Men that would make her high priestess of their savage god.

8

Treason Unmasked

MUZIMO loafed through the forest. He was glad to be alone, away from the noisy, boasting creatures that were men. True, The Spirit of Nyamwegi was given to boasting; but Muzimo never paid much attention to

him. Sometimes he chided him for behaving so much like
men; and as long as The Spirit of Nyamwegi could remember, he was quiet; but his memory was short. Only
when a certain stern expression entered the eyes of Muzimo
and he spoke in a low voice that was half growl, was The
Spirit of Nyamwegi quiet for long; but that occurred only
when there was important need for silence.

Muzimo and The Spirit of Nyamwegi had departed early
from the camp of the Utengas for the purpose of locating
and spying upon the village of the Leopard Men, but time
meant nothing to Muzimo. This thing that he had set out to
do, he would do when he was ready. So it was that the
morning was all but spent before Muzimo caught sight of
the village.

The warriors had already departed in search of the enemies from Watenga, and Muzimo had not seen them because he had taken a circuitous route from the camp to
the village. The girl had also been taken away to the
temple, though even had she still been there her presence
would have meant nothing to the ancestral spirit of Orando,
who was no more concerned with the fate of whites than
he was with the fate of Negroes.

The village upon which he looked from the concealing
verdure of a nearby tree differed little from the quiet native
village of Tumbai except that its palisade was taller and
stronger. There were a few men and women in its single
main street, the former lolling in the shade of trees, the latter busy with the endless duties of their sex, which they
lightened by the world-wide medium of gossip.

Muzimo was not much interested in what he saw, at least
at first. There was no great concourse of warriors. A hundred
Utengas, if they could surprise the village, could wreak vengeance upon it easily. He noted, however, that the gates
were thick and high, that they were closed, and that a guard
of warriors squatted near them in the shade of the palisade.
Perhaps, he thought, it would be better to take the place by
night when a few agile men might scale the palisade undetected and open the gates for their fellows. He finally decided that he would do that himself without assistance. For
Muzimo it would be a simple matter to enter the village
undetected.

Suddenly his eyes were arrested by a group before a large hut. There was a large man, whom he intuitively knew to be the chief, and there were several others with whom he was conversing; but it was not the chief who arrested his attention. It was one of the others. Instantly Muzimo recognized him, and his grey eyes narrowed. What was Lupingu doing in the village of the Leopard Men? It was evident that he was not a prisoner, for it was plainly to be seen that the conversation between the men was amicable.

Muzimo waited. Presently he saw Lupingu leave the party before the chief's hut and approach the gates. He saw the warriors on guard open them, and he saw Lupingu pass through them and disappear into the forest in the direction of the camp of the Utengas. Muzimo was puzzled. What was Lupingu going to do? What had he already done? Perhaps he had gone to spy upon the Leopard Men and was returning with information for Orando.

Silently Muzimo slipped from the tree in which he had been hiding, and swung through the trees upon the trail of Lupingu, who, ignorant of the presence of the Nemesis hovering above him, trotted briskly in the direction of the camp of the tribesmen he had betrayed.

Presently from a distance, far ahead, Muzimo heard sounds, sounds that the ears of Lupingu could not hear. They told him that many people were coming through the forest in his direction. Later he interpreted them as the sounds made by warriors marching hurriedly. They were almost upon him before Lupingu heard them. When he did he went off from the trail a short distance and hid in the underbrush.

Muzimo waited among the foliage above the trees. He had caught the scent of the oncoming men and had recognized none that was familiar to him. It was the scent of warriors, and mixed with it was the scent of fresh blood. Some of them wounded. They had been in battle.

Presently they came in sight; and he saw that they were not the Utengas, as his nostrils had already told him. He guessed that they were from the village of the Leopard Men, and that they were returning to it. This accounted for the small number of warriors that he had seen in the village. Where had they been? Had they been in battle with Orando's little force?

He counted them, roughly, as they passed below him. There were nearly three hundred of them, and Orando had but a hundred warriors. Yet he was sure that Orando had not been badly defeated, for he saw no prisoners nor were they bringing any dead warriors with them, not even their own dead, as they would have, if they were Leopard Men and had been victorious.

Evidently, whoever they had fought, and it must have been Orando, had repulsed them; but how had the Utengas fared? Their losses must have been great in battle with a force that so greatly outnumbered them. But all this was only surmise. Presently he would find the Utengas and learn the truth. In the meantime he must keep an eye on Lupingu who was still hiding at one side of the trail.

When the Leopard Men had passed, Lupingu came from his concealment, and continued on in the direction he had been going, while above him and a little in his rear swung Muzimo and The Spirit of Nyamwegi.

When they came at last to the place where the Utengas had camped, they found only grim reminders of the recent battle; the Utengas were not there. Lupingu looked about him, a pleased smile on his crafty face. His efforts had not been in vain; the Leopard Men had at least driven the Utengas away, even though it had been as evident to him as it had been to Muzimo that their victory had been far from decisive.

For a moment he hesitated, of two minds as to whether to follow his former companions, or return to the village and take part in the ceremonies at the temple at the installation of the white priestess; but at last he decided that the safer plan was to rejoin the Utengas, lest a prolonged absence should arouse their suspicions as to his loyalty. He did not know that the matter was not in his hands at all, or that a power far greater than his own lurked above him, all but reading his mind, a power that would have frustrated an attempt to return to the village of Gato Mgungu and carried him by force to the new camp of Orando.

Lupingu had jogged on along the plain trail of the re-treating Utengas for a couple of miles when he was halted by a sentry whom he recognized at once as the brother of the girl whose affections Nyamwegi had stolen from him. When the sentry saw that it was Lupingu, the traitor was permitted to pass; and a moment later he entered the camp, which he found bristling with spears, the nerve-shaken warriors having leaped to arms at the challenge of the sentry.

There were wounded men groaning upon the ground, and ten of the Utenga dead were stretched out at one side of the camp, where a burial party was digging a shallow trench in which to inter them.

A volley of questions was hurled at Lupingu as he sought out Orando, and the angry or suspicious looks that accompanied them warned him that his story must be a most convincing one if it were to avail him.

Orando greeted him with a questioning scowl. "Where have you been, Lupingu, while we were fighting?" he demanded.

"I, too, have been fighting," replied Lupingu glibly.

"I did not see you," countered Orando. "You were not there. You were not in camp this morning. Where were you? See that your tongue speaks no lies."

"My tongue speaks only true words," insisted Lupingu. "Last night I said to myself: 'Orando does not like Lupingu. There are many who do not like Lupingu. Because he advised them not to make war against the Leopard Men they do not like him. Now he must do something to show them that he is a brave warrior. He must do something to save them from the Leopard Men.'

"And so I went out from camp while it was still dark to search for the village of the Leopard Men, that I might spy upon them and bring word to Orando. But I did not find the village. I became lost, and while I was searching for it I met many warriors. I did not run. I stood and fought with them until I had killed three. Then some came from behind and seized me. They made me prisoner, and I learned that I was in the hands of the Leopard Men.

"Later they fought with you. I could not see the battle, as their guards held me far behind the fighting men; but after a while the Leopard Men ran away, and I knew that the Utengas had been victorious. In the excitement I escaped and hid. When they had all gone I came at once to the camp of Orando."

The son of Lobongo, the chief, was no fool. He did not believe Lupingu's story, but he did not guess the truth. The worst interpretation that he put on Lupingu's desertion was cowardice in the face of an impending battle; but that was something to be punished by the contempt of his fellow warriors and the ridicule of the women of his village when he returned to Kibbu.

Orando shrugged. He had other, more important matters to occupy his thoughts. "If you want to win the praise of warriors," he advised, "remain and fight beside them." Then he turned away.

With startling suddenness that shocked the frayed nerves of the Utengas, Muzimo and The Spirit of Nyamwegi dropped unexpectedly into their midst from the overhanging branches of a tree. Once again three score spears danced nervously, their owners ready to fight or fly as the first man set the example; but when they saw who it was their fears were calmed; and perhaps they felt a little more confidence, for the presence of two friendly spirits is most reassuring to a body of half defeated warriors fearful of the return of the enemy.

"You have had a battle," said Muzimo to Orando. "I saw the Leopard Men running away; but your men act as though they, too, had been defeated. I do not understand."

"They came to our camp and fell upon us while we were unprepared," explained Orando. "Many of our men were killed or wounded in their first charge, but the Utengas were brave. They rallied and fought the Leopard Men off, killing many, wounding many; then the Leopard Men ran away, for we were fighting more bravely than they.

"We did not pursue them, because they greatly outnumbered us. After the battle my men were afraid they might return in still greater numbers. They did not wish to fight any more. They said that we had won, and that now Nyamwegi was fully avenged. They want to go home. Therefore we fell back to this new camp. Here we bury our dead. Tomorrow we do what the gods decide. I do not know.

"What I *should* like to know, though, is how the Leopard Men knew we were here. They shouted at us and told us that the god of the Leopard Men had sent them to our camp to get much flesh for a great feast. They said that tonight they would eat us all. It was those words that frightened the Utengas and made them want to go home."

"Would you like to know who told the Leopard Men that you were coming and where your camp was?" asked Muzimo.

Lupingu's eyes reflected a sudden fear. He edged off toward the jungle. "Watch Lupingu," directed Muzimo, "lest he go again to 'spy upon the Leopard Men.'" The words were scarcely uttered before Lupingu bolted; but a dozen warriors blocked his way; and presently he was dragged back, struggling and protesting. "It was not a god that told the Leopard Men that the Utengas were coming," continued Muzimo. "I crouched in a tree above their village, and saw the one who told them talking to their chief. Very friendly were they, as though both were Leopard Men. I followed him when he left the village. I saw him hide when the retreating warriors passed in the jungle. I followed him to the camp of the Utengas. I heard his tongue speak lies to Orando. I am Muzimo. I have spoken."

Instantly hoarse cries for vengeance arose. Men fell upon Lupingu and knocked him about. He would have been killed at once had not Muzimo interfered. He seized the wretched man and shielded him with his great body, while The Spirit of Nyamwegi fled to the branches of a tree and screamed excitedly as he danced up and down in a perfect frenzy of rage, though what it was all about he did not know.

"Do not kill him," commanded Muzimo, sternly. "Leave him to me."

"The traitor must die," shouted a warrior.

"Leave him to me," reiterated Muzimo.

"Leave him to Muzimo," commanded Orando; and at last, disgruntled, the warriors desisted from their attempts to lay hands upon the wretch.

"Bring ropes," directed Muzimo, "and bind his wrists and his ankles."

When eager hands had done as Muzimo bid, the warriors formed a half circle before him and Lupingu, waiting expectantly to witness the death of the prisoner, which they believed would take the form of some supernatural and particularly atrocious manifestation.

They saw Muzimo lift the man to one broad shoulder. They saw him take a few running steps, leap as lightly into the air as though he bore no burden whatsoever, seize a low-hanging limb as he swung himself upward, and disappear amidst the foliage above, melting into the shadows of the coming dusk.

9

The Leopard God

NIGHT was approaching. The sun, half hidden by the tops of forest trees, swung downward into the west. Its departing rays turned the muddy waters of a broad river into the semblance of molten gold. A ragged white man emerged from a forest trail upon the outskirts of a broad field of manioc, at the far side of which a palisaded village cast long shadows back to meet the shadows of the forest where he stood with his two black companions. To his right the forest hemmed the field and came down to overhang the palisade at the rear of the village.

"Do not go on, Bwana," urged one of the natives. "It is the village of the Leopard Men."

"It is the village of old Gato Mgungu," retorted Old Timer. "I have traded with him in the past."

"Then you came with many followers and with guns; then Gato Mgungu was a trader. Today you come with only two *boys*; today you will find that old Gato Mgungu is a Leopard Man."

"Bosh!" exclaimed the white man. "He would not dare harm a white."

"You do not know them," insisted the black. "They would kill their own mothers for flesh if there was no one to see them do it."

"Every sign that we have seen indicates that the girl was

brought here," argued Old Timer. "Leopard Men or no Leopard Men, I am going into the village."

"I do not wish to die," said the Negro.

"Nor do I," agreed his fellow.

"Then wait for me in the forest. Wait until the shadow of the forest has left the palisade in the morning. If I have not returned then, go back to the camp where the young bwana waits and tell him that I am dead."

The natives shook their heads. "Do not go, Bwana. The white woman was not your wife, neither was she your mother nor your sister. Why should you die for a woman who was nothing to you?"

Old Timer shook his head. "You would not understand." He wondered if he himself understood. Vaguely he realized that the force that was driving him on was not governed by reason; back of it was something inherent, bred into his fiber through countless generations of his kind. Its name was duty. If there was another more powerful force actuating him he was not conscious of it. Perhaps there was no other. There were lesser forces, though, and one of them was anger and another, desire for revenge. But two days of tracking through the jungle had cooled these to the point where he would no longer have risked his life to gratify them. It was the less obvious but more powerful urge that drove him on.

"Perhaps I shall return in a few minutes," he said, "but if not, then until tomorrow morning!" He shook their hands in parting.

"Good luck, Bwana!"

"May the good spirits watch over you, Bwana!"

He strode confidently along the path that skirted the manioc field toward the gates set in the palisade. Savage eyes watched his approach. Behind him the eyes of his servitors filled with tears. Inside the palisade a warrior ran to the hut of Gato Mgungu.

"A white man is coming," he reported. "He is alone."

"Let him enter, and bring him to me," ordered the chief.

As Old Timer came close to the gates one of them swung open. He saw a few warriors surveying him more or less apathetically. There was nothing in their demeanor to suggest antagonism, neither was their greeting in any way friendly. Their manner was wholly perfunctory. He made the sign of peace, which they ignored; but that did not trouble him. He was not concerned with the attitude of warriors, only with that of Gato Mgungu, the chief. As he was, so would they be.

"I have come to visit my friend, Gato Mgungu," he announced.

"He is waiting for you," replied the warrior who had taken word of his coming to the chief. "Come with me."

Old Timer noted the great number of warriors in the village. Among them he saw wounded men and knew that there had been a battle. He hoped that they had been victorious. Gato Mgungu would be in better humor were such the case. The scowling, unfriendly glances of the villagers did not escape him as he followed his guide toward the hut of the chief. On the whole, the atmosphere of the village was far from reassuring; but he had gone too far to turn back, even had he been of a mind to do so.

Gato Mgungu received him with a surly nod. He was sitting on a stool in front of his hut surrounded by a number of his principal followers. There was no answering smile or pleasant word to Old Timer's friendly greeting. The aspect of the situation appeared far from roseate.

"What are you doing here?" demanded Gato Mgungu.

The smile had faded from the white man's face. He knew that this was no time for soft words. There was danger in the very air. He sensed it without knowing the reason for it; and he knew that a bold front, along, might release him from a serious situation.

"I have come for the white girl," he said.

Gato Mgungu's eyes shifted. "What white girl?" he demanded.

"Do not lie to me with questions,'" snapped Old Timer. "The white girl is here. For two days I have followed those who stole her from my camp. Give her to me. I wish to return to my people who wait for me in the forest."

"There is no white girl in my village," growled Gato Mgungu, "nor do I take orders from white men. I am Gato Mgungu, the chief. I give orders."

"You'll take orders from me, you old scoundrel," threatened the other, "or I'll have a force down on your village that'll wipe it off the map."

Gato Mgungu sneered. "I know you, white man. There are

two of you and six natives in your safari. You have few guns. You are poor. You steal ivory. You do not dare go where the white rulers are. They would put you in jail. You come with big words, but big words do not frighten Gato Mgungu; and now you are my prisoner."

"Well, what of it?" demanded Old Timer. "What do you think you're going to do with me?"

"Kill you," replied Gato Mgungu.

The white man laughed. "No you won't; not if you know what's good for you. The government would burn your village and hang you when they found it out."

"They will not find it out," retorted the chief. "Take him away. See that he does not escape."

Old Timer looked quickly around at the evil, scowling faces surrounding him. It was then that he recognized the chief, Bobolo, with whom he had long been upon good terms. Two warriors laid heavy hands upon him to drag him away. "Wait!" he exclaimed, thrusting them aside. "Let me speak to Bobolo. He certainly has sense enough to stop this foolishness."

"Take him away!" shouted Gato Mgungu.

Again the warriors seized him, and as Bobolo made no move to intercede in his behalf the white man accompanied his guard without further demonstration. After disarming him they took him to a small hut, filthy beyond description, and, tying him securely, left him under guard of a single sentry who squatted on the ground outside the low doorway; but they neglected to remove the pocket knife from a pocket in his breeches.

Old Timer was very uncomfortable. His bonds hurt his wrists and ankles. The dirt floor of the hut was uneven and hard. The place was alive with crawling, biting things. It was putrid with foul stenches. In addition to these physical discomforts the outlook was mentally distressing. He began to question the wisdom of his quixotic venture and to upbraid himself for not listening to the council of his two followers.

But presently thoughts of the girl and the horrid situation in which she must be, if she still lived, convinced him that even though he had failed he could not have done otherwise than he had. He recalled to his mind a vivid picture of her as he had last seen her, he recounted her perfections of face and figure, and he knew that if chance permitted him to escape from the village of Gato Mgungu he would face even greater perils to effect her rescue.

His mind was still occupied with thoughts of her when he heard someone in conversation with his guard, and a moment later a figure entered the hut. It was now night; the only light was that reflected from the cooking fires burning about the village and a few torches set in the ground before the hut of the chief. The interior of his prison was in almost total darkness. The features of his visitor were quite invisible. He wondered if he might be the executioner, come to inflict the death penalty pronounced by the chief; but at the first words he recognized the voice of Bobolo.

"Perhaps I can help you," said his visitor. "You would like to get out of here?"

"Of course. Old Mgungu must have gone crazy. What's the matter with the old fool, anyway?"

"He does not like white men. I am their friend. I will help you."

"Good for you, Bobolo," exclaimed Old Timer. "You'll never regret it."

"It cannot be done for nothing," suggested Bobolo

"Name your price."

"It is not my price," the black hastened to assure him; "it is what I shall have to pay to others."

"Well, how much?"

"Ten tusks of ivory."

Old Timer whistled. "Wouldn't you like a steam yacht and a Rolls Royce, too?"

"Yes," agreed Bobolo, willing to accept anything whether or not he knew what it was.

"Well, you don't get them; and, furthermore, ten tusks are too many."

Bobolo shrugged. "You know best, white man, what your life is worth." He arose to go.

"Wait!" exclaimed Old Timer. "You know it is hard to get any ivory these days."

"I should have asked for a hundred tusks; but you are a friend, and so I asked only ten."

"Get me out of here and I will bring the tusks to you when I get them. It may take time, but I will bring them."

Bobolo shook his head. "I must have the tusks first. Send word to your white friend to send me the tusks; then you will be freed."

"How can I send word to him? My men are not here."

"I will send a messenger."

"All right, you old horse-thief," consented the white. "Untie my wrists and I'll write a note to him."

"That will not do. I would not know what the paper that talks said. It might say things that would bring trouble to Bobolo."

"You're darn right it would," soliloquized Old Timer. "If I could get the notebook and pencil out of my pocket The Kid would get a message that would land you in jail and hang Gato Mgungu into the bargain." But aloud he said, "How will he know that the message is from me?"

"Send something by the messenger that he will know is yours. You are wearing a ring. I saw it today."

"How do I know you will send the right message?" demurred Old Timer. "You might demand a hundred tusks."

"I am your friend. I am very honest. Also, there is no other way. Shall I take the ring?"

"Very well; take it."

The Negro stepped behind Old Timer and removed the ring from his finger. "When the ivory comes you will be set free," he said as he stooped, and passed out of the hut.

"I don't take any stock in the old fraud," thought the white man, "but a drowning man clutches at a straw."

Bobolo grinned as he examined the ring by the light of a fire. "I am a bright man," he muttered to himself. "I shall have a ring as well as the ivory." As for freeing Old Timer, that was beyond his power; nor had he any intention of even attempting it. He was well contented with himself when he joined the other chiefs who were sitting in council with Gato Mgungu.

They were discussing, among other things, the method of dispatching the white prisoner. Some wished to have him slain and butchered in the village that they might not have to divide the flesh with the priests and the Leopard God at the temple. Others insisted that he be taken forthwith to the high priest that his flesh might be utilized in the ceremonies accompanying the induction of the new white high priestess There was a great deal of oratory, most of which was in-apropos; but that is ever the way of men in conferences. Black or white they like to hear their own voices.

Gato Mgungu was in the midst of a description of heroic acts that he had performed in a battle that had been fought twenty years previously when he was silenced by a terrifying interruption. There was a rustling of the leaves in the tree that overhung his hut; a heavy object hurtled down into the center of the circle formed by the squatting councilors, and as one man they leaped to their feet in consternation. Expressions of surprise, awe, or terror were registered upon every countenance. They turned affrighted glances upward into the tree, but nothing was visible there among the dark shadows; then they looked down at the thing lying at their feet. It was the corpse of a man, its wrists and ankles bound, its throat cut from ear to ear.

"It is Lupingu, the Utenga," whispered Gato Mgungu "He brought me word of the coming of the son of Lobongo and his warriors."

"It is an ill omen," whispered one.

"They have punished the traitor," said another.

"But who could have carried him into the tree and thrown him down upon us?" demanded Bobolo.

"He spoke today of one who claimed to be the *muzimo* of Orando," explained Gato Mgungu, "a huge white man whose powers were greater than the powers of Sobito, the witch-doctor of Tumbai."

"We have heard of him from another," interjected a chief.

"And he spoke of another," continued Gato Mgungu, "that is the spirit of Nyamwegi of Kibbu, who was killed by children of the Leopard God. This one has taken the form of a little monkey."

"Perhaps it was the *muzimo* that brought Lupingu here," suggested Bobolo. "It is a warning. Let us take the white man to the high priest to do with as he sees fit. If he kills him the fault will not be ours."

"Those are the words of a wise man." The speaker was one who owed a debt to Bobolo.

"It is dark," another reminded them; "perhaps we had better wait until morning."

"Now is the time," said Gato Mgungu. "If the *muzimo* is white and is angry because we have made this white man prisoner, he will hang around the village as long as we keep the other here. We will take him to the temple. The high priest and the Leopard God are stronger than any *muzimo*."

Hidden amidst the foliage of a tree Muzimo watched the natives in the palisaded village below. The Spirit of Nyamwegi, bored by the sight, disgusted with all this wandering about by night, had fallen asleep in his arms, Muzimo saw the warriors arming and forming under the commands of their chiefs. The white prisoner was dragged from the hut in which he had been imprisoned, the bonds were removed from his ankles, and he was hustled under guard toward the gateway through which the warriors were now debouching upon the river front. Here they launched a flotilla of small canoes (some thirty of them) each with a capacity of about ten men, for there were almost three hundred warriors of the Leopard God in the party, only a few having been left in the village to act as a guard. The large war canoes, seating fifty men, were left behind, bottom up, upon the shore.

As the last canoe with its load of painted savages drifted down the dark current, Muzimo and The Spirit of Nyamwegi dropped from the tree that had concealed them and followed along the shore. An excellent trail paralleled the river; and along this Muzimo trotted, keeping the canoes always within hearing.

The Spirit of Nyamwegi, aroused from sound sleep to follow many more of the hated Gomangani than he could count, was frightened and excited. "Let us turn back," he begged. "Why must we follow all these Gomangani who will kill us if they catch us, when we might be sleeping safely far away in a nice large tree?"

"They are the enemies of Orando," explained Muzimo. "We follow to see where they are going and what they are going to do."

"I do not care where they are going or what they are going to do," whimpered The Spirit of Nyamwegi; "I am sleepy. If we go on, Sheeta will get us or Sabor or Numa; if not they, then the Gomangani. Let us go back."

"No," replied the white giant. "I am a *muzimo*. *Muzimos* must know everything. Therefore I must go about by night as well as by day watching the enemies of Orando. If you do not wish to come with me climb a tree and sleep."

The Spirit of Nyamwegi was afraid to go on with Muzimo, but he was more afraid to remain alone in this strange forest; so he said nothing more about the matter as Muzimo trotted along the dark trail beside the dark, mysterious river.

They had covered about two miles when Muzimo became aware that the canoes had stopped, and a moment later he came to the bank of a small affluent of the larger stream. Into this the canoes were moving slowly in single file. He watched them, counting, until the last had entered the sluggish stream and disappeared in the darkness of the overhanging verdure; then, finding no trail, he took to the trees, following the canoes by the sound of the dipping paddles beneath him.

It chanced that Old Timer was in a canoe commanded by Bobolo, and he took advantage of the opportunity to ask the chief whither they were taking him and why; but Bobolo cautioned him to silence, whispering that at present no one must know of his friendship for the prisoner. "Where you are going you will be safer; your enemies will not be able to find you," was the most that he would say.

"Nor my friends either," suggested Old Timer; but to that Bobolo made no answer.

The surface of the stream beneath the trees, which prevented even the faint light of a moonless sky from reaching it, was shrouded in utter darkness. Old Timer could not see the man next to him, nor his hand before his face. How the paddlers guided their caft along this narrow, tortuous river appeared little less than a miracle to him, yet they moved steadily and surely toward their destination. He wondered what that destination might be. There seemed something mysterious and uncanny in the whole affair. The river itself was mysterious. The unwonted silence of the warriors accentuated the uncanniness of the situation. Everything combined to suggest to his imagination a company of dead men paddling up a river of death, three hundred Charons escorting his dead soul to Hell. It was not a pleasant thought; he sought to thrust it from his mind, but there was none more pleasant to replace it. It seemed to Old Timer that his fortunes never before had been at such low ebb.

"At least," he soliloquized, "I have the satisfaction of knowing that things could get no worse."

One thought which recurred persistently caused him the most concern. It was of the girl and her fate. While he was not convinced that she had not been in the village while he was captive there, he felt that such had not been the case. He realized that his judgment was based more upon intuition than reason, but the presentiment was so strong that it verged upon conviction. Being positive that she had been brought to the village only a short time before his arrival, he sought to formulate some reasonable conjecture as to the disposition the savages had made of her. He doubted that they had killed her as yet. Knowing, as he did, that they were cannibals, he was positive that the killing of the girl, if they intended to kill her, would be reserved for a spectacular ceremony and followed by a dance and an orgy. There had not been time for such a celebration since she had been brought to the village; therefore it seemed probable that she had preceded him up this mysterious river of darkness.

He hoped that this last conjecture might prove correct, not only because of the opportunity it would afford to rescue her from her predicament (provided that lay within his power) but because it would bring him near her once more where, perchance, he might see or even touch her. Absence had but resulted in stimulating his mad infatuation for her. Mere contemplation of her charms aroused to fever heat his longing for her, redoubled his anger against the savages who had abducted her.

His mind was thus occupied by these complex emotions when his attention was attracted by a light just ahead upon the right bank of the stream. At first he saw only the light, but presently he perceived human figures dimly illuminated by its rays and behind it the outlines of a large structure. The number of the figures increased rapidly and more lights appeared. He saw that the former were the crews of the canoes which had preceded his and the latter torches borne by people coming from the structure, which he now saw was a large building.

Presently his own canoe pulled in to the bank, and he was hustled ashore. Here, among the warriors who had come from the village, were savages clothed in the distinctive apparel of the Leopard Men. It was these who had emerged from the building, carrying torches. A few of them wore hideous masks. They were the priests of the Leopard God.

Slowly there was dawning upon the consciousness of the white man the realization that he had been brought to that mysterious temple of the Leopard Men of which he had heard frightened, whispered stories from the lips of terrified natives upon more than a single occasion, and which he had come to consider more fabulous than real. The reality of it, however, was impressed upon him with overpowering certainty when he was dragged through the portals of the building into it barbaric interior.

Lighted by many torches, the scene was one to be indelibly impressed upon the memory of a beholder. Already the great chamber was nearly filled with the warriors from the village of Gato Mgungu. They were milling about several large piles of leopard skins presided over by masked priests who were issuing these ceremonial costumes to them. Gradually the picture changed as the warriors donned the garb of their savage order, until the white man saw about him only the black and yellow hides of the carnivores; the curved, cruel, steel talons; and the black faces, hideously painted, partially hidden by the leopard head helmets.

The wavering torchlight played upon carved and painted idols; it glanced from naked human skulls, from gaudy shields and grotesque masks hung upon the huge pillars that supported the roof of the building. It lighted, more brilliantly than elsewhere, a raised dais at the far end of the chamber, where stood the high priest upon a smaller platform at the back of the dais. Below and around him were grouped a number of lesser priests; while chained to a heavy post near him was a large leopard, bristling and growling at the massed humanity beneath him, a devil-faced leopard that seemed to the imagination of the white man to personify the savage bestiality of the cult it symbolized.

The man's eyes ranged the room in search of the girl, but

she was nowhere to be seen. He shuddered at the thought that she might be hidden somewhere in this frightful place, and would have risked everything to learn, had his guards given him the slightest oppportunity. If she were here her case was hopeless, as hopeless as he now realized his own to be; for since he had become convinced that he had been brought to the temple of the Leopard Men, allowed to look upon their holy of holies, to view their most secret rites, he had known that no power on earth could save him; and that the protestations and promises of Bobolo had been false, for no one other than a Leopard Man could look upon these things and live.

Gato Mgungu, Bobolo, and the other chiefs had taken their places in front of the common warriors at the foot of the dais. Gato Mgungu had spoken to the high priest, and now at a word from the latter his guards dragged Old Timer forward and stood with him at the right of the dais. Three hundred pairs of evil eyes, filled with hatred, glared at him— savage eyes, hungry eyes.

The high priest turned toward the snarling, mouthing leopard. "Leopard God," he cried in a high, shrill voice, "the children of the Leopard God have captured an enemy of his people. They have brought him here to the great temple. What is the will of the Leopard God?"

There was a moment's silence during which all eyes were fixed upon the high priest and the leopard. Then a weird thing happened, a thing that turned the skin of the white man cold and stiffened the hairs upon his scalp. From the snarling mouth of the leopard came human speech. It was incredible, yet with his own ears he heard it.

"Let him die that the children of the Leopard God may be fed!" The voice was low and husky and merged with bestial growls. "But first bring forth the new high priestess of the temple that my children may look upon her whom my brother commanded Lulimi to bring from a far country."

Lulimi, who by virtue of his high priestly rank stood nearest to the throne of the high priest, swelled visibly with pride. This was the big moment for which he had waited. All eyes were upon him. He trod a few steps of a savage dance, leaped high into the air, and voiced a hideous cry that echoed through the lofty rafters far above. The lay brothers were impressed; they would not soon forget Lulimí. But instantly their attention was distracted from Lulimi to the doorway at the rear of the dais. In it stood a girl, naked but for a few ornaments. She stepped out upon the dais, to be followed immediately by eleven similarly garbed priestesses. Then there was a pause.

Old Timer wondered which of these was the new high priestess. There was little difference between them other than varying degrees of age and ugliness. Their yellow teeth were filed to sharp points; the septa of their noses were pierced, and through these holes were inserted ivory skewers; the lobes of their ears were stretched to their shoulders by heavy ornaments of copper, iron, brass, and ivory; their faces were painted a ghoulish blue and white.

Now the Leopard God spoke again. "Fetch the high priestess!" he commanded, and with three hundred others Old Timer centered his gaze again upon the aperture at the back of the dais. A figure, dimly seen, approached out of the darkness of the chamber beyond until it stood in the doorway, the flare of the torches playing upon it.

The white man stifled a cry of astonishment and horror. The figure was that of the girl whom he sought.

10

While the Priests Slept

A S Kali Bwana was pushed into the doorway at the rear of the dais by the old hag who was her chief guardian, she paused in consternation and horror at the sight which met her eyes. Directly before her stood the high priest, terrifying in his weird costume and horrid mask, and near him a great leopard, nervous and restless on its chain. Beyond these was a sea of savage, painted faces and grotesque masks, discernible vaguely in the light of torches against a background of leopard skins.

The atmosphere of the room was heavy with the acrid

stench of bodies. A wave of nausea surged over the girl; she reeled slightly and placed the back of one hand across her eyes to shut out the terrifying sight.

The old woman behind her whispered angrily and shoved her forward. A moment later Imigeg, the high priest, seized her hand and drew her to the center of the smaller, higher dais beside the growling leopard. The beast snarled and sprang at her; but Imigeg had anticipated such an emergency, and the leopard was brought to a sudden stop by its chain before its raking talons touched the soft flesh of the shrinking girl.

Old Timer shuddered as the horror of her position impressed itself more deeply upon his consciousness. His rage against the men and his own futility left him weak and trembling. His utter helplessness to aid her was maddening, as the sight of her redoubled the strength of his infatuation. He recalled the harsh and bitter things he had said to her, and he flushed with shame at the recollection. Then the eyes of the girl, now taking in the details of the scene before her, met his. For a moment she regarded him blankly; then she recognized him. Surprise and incredulity were written upon her countenance. At first she did not realize that he, too, was a prisoner. His presence recalled his boorish and ungallant attitude toward her at their first meeting. She saw in him only another enemy; yet the fact that he was a white man imparted a new confidence. It did not seem possible that even he would stand idly by and permit a white woman to be imprisoned and maltreated by Negroes. Slowly, then, it dawned upon her that he was a prisoner as well as she; and though the new hope waned, there still remained a greater degree of confidence than she had felt before.

She wondered what queer trick of fate had brought them together again thus. She could not know, nor even dream, that he had been captured in an effort to succor her. Perhaps had she known and known, too, the impulse that had actuated him, even the slight confidence that his presence imparted to her would have been dissipated; but she did not know. She only realized that he was a man of her own race, and that because he was there she felt a little braver.

As Old Timer watched the slender, graceful figure and beautiful face of the new high priestess of the Leopard God,

other eyes surveyed and appraised her. Among these were
the eyes of Bobolo—savage, bloodshot eyes; greedy, lustful
eyes. Bobolo licked his lips hungrily. The savage chief
was hungry, but not for food.

The rites of installation were proceeding. Imigeg held the
center of the stage. He jabbered incessantly. Sometimes he
addressed an underpriest or a priestess, again the Leopard
God; and when the beast answered, it never failed to elicit a
subdued gasp of awe from the assembled warriors, though
the white girl and Old Timer were less mystified or impressed after their first brief surprise.

There was another listener who also was mystified by the
talking leopard, but who, though he had never heard of a
ventriloquist, pierced the deception with his uncanny per-
ceptive faculties as, perched upon a tiebeam of the roof that
projected beyond the front wall of the building, he looked
through an opening below the ridgepole at the barbaric scene
being enacted beneath him.

It was Muzimo; and beside him, trembling at the sight of
so many leopards, perched The Spirit of Nyamwegi. "I am
afraid," he said; "Nkima is afraid. Let us go back to the land
that is Tarzan's. Tarzan is king there; here no one knows
him, and he is no better than a Gomangani."

"Always you speak of Nkima and Tarzan," complained
Muzimo. "I have never heard of them. You are The Spirit
of Nyamwegi and I am Muzimo. How many times must I
tell you these things?"

"You are Tarzan, and I am Nkima," insisted the little
monkey. "You are a Tarmangani."

"I am the spirit of Orando's ancestor," insisted the other.
"Did not Orando say so?"

"I do not know," sighed The Spirit of Nyamwegi wearily;
"I do not understand the language of the Gomangani. All I
know is that I am Nkima, and that Tarzan has changed.
He is not the same since the tree fell upon him. I also know
that I am afraid. I want to go away from here."

"Presently," promised Muzimo. He was watching the scene
below him intently. He saw the white man and the white
girl, and he guessed the fate that awaited them, but it did
not move him to compassion, nor arouse within him any sense
of blood-responsibility. He was the ancestral spirit of Orando,

the son of a chief; the fate of a couple of strange Tarmangani meant nothing to him. Presently, however, his observing eyes discovered something which did arouse his keen interest. Beneath one of the hideous priest-masks he caught a glimpse of familiar features. He was not surprised, for he had been watching this particular priest intently for some time, his attention having been attracted to him by something familiar in his carriage and conformation. The shadow of a smile touched the lips of Muzimo. "Come!" he whispered to The Spirit of Nyamwegi, as he clambered to the roof of the temple.

Sure-footed as a cat he ran along the ridgepole, the little monkey at his heels. Midway of the building he sprang lightly down the sloping roof and launched himself into the foliage of a nearby tree, and as The Spirit of Nyamwegi followed him the two were engulfed in the Erebusan darkness of the forest.

Inside the temple the priestesses had lighted many fires upon the large clay dais and swung cooking pots above them on crude tripods, while from a rear room of the temple the lesser priests had brought many cuts of meat, wrapped in plantain leaves. These the priestesses placed in the cooking pots, while the priests returned for gourds and jugs of native beer, which were passed among the warriors.

As the men drank they commenced to dance. Slowly at first, their bodies bent foward from the hips, their elbows raised, they stepped gingerly, lifting their feet high. In their hands they grasped their spears and shields, holding them awkwardly because of the great, curved steel talons affixed to their fingers. Restricted by lack of space upon the crowded floor, each warrior pivoted upon the same spot, pausing only to take long drinks from the beer jugs as they were passed to him. A low, rhythmic chant accompanied the dance, rising in volume and increasing in tempo as the temp of the dance steps increased, until the temple floor was a mass of howling, leaping savages.

Upon the upper dais the Leopard God, aroused to fury by the din and movement about him and the scent of the flesh that was cooking in the pots, strained at his chain, snarling and growling in rage. The high priest, stimulated by the contents of a beer pot, danced madly before the frenzied carnivore, leaping almost within reach of its raking talons, then springing away again as the infuriated beast struck at him. The white girl shrank to the far side of the dais, her brain reeling to the hideous pandemonium surrounding her, half numb from fear and apprehension. She had seen the meat brought to the cooking pots but had only vaguely guessed the nature of it until a human hand had fallen from its wrappings of plaintain leaves. The significance of the grisly object terrified and sickened her.

The white man watching the scene about him looked most often in her direction. Once he had tried to speak to her; but one of his guards had struck him heavily across the mouth, silencing him. As the drinking and the dancing worked the savages into augmented fury, his concern for the safety of the girl increased. He saw that religious and al-coholic drunkenness were rapidly robbing them of what few brains and little self-control Nature had vouchsafed them, and he trembled to think of what excesses they might com-mit when they had passed beyond even the restraint of their leaders; nor did the fact that the chiefs, the priests, and the priestesses were becoming as drunk as their followers tend but to aggravate his fears.

Bobolo, too, was watching the white girl. In his drunken brain wild schemes were forming. He saw her danger, and he wished to save her for himself. Just how he was going to possess her was not entirely clear to his muddled mind, yet it clung stubbornly to the idea. Then his eyes changed to alight on Old Timer, and a scheme evolved hazily through the beer fumes.

The white man wished to save the white woman. This fact Bobolo knew and recalled. If he wished to save her he would protect her. The white man also wished to escape. He thought Bobolo was his friend. Thus the premises formed slowly in his addled brain. So far, so good! The white man would help him abduct the high priestess, but that could not be effected until practically everyone was too drunk to prevent the accomplishment of his plan or remember it afterward. He would have to wait for the proper moment to arrive, but in the meantime he must get the girl out of this chamber and hide her in one of the other rooms of the tem-ple. Already the priestesses were mingling freely with the excited, drunken warriors; presently the orgy would be in full swing. After that it was possible that no one might save her; not even the high priest, who was now quite as drunk as any of them.

Bobolo approached Old Timer and spoke to his guards. "Go and join the others," he told them. "I will watch the prisoner."

The men, already half drunk, needed no second invitation. The word of a chief was enough; it released them from all responsibility. In a moment they were gone. "Quick!" urged Bobolo, grasping Old Timer by the arm. "Come with me."

The white man drew back. "Where?" he demanded.

"I am going to help you to escape," whispered Bobolo.

"Not without the white woman," insisted the other.

This reply fitted so perfectly with Bobolo's plans that he was delighted. "I will arrange that, too; but I must get you out of here into one of the back rooms of the temple. Then I shall come back for her. I could not take you both at the same time. It is very dangerous. Imigeg would have me killed if he discovered it. You must do just as I say."

"Why do you take this sudden interest in our welfare?" demanded the white, suspiciously.

"Because you are both in danger here," replied Bobolo. "Everyone is very drunk, even the high priest. Soon there would be no one to protect either of you, and you would be lost. I am your friend. It is well for you that Bobolo is your friend and that he is not drunk."

"Not very!" thought Old Timer as the man staggered at his side toward a doorway in the rear partition of the chamber.

Bobolo conducted him to a room at the far end of the temple. "Wait here," he said. "I shall go back and fetch the girl."

"Cut these cords at my wrists," demanded the white. "They hurt."

Bobolo hesitated, but only for a moment. "Why not?" he asked. "You do not have to try to escape, because I am going to take you away myself; furthermore you could not escape alone. The temple stands upon an island surrounded by the river and swamp land alive with crocodiles. No trails lead from it other than the river. Ordinarily there are no canoes here, lest some of the priests or priestesses might escape. They, too, are prisoners. You will wait until I am ready to take you away from here."

"Of course I shall. Hurry, now, and bring the white woman."

Bobolo returned to the main chamber of the temple, but this time he approached it by way of the door that let upon the upper dais at its rear. Here he paused to reconnoiter. The meat from the cooking pots was being passed among the warriors, but the beer jugs were still circulating freely. The high priest lay in a stupor at the far side of the upper dais. The Leopard God crouched, growling, over the thigh bone of a man. The high priestess leaned against the partition close to the doorway where Bobolo stood. The chief touched her upon the arm. With startled eyes she turned toward him.

"Come," he whispered and beckoned her to follow.

The girl understood only the gesture, but she had seen this same man lead her fellow prisoner away from the foot of the dais but a moment before; and instantly she concluded that by some queer freak of fate this man might be friendly. Certainly there had been nothing threatening or unfriendly in his facial expressions as he had talked to the white man. Reasoning thus, she followed Bobolo into the gloomy chambers in the rear of the temple. She was afraid, and how close to harm she was only Bobolo knew. Excited to desire by propinquity and impelled to rashness by drink, he suddenly thought to drag her into one of the dark chambers that lined the corridor along which he was conducting her; but as he turned to seize her a voice spoke at his elbow. "You got her more easily than I thought possible." Bobolo wheeled. "I followed you," continued Old Timer, "thinking you might need help."

The chief grunted angrily, but the surprise had brought him to his senses. A scream or the noise of a scuffle might have brought a guardian of the temple to investigate, which would have meant death for Bobolo. He made no reply, but led them back to the room in which he had left Old Timer.

"Wait here for me," he cautioned them. "If you are discovered do not say that I brought you here. If you do

I shall not be able to save you. Say that you were afraid and came here to hide." He turned to go.

"Wait," said Old Timer. "Suppose we are unable to get this girl away from here; what will become of her?"

Bobolo shrugged. "We have never before had a white priestess. Perhaps she is for the Leopard God, perhaps for the high priest, Who knows?" Then he left them.

" 'Perhaps for the Leopard God, perhaps for the high priest,' " repeated Kali Bwana when the man had translated the words. "Oh, how horrible!"

The girl was standing very close to the white man. He could feel the warmth of her almost naked body. He trembled, and when he tried to speak his voice was husky with emotion. He wanted to seize her and crush her to him. He wanted to cover her soft, warm lips with kisses. What stayed him he did not know. They were alone at the far extremity of the temple, the noises of the savage orgy in the main chamber of the building would have drowned any outcry that she might make; she was absolutely at his mercy, yet he did not touch her.

"Perhaps we shall escape soon," he said. "Bobolo has promised to take us away."

"You know him and can trust him?" she asked.

"I have known him for a couple of years," he replied, "but I do not trust him. I do not trust any of them. Bobolo is doing this for a price. He is an avaricious old scoundrel."

"What is the price?"

"Ivory."

"But I have none."

"Neither have I," he admitted, "but I'll get it."

"I will pay you for my share," she offered. "I have money with an agent at rail-head."

He laughed. "Let's cross that bridge when we get to it, if we ever do."

"That doesn't sound very reassuring."

"We are in a bad hole," he explained. "We mustn't raise our hopes too high. Right now our *only* hope seems to lie in Bobolo. He is a Leopard Man and a scoundrel, in addition to which he is drunk—a slender hope at best."

Bobolo, returning slightly sobered to the orgy, found him-

self suddenly frightened by what he had done. To bolster
his waning courage he seized upon a large jug of beer and
drained it. The contents exercised a magical effect upon Bobolo, for when presently his eyes fell upon a drunken priestess reeling in a corner she was transformed into a much-
to-be-desired houri. An hour later Bobolo was fast asleep in
the middle of the floor.

The effects of the native beer wore off almost as rapidly
as they manifested themselves in its devotees, with the result that in a few hours the warriors commenced to bestir
themselves. They were sick and their heads ached. They
wished more beer; but when they demanded it they learned
that there was no more, nor was there any food. They had
consumed all the refreshments, liquid and solid.

Gato Mgungu had never had any of the advantages of
civilization (He had never been to Hollywood); but he knew
what to do under the circumstances, for the psychology of
celebrators is doubtless the same in Africa as elsewhere.
When there is nothing more to eat or drink, it must be time
to go home. Gato Mgungu gathered the other chiefs and
transmitted this philosophical reflection to them. They agreed,
Bobolo included. His brain was slightly befogged. He had
already forgotten several events of the past evening, including the houri-like priestess. He knew that there was something important on his mind, but he could not recall just
what it was; therefore he herded his men to their canoes just
as the other chiefs and headmen were doing.

Presently he was headed down river, part of a long pro-
cession of war canoes filled with headaches. Back in the
temple lay a few warriors who had still been too drunk to
stand. For these they had left a single canoe. These men
were strewn about the floor of the temple, asleep. Among
them were all of the lesser priests and the priestesses. Imigeg was curled up on one corner of the dais fast asleep.
The Leopard God, his belly filled, slept also.

Kali Bwana and Old Timer, waiting impatiently in the
dark room at the rear of the temple for the return of Bobolo,
had noted the increasing quiet in the front chamber of the
building; then they had heard the preparations for departure
as all but a few made ready to leave. They heard the
shuffling of feet as the warriors passed out of the building;

they heard the shouts and commands at the river bank that told the white man that the natives were launching their canoes. After that there had been silence.

"Bobolo ought to be coming along," remarked the man.

"Perhaps he has gone away and left us," suggested Kali Bwana.

They waited a little longer. Not a sound came from any part of the temple nor from the grounds outside. The silence of death reigned over the holy of holies of the Leopard God. Old Timer stirred uneasily. "I am going to have a look out there," he said. "Perhaps Bobolo *has* gone, and if he has we want to know it." He moved toward the doorway. "I shall not be gone long," he whispered. "Do not be afraid."

As the girl waited in the darkness her mind dwelt upon the man who had just left her. He seemed changed since the time of their first meeting. He appeared more solicitous as to her welfare and much less brusque and churlish. Yet she could not forget the harsh things he had said to her upon that other occasion. She could never forgive him, and in her heart she still half feared and mistrusted him. It galled her to reflect that in the event of their escape she would be under obligation to him, and as these thoughts occupied her mind Old Timer crept stealthily along the dark corridor toward the small doorway that opened upon the upper dais.

Only a suggestion of light came through it now to guide his footsteps, and when he reached it he looked out into an almost deserted room. The embers of the cooking fires were hidden by white ashes; only a single torch remained that had not burned out. Its smoky flame burned steadily in the quiet air, and in its feeble light he saw the sleepers sprawled upon the floor. In the dim light he could not distinguish the features of any; so he could not know if Bobolo were among them. One long searching look he gave that took in the whole interior of the chamber, a look that assured him that no single conscious person remained in the temple; then he turned and hastened back to the girl.

"Did you find him?" she asked.

"No. I doubt that he is here. Nearly all of them have left, except just a few who were too drunk to leave. I think it is our chance."

"What do you mean?"

"There is no one to prevent our escaping. There may be no canoe. Bobolo told me that no canoe was ever left here, for fear that the priests or priestesses might escape. He may have been lying, but whether he was or not we may as well take the chance. There is no hope for either of us if we remain here. Even the crocodiles would be kinder to you than these fiends."

"I will do whatever you say," she replied, "but if at any time I am a burden, if my presence might hinder your escape, do not consider me. Go on without me. Remember that you are under no obligation to me, nor—' She hesitated and stopped.

"Nor what?" he asked.

"Nor do I wish to be under obligation to you. I have not forgotten the things that you said to me when you came to my camp."

He hesitated a moment before replying; then he ignored what she had said. "Come!" he commanded brusquely. "We have no time to waste."

He walked to a window in the rear wall of the room and looked out. It was very dark. He could see nothing. He knew that the building was raised on piles and that the drop to the ground might prove dangerous; but he also knew that a verandah stretched along one side of the structure. Whether it continued around to the rear of the building where this room was located he could not know. To go out through the main room among all those savages was too fraught with risk. An alternative was to find their way to one of the rooms overlooking the verandah that he knew was there on the river side of the building.

"I think we'll try another room," he whispered. "Give me your hand, so that we shall not become separated."

She slipped her hand into his. It was tender and warm. Once again the mad urge of his infatuation rose like a great tide within him, so that it was with difficulty that he controlled himself, yet by no sign did he betray his passion to the girl. Quietly they tiptoed into the dark corridor, the man groping with his free hand until he found a doorway. Gingerly they crossed the room beyond in search of a window.

What if this were the apartment of some temple inmate who had left the orgy to come here and sleep! The thought brought cold sweat to the man's brow, and he swore in his heart that he would slay any creature that put itself in the way of the rescue of the girl; but fortunately the apartment was uninhabited, and the two came to the window unchallenged. The man threw a leg over the sill, and a moment later stood upon the verandah beyond; then he reached in and assisted the girl to his side.

They were near the rear of the building. He dared not chance detection by going to the stairway that led to the ground from the front entrance to the temple. "We shall have to climb down one of the piles that support the building," he explained. "It is possible that there may be a guard at the front entrance. Do you think that you can do it?"

"Certainly," she replied.

"I'll go first," he said. "If you slip I'll try to hold you."

"I shall not slip; go ahead."

The verandah had no railing. He lay down and felt beneath its edge until he found the top of a pile. "Here," he whispered, and lowered himself over the edge.

The girl followed. He dropped a little lower and guided her legs until they had found a hold upon the pile, which was the bole of a young tree about eight inches in diameter. Without difficulty they reached the ground, and again he took her hand and led her to the bank of the river. As they moved down stream parallel with the temple he sought for a canoe, and when they had come opposite the front of the building he could scarce restrain an exclamation of relief and delight when they came suddenly upon one drawn up on the shore, partially out of the water.

Silently they strained to push the heavy craft into the river. At first it seemed that their efforts would prove of no avail; but at last it started to slip gently downward, and once it was loosened from the sticky mud of the bank that same medium became a slipper slide down which it coasted easily.

He helped her in, shoved the canoe out into the sluggish stream, and jumped in after her; then with a silent prayer of thanksgiving they drifted silently down toward the great river.

11

Battle

INTO the camp of the sleeping Utengas dropped Muzimo and The Spirit of Nyamwegi an hour after midnight. No sentry had seen them pass, a fact which did not at all surprise the sentries, who knew that spirits pass through the forest unseen at all times if they choose to do so.

Orando, being a good soldier, had just made the rounds of his sentry posts and was still awake when Muzimo located him. "What news have you brought me, O Muzimo?" demanded the son of Lobongo. "What word of the enemy?"

"We have been to his village," replied Muzimo, "The Spirit of Nyamwegi, Lupingu, and I."

"And where is Lupingu?"

"He remained there after carrying a message to Gato Mgungu."

"You gave the traitor his liberty!" exclaimed Orando.

"It will do him little good. He was dead when he entered the village of Gato Mgungu."

"How then could he carry a message to the chief?'

"He carried a message of terror that the Leopard Men understood. He told them that traitors do not go unpunished. He told them that the power of Orando is great."

"And what did the Leopard Men do?"

"They fled to their temple to consult the high priest and the Leopard God. We followed them there; but they did not learn much from the high priest or the Leopard God, for they all got very drunk upon beer—all except the Leopard, and he cannot talk when the high priest cannot talk. I came to tell you that their village is now almost deserted except for the women, the children, and a few warriors. This would be a good time to attack it, or to lie in ambush near it awaiting the return of the warriors from the temple. They will be sick, and men do not fight so well when they are sick."

"Now is a good time," agreed Orando, clapping his palms together to awaken the sleepers near him.

"In the temple of the Leopard God I saw one whom you know well," remarked Muzimo as the sleepy headmen aroused their warriors. "He is a priest of the Leopard God."

"I know no Leopard Men," replied Orando.

"You knew Lupingu, although you did not know that he was a Leopard Man," Muzimo reminded him; "and you know Sobito. It was he whom I saw behind the mask of a priest. He is a Leopard Man."

Orando was silent for a moment. "You are sure?" he asked.

"Yes."

"When he went to consult the spirits and the demons, and was gone from the village of Tumbai for many days, he was with the Leopard Men instead," said Orando. "Sobito is a traitor. He shall die."

"Yes," agreed Muzimo, "Sobito shall die. He should have been killed long ago."

Along the winding forest trail Muzimo guided the warriors of Orando toward the village of Gato Mgungu. They moved as rapidly as the darkness and the narrow trail would permit, and at length he halted them at the edge of the field of manioc that lies between the forest and the village. After that they crept silently down toward the river when Muzimo had ascertained that the Leopard Men had not returned from the temple. There they waited, hiding among the bushes that grew on either side of the landing place, while Muzimo departed to scout down the river.

He was gone but a short time when he returned with word that he had counted twenty-nine canoes paddling up stream toward the village. "Though thirty canoes went down river to the temple," he explained to Orando, "these must be the Leopard Men returning."

Orando crept silently among his warriors, issuing instructions, exhorting them to bravery. The canoes were approaching. They could hear the paddles now, dipping, dipping, dipping. The Utengas waited—tensed, eager. The first canoe touched the bank and its warriors leaped out. Before they had drawn their heavy craft out on the shore the second

canoe shot in. Still the Utengas awaited the sign of their
leader. Now the canoes were grounding in rapid succession.
A line of warriors was stringing out toward the village gate.
Twenty canoes had been drawn up on the shore when
Orando gave the signal, a savage battle cry that was taken
up by ninety howling warriors as spears and arrows show-
ered into the ranks of the Leopard Men.

The charging Utengas broke through the straggling line
of the enemy. The Leopard Men, taken wholly by surprise, thought only of flight. Those who had been cut off
at the river sought to launch their canoes and escape; those
who had not yet landed turned their craft down stream. The
remainder fled toward the village, closely pursued by the
Utengas. At the closed gates, which the defenders feared to
open, the fighting was fierce; at the river it was little better
than a slaughter as the warriors of Orando cut down the terrified Leopard Men struggling to launch their canoes.

When it was too late the warriors left to guard the village
opened the gates with the intention of making a sortie against
the Utengas. Already the last of their companions had been
killed or had fled, and when the gates swung open a howling band of Utengas swarmed through.

The victory was complete. No living soul was left within
the palisaded village of Gato Mgungu when the blood-
spattered warriors of Orando put the torch to its thatched
huts.

From down the river the escaping Leopard Men saw the
light of the flames billowing upward above the trees that
lined the bank, saw their reflection on the surface of the
broad river behind them, and knew the proportions of the
defeat that had overwhelmed them. Gato Mgungu, squatting
in the bottom of his canoe, saw the flames from his burning
village, saw in them, perhaps the waning of his savage,
ruthless power. Bobolo saw them and, reading the same story,
knew that Gato Mgungu need no longer be feared. Of all
that band of fleeing warriors Bobolo was the least depressed.

By the light of the burning village Orando took stock of
his losses, mustering his men and searching out the dead
and wounded. From a tree beyond the manioc field a little
monkey screamed and chattered. It was The Spirit of Nyamwegi calling to Muzimo, but Muzimo did not answer.

Among the dead and wounded Orando found him like mortal clay stretched out upon his back from a blow upon the head.

The son of the chief was surprised and grieved; his followers were shocked. They had been certain that Muzimo was of the spirit world and therefore immune from death. Suddenly they realized that they had won the battle without his aid. He was a fraud. Filled with blood lust, they would have vented their chagrin through spear thrusts into his lifeless body; but Orando stopped them.

"Spirits do not always remain in the same form," he reminded them. "Perhaps he has entered another body or, unseen, is watching us from above. If that is so he will avenge any harm that you do this body he has quitted." In the light of their knowledge this seemed quite possible to the Utengas; so they desisted from their proposed mutilation and viewed the body with renewed awe. "Furthermore," continued Orando, "man or ghost, he was loyal to me; and those of you who saw him fight know that he fought bravely and well."

"That is so," agreed a warrior.

"Tarzan! Tarzan!" shrieked The Spirit of Nyamwegi from the tree at the edge of the manioc field. "Tarzan of the Apes, Nkima is afraid!"

The white man paddled the stolen canoe down the sluggish stream toward the great river depending upon the strong current for aid to carry him and the girl to safety. Kali Bwana sat silent in the bottom of the craft. She had torn the barbaric headdress from her brow and the horrid necklace of human teeth from her throat, but she retained the bracelets and anklets, although why it might have been difficult for her to explain. Perhaps it was because, regardless of her plight and all that she had passed through, she was still a woman—a beautiful woman. That is something which one does not easily forget.

Old Timer felt amost certain of success. The Leopard Men who had preceded him down the stream must have been returning to their village; there was no reason to expect that they would return immediately. There was no canoe at the temple; therefore there could be no pursuit, for Bobolo had assured him that there were no trails through the forest leading to the temple of the Leopard Men. He was almost jubilant as the canoe moved slowly into the mouth of the stream and he saw the dark current of the river stretching before him.

Then he heard the splash of paddles, and his heart seemed to leap into his throat. Throwing every ounce of his muscle and weight into the effort, he turned the prow of the canoe toward the right bank, hoping to hide in the dense shadows, undiscovered, until the other craft had passed. It was very dark, so dark that he had reason to believe that his plan would succeed.

Suddenly the oncoming canoe loomed out of the darkness. It was only a darker blur against the darkness of the night. Old Timer held his breath. The girl crouched low behind a gunwale lest her blonde hair and white skin might be visible to the occupants of the other boat even in the darkness that engulfed all other objects. The canoe passed on up the stream.

The broad river lay just ahead now; there, there would be less danger of detection. Old Timer dipped his paddle and started the canoe again upon its interrupted voyage. As the current caught it, it moved more rapidly. They were out upon the river! A dark object loomed ahead of them. It seemed to rise up out of the water directly in front of their craft. Old Timer plied his paddle in an effort to alter the course of the canoe, but too late. There was a jarring thud as it struck the object in its path, which the man had already recognized as a canoe filled with warriors.

Almost simultaneously another canoe pulled up beside him. There was a babel of angry questions and commands. Old Timer recognized the voice of Bobolo. Warriors leaped into the canoe and seized him, fists struck him, powerful fingers dragged him down. He was overpowered and bound.

Again he heard the voice of Bobolo. "Hurry! We are being pursued. The Utengas are coming!"

Brawny hands grasped the paddles. Old Timer felt the canoe shoot forward, and a moment later it was being driven frantically up the smaller river toward the temple. The heart of the white man went cold with dread. He had had the girl upon the threshold of escape. Such an opportunity would never come again. Now she was doomed. He did not think of his own fate. He thought only of the girl. He searched through the darkness with his eyes, but he could not find her; then he spoke to her. He wanted to comfort her. A new emotion had suddenly taken possession of him. He thought only of her safety and comfort. He did not think of himself at all.

He called again, but she did not answer. "Be quiet!" growled a warrior near him.

"Where is the girl?" demanded the white man.

"Be quiet," insisted the warrior. "There is no girl here."

As the canoe in which Bobolo rode swung alongside that in which the girl and the white man were attempting to escape, it had brought the chief close to the former, so close that even in the darkness of the night he had seen her white skin and her blonde hair. Instantly he had recognized his opportunity and seized it. Reaching over the gunwales of the two canoes he had dragged her into his own; then he had voiced the false alarm that he knew would send the other canoes off in a panic.

The warriors with him were all his own men. His village lay on the left bank of the river farther down. A low-voiced command sent the canoe out into the main current of the river, and willing hands sped it upon its course.

The girl, who had passed through so much, who had seen escape almost assured, was stunned by the sudden turn of events that had robbed her of the only creature to whom she might look for aid and crushed hope from her breast.

To Old Timer, bound and helpless, the return journey to the temple was only a dull agony of vain regrets. It made little difference to him now what they did to him. He knew that they would kill him. He hoped that the end would come speedily, but he knew enough about the methods of cannibals to be almost certain that death would be slow and horrible.

As they dragged him into the temple he saw the floor strewn with the bodies of the drunken priests and priestesses. The noise of the entrance aroused Imigeg, the high priest. He rubbed his eyes sleepily and then rose unsteadily to his feet.

"What has happened?" he demanded.

Gato Mgungu strode into the room at the moment, his canoe having followed closely upon that in which Old Timer had been brought back. "Enough has happened," he snapped. "While you were all drunk this white man escaped. The

Utengas have killed my warriors and burned my village. What is the matter with your medicine, Imigeg? It is no good."

The high priest looked about him, a dazed expression in his watery eyes. "Where is the white priestess?" he cried. "Did she escape?"

"I saw only the white man," replied Gato Mgungu.

"The white priestess was there, too," volunteered a warrior. "Bobolo took her into his canoe."

"Then she should be along soon," offered Gato Mgungu. "Bobolo's canoe cannot have been far behind mine."

"She shall not escape again," said Imigeg, "nor shall the man. Bind him well, and put him in the small room at the rear of the temple."

"Kill him!" cried Gato Mgungu. "Then he cannot run away again."

"We shall kill him later," replied Imigeg, who had not relished Gato Mgungu's irreverent tone or his carping criticism and desired to reassert his authority.

"Kill him now," insisted the chief, "or he will get away from you again; and if he does, the white men will come with their soldiers and kill you and burn the temple."

"I am high priest," replied Imigeg haughtily. "I take orders from no one but the Leopard God. I shall question him. What he says I shall do." He turned toward the sleeping leopard and prodded it with a sharp-pointed pole. The great cat leaped to its feet, its face convulsed by a horrid snarl. "The white man escaped," explained Imigeg to the leopard. "He has been captured again. Shall he die tonight?"

"No," replied the leopard. "Tie him securely and place him in the small room at the rear of the temple; I am not hungry."

"Gato Mgungu says to kill him now," continued Imigeg.

"Tell Gato Mgungu that I speak only through Imigeg, the high priest. I do not speak through Gato Mgungu. Because Gato Mgungu had evil in his mind I have caused his warriors to be slain and his village to be destroyed. If he thinks evil again he shall be destroyed that the children of the Leopard God may eat. I have spoken."

"The Leopard God has spoken," said Imigeg.

Gato Mgungu was deeply impressed and thoroughly frightened. "Shall I take the prisoner to the back of the temple and see that he is safely bound?" he asked.

"Yes," replied Imigeg, "take him, and see to it that you bind him so that he cannot escape."

12

The Sacrifice

TARZAN! Tarzan!" shrieked The Spirit of Nyamwegi from the tree at the edge of the manioc field. "Tarzan of the Apes, Nkima is afraid!"

The white giant lying upon the ground opened his eyes and looked about him. He saw Orando and many warriors gathered about. A puzzled expression overspread his countenance. Suddenly he leaped to his feet.

"Nkima! Nkima!" he called in the language of the great apes. "Where are you, Nkima? Tarzan is here!"

The little monkey leaped from the tree and came bounding across the field of manioc. With a glad cry he leaped to the shoulder of the white man and throwing his arms about the bronzed neck pressed his cheek close to that of his master; and there he clung, whimpering with joy.

"You see," announced Orando to his fellows, "Muzimo is not dead."

The white man turned to Orando. "I am not Muzimo," he said; "I am Tarzan of the Apes." He touched the monkey. "This is not The Spirit of Nyamwegi; it is Nkima. Now I remember everything. For a long time I have been trying to remember but until now I could not—not since the tree fell upon me."

There was none among them who had not heard of Tarzan of the Apes. He was a legend of the forest and the jungle that had reached to their far country. Like the spirits and the demons which they never saw, they had never expected to see him. Perhaps Orando was a little disappointed, yet, on the whole, it was a relief to all of them to discover that this was a man of flesh and blood, motivated by the same forces that actuated them, subject to the same laws of Nature that controlled them. It had always been a bit disconcerting never to be sure in what strange form the ancestral spirit of Orando might choose to appear, nor to know of a certainty that he would turn suddenly from a benign to a malign force; and so they accepted him in his new rôle, but with this difference: where formerly he had seemed the creature of Orando, doing his bidding as a servant does the bidding of his master, now he seemed suddenly clothed in the dignity of power and authority. The change was so subtly wrought that it was scarcely apparent and was due, doubtless, to the psychological effect of the reawakened mentality of the white man over that of his black companions.

They made camp beside the river near the ruins of Gato Mgungu's village, for there were fields of manioc and plantain that, with the captured goats and chickens of the Leopard Men, insured full bellies after the lean fare of the days of marching and fighting.

During the long day Tarzan's mind was occupied with many thoughts. He had recalled now why he had come into this country, and he marvelled at the coincidence of later events that had guided his footsteps along the very paths that he had intended trodding before accident had robbed him of the memory of his purpose. He knew now that depredations by Leopard Men from a far country had caused him to get forth upon a lonely reconnaissance with only the thought of locating their more or less fabled stronghold and temple. That he should be successful in both finding these and reducing one of them was gratifying in the extreme, and he felt thankful now for the accident that had been responsible for the results.

His mind was still not entirely clear on certain details; but these were returning gradually, and as evening fell and the evening meal was under way he suddenly recalled the white man and the white girl whom he had seen in the temple of the Leopard God. He spoke to Orando about them, but he knew nothing of them.

"If they were in the temple they probably have been killed he knew nothing of them.

Tarzan sat immersed in thought for a long time. He did not know these people, yet he felt a certain obligation to them because they were of his race. Finally he arose and called Nkima, who was munching on a plantain that a warrior was sharing with him.

"Where are you going?" asked Orando.

"To the temple of the Leopard God," replied Tarzan.

*   *   *   *   *   *   *

Old Timer had lain all day securely bound and without food or water. Occasionally a priest or a priestess had looked in to see that he had not escaped or loosened his bonds, but otherwise he had been left alone. The inmates of the temple had stirred but little during the day, most of them being engaged in sleeping off the effects of the previous night's debauch; but with the coming of night the prisoner heard increased evidence of activity. There were sounds of chanting from the temple chamber, and above the other noises the shrill voice of the high priest and the growls of the leopard. His thoughts during those long hours were often of the girl. He had heard the warrior tell Imigeg that Bobolo had captured her, and supposed that she was again being forced to play her part on the dais with the Leopard God. At least he might see her again (that would be something), but hope that he might rescue her had ebbed so low that it might no longer be called hope.

He was trying to reason against his better judgment that having once escaped from the temple they could do so again, when a priest entered the room, bearing a torch. He was an evil-appearing old fellow, whose painted face accentuated the savagery of the visage. He was Sobito, the witch-doctor of Tumbai. Stooping, he commenced to untie the cords that secured the white man's ankles.

"What are they going to do to me?" demanded Old Timer.

A malevolent grin bared Sobito's yellow fangs. "What do you suppose, white man?"

Old Timer shrugged. "Kill me, I suppose."

"Not too quickly," explained Sobito. "The flesh of those who die slowly and in pain is tender."

"You old devil!" exclaimed the prisoner.

Sobito licked his lips. He delighted in inflicting torture

either physical or mental. Here was an opportunity he could not forego. "First your arms and legs will be broken," he explained; "then you will be placed upright in a hole in the swamp and fastened so that you cannot get your mouth or nose beneath the surface and drown yourself. You will be left there three days, by which time your flesh will be tender." He paused.

"And then?" asked the white. His voice was steady. He had determined that he would not give them the added satisfaction of witnessing his mental anguish, and when the time came that he must suffer physically he prayed that he might have the strength to endure the ordeal in a manner that would reflect credit upon his race. Three days! God, what a fate to anticipate!

"And then?" repeated Sobito. "Then you will be carried into the temple, and the children of the Leopard God will tear you to pieces with their steel claws. Look!" He exhibited the long, curved weapons which dangled from the ends of the loose leopard skin sleeves of his garment.

"After which you will eat me, eh?"

"Yes."

"I hope you choke."

Sobito had at last untied the knots that had secured the bonds about the white man's ankles. He gave him a kick and told him to rise.

"Are you going to kill and eat the white girl, too?" demanded Old Timer.

"She is not here. Bobolo has stolen her. Because you helped her to escape, your suffering shall be greater. I have already suggested to Imigeg that he remove your eyeballs after your arms and legs are broken. I forgot to tell you that we shall break each of them in three or four places.

"Your memory is failing," commented Old Timer, "but I hope that you have not forgotten anything else."

Sobito grunted. "Come with me," he commanded, and led the white man through the dark corridor to the great chamber where the Leopard Men were gathered.

At sight of the prisoner a savage cry broke from a hundred and fifty throats, the leopard growled, the high priest danced upon the upper dais, the hideous priestesses screamed and leaped forward as though bent upon tearing the white man to pieces. Sobito pushed the prisoner to the summit of the lower dais and dragged him before the high priest. "Here is the sacrifice!" he screamed.

"Here is the sacrifice!" cried Imigeg, addressing the Leopard God. "What are your commands, O father of the leopard children?"

The bristling muzzle of the great beast wrinkled into a snarl as Imigeg prodded him with his sharp pole, and from the growling throat the answer seemed to come. "Let him be broken, and on the third night let there be a feast!"

"And what of Bobolo and the white priestess?" demanded Imigeg.

"Send warriors to fetch them to the temple that Bobolo may be broken for another feast. The white girl I give to Imigeg, the high priest. When he tires of her we shall feast again."

"It is the word of the Leopard God," cried Imigeg. "As he commands, it shall be done."

"Let the white man be broken," growled the leopard, "and on the third night let my children return that each may be made wise by eating the flesh of a white man. When you have eaten of it the white man's weapons can no longer harm you. Let the white man be broken!"

"Let the white man be broken!" shrieked Imigeg.

Instantly a half dozen priests leaped forward and seized the prisoner, throwing him heavily to the clay floor of the dais, and here they pinioned him, stretching his arms and legs far apart, while four priestesses armed with heavy clubs rushed forward. A drum commenced to boom somewhere in the temple, weirdly, beating a cadence to which the priestesses danced about the prostrate form of their victim.

Now one rushed in and flourished her club above the prisoner; but a priest pretended to protect him, and the woman danced out again to join her companions in the mad whirl of the dance. Again and again was this repeated, but each succeeding time the priests seemed to have greater difficulty in repulsing the maddened women.

That it was all acting (part of a savage ceremony) the white man realized almost from the first, but what it was supposed to portray he could not imagine. If they had hoped to wring some evidence of fear from him, they failed. Lying upon his back, he watched them with no more apparent concern than an ordinary dance might have elicited.

Perhaps it was because of his seeming indifference that they dragged the dance out to great lengths, that they howled the louder, and that the savagery of their gestures and their screams beggared description; but the end, he knew, was inevitable. The fate that Sobito had pictured had been no mere idle threat. Old Timer had long since heard that among some cannibal tribes this method of preparing human flesh was the rule rather than the exception. The horror of it, like a loathsome rat, gnawed at the foundations of the citadel of his reason. He sought to keep his mind from contemplation of it, lest he go mad.

The warriors, aroused to frenzy by the dancing and the drum, urged the priestesses on. They were impatient for the climax of the cruel spectacle. The high priest, master showman, sensed the temper of his audience. He made a signal, and the drumming ceased. The dancing stopped. The audience went suddenly quiet. Silence even more terrifying than the din which had preceded it enveloped the chamber. It was then that the priestesses, with raised clubs, crept steathily toward their helpless victim.

13

Down River

KALI BWANA crouched in the bottom of the canoe; she heard the rhythmic dip of the paddles as powerful arms sent the craft swiftly down stream with the current. She knew that they were out on the bosom of the large river, that they were not returning to the temple nor up stream to the village of Gato Mgungu. Where, then, to what new trials was fate consigning her?

Bobolo leaned toward her and - whispered, "Do not be afraid. I am taking you away from the Leopard Men."

She understood just enough of the tribal dialect that he

employed to catch the sense of what he had said. "Who are you?" she asked.

"I am Bobolo, the chief," he replied.

Instantly she recalled that the white man had hoped for aid from this man, for which he was to pay him in ivory. Her hopes rose. Now she could purchase safety for both of them. "Is the white man in the canoe?" she asked.

"No," replied Bobolo.

"You promised to save him," she reminded him.

"I could save but one," replied Bobolo.

"Where are you taking me?"

"To my village. There you will be safe. Nothing can harm you."

"Then you will take me on down river to my own people?" she asked.

"Maybe so after a while," he answered. "There is no hurry. You stay with Bobolo. He will be good to you, for Bobolo is a very big chief with many huts and many warriors. You shall have lots of food; lots of slaves; no work."

The girl shuddered, for she knew the import of his words. "No!" she cried. "Oh, please let me go. The white man said that you were his friend. He will pay you; I will pay you."

"He will never pay," replied Bobolo. "If he is not already dead, he will be in a few days."

"But I can pay," she pleaded. "Whatever you ask I will pay you if you will deliver me safely to my own people."

"I do not want pay," growled Bobolo; "I want you."

She saw that her situation was without hope. In all this hideous land the only person who knew of her danger and might have helped her was either dead or about to die, and she could not help herself. But there *was* a way out! The idea flashed suddenly to her mind. *The river!*

She must not permit herself to dwell too long upon the idea—upon the cold, dark waters, upon the crocodiles, lest her strength fail her. She must act instantly, without thought. She leaped to her feet, but Bobolo was too close. Upon the instant he guessed her intention and seized her, throwing her roughly to the bottom of the canoe. He was very angry and struck her heavily across the face; then he bound her, securing her wrists and her ankles.

"You will not try that again," he growled at her.

"I shall find some other way then," she replied defiantly.
"You shall not have me. It will be better for you to accept my
offer, as otherwise you shall have neither me nor the pay."

"Be quiet, woman," commanded Bobo Lo; "I have heard
enough," and he struck her again.

For four hours the canoe sped swiftly onward; the ebon
paddlers, moving in perfect rhythm, seemed tireless. The
sun had risen, but from her prone position in the bottom of
the craft the girl saw nothing but the swaying bodies
of the paddlers nearest her, the degraded face of Bobolo,
and the brazen sky above.

At last she heard the sound of voices shouting from the
shore. There were answering shouts from the crew of the
canoe, and a moment later she felt its prow touch the bank.
Then Bobolo removed the bonds from her wrists and ankles
and helped her to her feet. Before her, on the river bank,
were hundreds of savages; men, women, and children. Beyond
them was a village of grass-thatched, beehive huts, surrounded
by a palisade of poles bound together with lianas.

When the eyes of the villagers alighted upon the white
prisoner there was a volley of shouts and questions; and as
she stepped ashore she was surrounded by a score of curious
savages, among whom the women were the most unfriendly.
She was struck and spat upon by them; and more serious harm
would have been done her had not Bobolo stalked among them,
striking right and left with the shaft of his spear.

Trailed by half the village, she was led into the compound
to the hut of the chief, a much larger structure than any
of the others, flanked by several two-room huts, all of which
were enclosed by a low palisade. Here dwelt the chief and
his harem with their slaves. At the entrance to the chief's
compound the rabble halted, and Kali Bwana and Bobolo
entered alone. Instantly the girl was surrounded again by
angry women, the wives of Bobolo. There were fully a dozen
of them; and they ranged in age from a child of fourteen
to an ancient, toothless hag, who, despite the infirmities of
age, appeared to dominate the others.

Again Bobolo had recourse to his spear to save his captive
from serious harm. He belabored the most persistent of them

unmercifully until they fell back out of reach of his weapon, and then he turned to the old woman.

"Ubooga," he said, addressing her, "this is my new wife. I place her in your care. See that no harm comes to her. Give her two women-slaves. I shall send men-slaves to build a hut for her close to mine."

"You are a fool," cried Ubooga. "'She is white. The women will not let her live in peace, if they let her live at all, nor will they let you live in peace until she is dead or you get rid of her. You were a fool to bring her, but then you were always a fool."

"Hold your tongue, old woman!" cried Bobolo. "I am chief. If the women molest her I will kill them—and you, too," he added.

"Perhaps you will kill the others," screamed the old hag, "but you will not kill me. I will scratch out your eyes and eat your heart. You are the son of a pig. Your mother was a jackal. You, a chief! You would have been the slave of a slave had it not been for me. Who are you! Your own mother did not know who your father was. "You—" But Bobolo had fled.

With her hands on her hips the old termagant turned toward Kali Bwana and surveyed her, appraising her from head to feet. She noted the fine leopard skin garment and the wealth of bracelets and anklets. "Come, you!" she screamed and seized the girl by the hair.

It was the last straw. Far better to die now than to prolong the agony through brutal abuse and bitter insult. Kali Bwana swung a blow to the side of Ubooga's head that sent her reeling. The other women broke into loud laughter. The girl expected that the old woman would fall upon her and kill her, but she did nothing of the kind. Instead she stood looking at her; her lower jaw dropped, her eyes wide in astonishment. For a moment she stood thus, and then she appeared to notice the laughter and taunts of the other women for the first time. With a maniacal scream she seized a stick and charged them. They scattered - like frightened rabbits seeking their burrows, but not before the stick had fallen heavily upon a couple of them as Ubooga, screaming curses, threatened them with the anger of Bobolo.

When she returned to the white girl she merely nodded her head in the direction of one of the huts and said "Come" again, but this time in a less peremptory tone; in other ways, too, her attitude seemed changed and far less unfriendly, or perhaps it would be better to say less threatening. That the terrible old woman could be friendly to any one seemed wholly beyond the range of possibility.

Having installed the girl in her own hut, under the protection of two women slaves, Ubooga hobbled to the main entrance of the chief's compound, possibly in the hope of catching a glimpse of Bobolo, concerning whom she had left a number of things unsaid; but Bobolo was nowhere to be seen. There was, however, a warrior who had returned with the chief from up river squatting before a nearby hut while his wife prepared food for him.

Ubooga, being a privileged character and thus permitted to leave the sacred precincts of the harem crossed over and squatted down near the warrior.

"Who is the white girl?" demanded the old woman.

The warrior was a very stupid fellow, and the fact that he had recently been very drunk and had had no sleep for two nights lent him no greater acumen. Furthermore, he was terribly afraid of Ubooga, as who was not? He looked up dully out of red-rimmed, bloodshot eyes.

"She is the new white priestess of the Leopard God," he said.

"Where did Bobolo get her?" persisted Ubooga.

"We had come from the battle at Gato Mgungu's village, where we were defeated, and were on our way with Gato Mgungu back to the temp—" He stopped suddenly. "I don't know where Bobolo got her," he ended sullenly.

A wicked, toothless grin wrinkled Ubooga's unlovely features. "I thought so," she cackled enigmatically and, rising, hobbled back to the chief's compound.

The wife of the warrior looked at him with disgust. "So you are a Leopard Man!" she whispered accusingly.

"It is a lie," he cried; "I said nothing of the sort."

"You did," contradicted his wife, "and you told Ubooga that Bobolo is a Leopard Man. This will not be well for Bobolo or for you."

"Women who talk too much sometimes have their tongues cut out," he reminded her.

"It is you who have talked too much," she retorted. "I have said nothing. I shall say nothing. Do you think that I want the village to know that my man is a Leopard Man?" There was deep disgust in her tone.

The order of Leopard Men is a secret order. There are few villages and no entire tribes composed wholly of Leopard Men, who are looked upon with disgust and horror by all who are not members of the feared order. Their rites and practices are viewed with contempt by even the most degraded of tribes, and to be proved a Leopard Man is equivalent to the passing of a sentence of exile or death in practically any community.

Ubooga nursed the knowledge she had gained, metaphorically cuddling it to her breast. Squatting down before her hut, she mumbled to herself; and the other women of the harem who saw her were frightened, for they saw that Ubooga smiled, and when Ubooga smiled they knew that something unpleasant was going to happen to some one. When Bobolo entered the compound they saw that she smiled more broadly, and they were relieved, knowing that it was Bobolo and not they who was to be the victim.

"Where is the white girl?" demanded Bobolo as he halted before Ubooga. "Has any harm befallen her?"

"Your priestess is quite safe, Leopard Man," hissed Ubooga, but in a voice so low that only Bobolo might hear.

"What do you mean, you old she-devil?" Bobolo's face turned a livid blue from rage.

"For a long time I have suspected it," cackled Ubooga. "Now I know it."

Bobolo seized his knife and grasped the woman by the hair, dragging her across one knee. "You said I did not dare to kill you," he growled.

"Nor do you. Listen. I have told another, who will say nothing unless I command it, or unless I die. If I die the whole village will know it, and you will be torn to pieces. Now kill me, if you dare!"

Bobolo let her fall to the ground. He did not know that Ubooga had lied to him, that she had told no one. He may have surmised as much; but he dared not take the chance, for he knew that Ubooga was right. His people would tear him to pieces should they discover he was a Leopard Man, nor would the other culprits in the tribe dare come to his defense. To divert suspicion from themselves they would join his executioners. Bobolo was very much worried.

"Who told you?" he demanded. "It is a lie, whoever told you."

"The girl is high priestess of the Leopard God," taunted Ubooga. "After you left the village of Gato Mgungu, following the fight in which you were defeated, you returned to the temple with Gato Mgungu who all men know is the chief of the Leopard Men. There you got the girl."

"It is a lie. I stole her from the Leopard Men. I am no Leopard Man."

"Then return her to the Leopard Men, and I will say nothing about the matter. I will tell no one that you are such a good friend of Gato Mgungu that you fight with him against his enemies, for then everyone will know that you must be a Leopard Man."

"It is a lie," repeated Bobolo, who could think of nothing else to say.

"Lie or no lie, will you get rid of her?"

"Very well," said Bobolo; "in a few days."

"Today," demanded Ubooga. "Today, or I will kill her tonight."

"Today," assented Bobolo. He turned away.

"Where are you going?"

"To get someone to take her back where the Leopard Men can find her."

"Why don't you kill her?"

"The Leopard Men would kill me if I did. They would kill many of my people. First of all they would kill my women if I killed theirs."

"Go and get someone to take her away," said Ubooga, "but see that there is no trickery, you son of a wart hog, you pig, you——"

Bobolo heard no more. He had fled into the village. He was very angry, but he was more afraid. He knew that what Ubooga had said was true; but, on the other hand, his passion still ran high for the white girl. He must try to find some means to preserve her for himself; in case he failed, however, there were other uses to which she could be put. Such were the thoughts which occupied his mind as he walked the length of the village street toward the hut of his old crony Kapopa, the witch doctor, upon more than one occasion a valuable ally.

He found the old man engaged with a customer who desired a charm that would kill the mother of one of his wives, for which Kapopa had demanded three goats—in advance. There was considerable haggling, the customer insisting that his mother-in-law was not worth one goat, alive, which, he argued, would reduce her value when dead to not more than a single chicken; but Kapopa was obdurate, and finally the man departed to give the matter further thought.

Bobolo plunged immediately into the matter that had brought him to the witch-doctor. "Kapopa knows," he commenced, "that when I returned from up the river I brought a white wife with me."

Kapopa nodded. "Who in the village does not?"

"Already she has brought me much trouble," continued Bobolo.

"And you wish to be rid of her."

"I do not. It is Ubooga who wishes to rid me of her."

"You wish a charm to kill Ubooga?"

"I have already paid you for three such charms," Bobolo reminded him, "and Ubooga still lives. I do not wish another. Your medicine is not so strong as Ubooga."

"What do you wish?"

"I will tell you. Because the white girl is a priestess of the Leopard God, Ubooga says that I must be a Leopard Man, but that is a lie. I stole her from the Leopard Men. Everyone knows that I am not a Leopard Man."

"Of course," assented Kapopa.

"But Ubooga says that she will tell everyone that I am a Leopard Man if I do not kill the girl or send her away. What can I do?"

Kapopa sat in silence for a moment; then he rummaged in a bag that lay beside him. Bobolo fidgeted. He knew that when Kapopa rummaged in that bag it was always expensive. Finally the witch-doctor drew forth a little bundle wrapped in dirty cloth. Very carefully he untied the strings and spread the cloth upon the ground, revealing its contents, a few short twigs and a figurine carved from bone. Kapopa set the figurine in an upright position facing him, shook the twigs between his two palms, and cast them before the idol. He examined the position of the twigs carefully, scratched his head for a moment, then gathered them up, cast them again. Once more he studied the situation in silence. Presently he looked up.

"I now have a plan," he announced.

"How much will it cost?" demanded Bobolo. "Tell me that first."

"You have a daughter," said Kapopa.

"I have many of them," rejoined Bobolo.

"I do not want them all."

"You may have your choice if you will tell me how I may keep the white girl without Ubooga knowing it."

"It can be done," announced Kapopa. "In the village of the little men there is no witch-doctor. For a long time they have been coming to Kapopa for their medicine. They will do whatever Kapopa asks."

"I do not understand," said Bobolo.

"The village of the little men is not far from the village of Bobolo. We shall take the white girl there. For a small payment of meal and a few fish at times they will keep her there for Bobolo until Ubooga dies. Some day she must die. Already she has lived far too long. In the meantime Bobolo can visit his wife in the village of the little men."

"You can arrange this with the little men?"

"Yes. I shall go with you and the white girl, and I will arrange everything."

"Good," exclaimed Bobolo. "We will start now; when we return you may go to the harem of Bobolo and select any of his daughters that you choose."

Kapopa wrapped up the twigs and the idol and replaced them in his pouch; then he got his spear and shield. "Fetch the white girl," he said.

14

The Return of Sobito

THE wavering light of the smoky torches illuminated the interior of the temple of the Leopard God, revealing the barbaric, savage drama being enacted there; but outside it was very dark, so dark that the figure of a man moving swiftly along the river bank might scarcely have been seen at a distance of fifty feet. He stepped quickly and silently among the canoes of the Leopard Men, pushing them out into the current of the stream. When all had been turned adrift save one, he dragged that up the river and partially beached it opposite the rear of the temple; then he ran toward the building, scaled one of the piles to the verandah, and a moment later paused upon the tiebeam just beneath the overhanging roof at the front of the building, where, through an opening, he could look down upon the tragic scene within.

He had been there a few moments before, just long enough to see and realize the precarious position of the white prisoner. Instantly his plan had been formed, and he had dropped swiftly to the river bank to put a part of it into immediate execution. Now that he was back he realized that a few seconds later he would have been too late. A sudden silence had fallen upon the chamber below. The priestesses of the Leopard God were sneaking stealthily toward their prostrate victim. No longer did the lesser priests make the purely histrionic pretense of protection. The end had come.

Through the aperture and into the interior of the temple swung Tarzan of the Apes. From tiebeam to tiebeam he leaped, silent as the smoke rising from the torches below. He saw that the priestesses were almost upon the white prisoner, that, swift as he was, he might not be able to reach the man's side in time. It was a bold, mad scheme that had formed in the active brain of the ape-man, and one that depended for success largely upon its boldness. Now it seemed that it was foredoomed to failure even before it could be put into execution.

The sudden silence, following the din of drums and yells and dancing feet, startled the tense nerves of the pinioned prisoner. He turned his eyes from side to side and saw the priestesses creeping toward him. Something told him that the final, hideous horror was upon him now. He steeled himself to meet the agony of it, lest his tormentors should have the added gratification of witnessing the visible effects of his suffering. Something inherent, something racial rebelled at the thought of showing fear or agony before these creatures of an inferior race.

The priestesses were almost upon him when a voice high

above them broke the deathly silence. "Sobito! Sobito! Sobito!" it boomed in hollow accents from the rafters of the
temple. "I am the *muzimo* of Orando, the friend of Nyamwegi. I have come for you. With The Spirit of Nyamwegi,
I have come for you!"

Simultaneously a giant white man, naked but for a loin
cloth, ran down one of the temple pillars like an agile monkey
and leaped to the lower dais. The startling interruption momentarily paralyzed the natives, partially from astonishment
and partially from fear. Sobito was speechless. His knees
trembled beneath him; then, recovering himself, he fled
screaming from the dais to the protection of the concourse of
warriors on the temple floor.

Old Time, no less astonished than the Negroes, looked
with amazement upon the scene. He expected to see the
strange white man pursue Sobito, but he did nothing of
the sort. Instead, he turned directly toward the prisoner.

"Be ready to follow me," commanded the stranger. "I
shall go out through the rear of the temple." He spoke in
low tones and in English; then, as swiftly, he changed to the
dialect of the district. "Capture Sobito and bring him to me,"
he shouted to the warriors below the dais. "Until you fetch
him I shall hold this white man as hostage."

Before there could be either reply or opposition, he leaped
to the side of Old Timer, hurled the terrified priests from
him, and seizing him by the hand jerked him to his feet.
He spoke no further word but turned and ran swiftly across
the lower dais, leaped to the higher one where Imigeg
shrank aside as they passed, and disappeared from the
sight of the Leopard Men through the doorway at its rear.
There he paused for a moment and stopped Old Timer.

"Where is the white girl?" he demanded. "We must take
her with us."

"She is not here," replied old Timer; "a chief stole her
and, I imagine, took her down river to his village."

"This way, then," directed Tarzan, darting into a doorway on their left.

A moment later they were on the verandah, from which
they gained the ground by way of one of the piles that supported the building; then the ape-man ran quickly toward the

river, followed closely by Old Timer. At the edge of the river Tarzan stopped beside a canoe.

"Get into this," he directed; "it is the only one left here. They cannot follow you. When you reach the main river you will have such a start that they cannot overtake you."

"Aren't you coming with me?"

"No," he replied and started to shove the craft out into the stream. "Do you know the name of the chief who stole the girl?" he asked.

"It was Bobolo."

Tarzan pushed the canoe away from the bank.

"I can't thank you, old man," said Old Timer; "there just aren't the right words in the English language."

The silent figure on the river bank made no reply, and a moment later, as the current caught the canoe, it was swallowed up in the darkness. Then Old Timer seized a paddle and sought to accelerate the speed of the craft, that he might escape as quickly as possible from this silent river of mystery and death.

The canoe had scarcely disappeared in the darkness when Tarzan of the Apes turned back toward the temple. Once again he scaled a pile to the verandah and reëntered the rear of the building. He heard screaming and scuffling in the fore part of the temple, and a grim smile touched his lips as he recognized the origin of the sounds. Advancing quickly to the doorway that opened upon the upper dais he saw several warriors dragging the kicking, screaming Sobito toward him; then he stepped out upon the dais beside the Leopard God. Instantly all eyes were upon him, and fear was in every eye. The boldness of his entrance into their holy of holies, his affrontery, the ease with which he had taken their prisoner from them had impressed them, while the fact that Sobito, a witch-doctor, had fled from him in terror had assured them of his supernatural origin.

"Bind his hands and feet," commanded Tarzan, "and deliver him to me. The Spirit of Nyamwegi watches, waiting whom he shall kill; so delay not."

Hastily the warriors dragging Sobito secured his wrists and ankles; then they lifted him to their shoulders and carried him through the doorway at the side of the dais to the rear chambers of the temple. Here Tarzan met them.

"Leave Sobito with me," he directed.

"Where is the white prisoner you seized as hostage?" demanded one more courageous than his fellows.

"Search for him in the last room at the far end of the temple," said the ape-man; but he did not say that they would find him there. Then he lifted Sobito to his shoulder and stepped into the room through which he had led Old Timer to freedom, and as the warriors groped through the darkness in search of their victim the ape-man carried Sobito, screaming from fright, out into the forest.

For a long time the silent, terrified listeners in the temple of the Leopard God heard the eerie wails of the witch-doctor of Tumbai growing fainter in the distance; then the warriors returned from their search of the temple to report that the prisoner was not there.

"We have been tricked!" cried Imigeg. "The *muzimo* of Orando, the Utenga, has stolen our prisoner."

"Perhaps he escaped while the *muzimo* was taking Sobito," suggested Gato Mgungu.

"Search the island," cried another chief.

"The canoes!" exclaimed a third.

Instantly there was a rush for the river, and then the Leopard Men realized the enormity of the disaster that had befallen them, for not a canoe was left of all those that had brought them to the temple. Their situation was worse than it might appear at first glance. Their village had been burned and those of their fellows who had not accompanied them to the temple were either dead or scattered; there was no path through the tangled mazes of the jungle; but worse still was the fact that religious superstition forbade them from entering the dismal stretch of forest that extended from the island to the nearest trail that they might utilize. The swamps about them and the river below them were infested with crocodiles. The supply of food at the temple was not sufficient to support them for more than a few days. They were cannibals, and the weaker among them were the first to appreciate the significance of that fact.

The warriors of Orando squatted about their fires in their camp beside the manioc field of Gato Mgungu. Their bellies were full, and they were happy. Tomorrow they would start upon the return march to their own country. Already they were anticipating the reception that awaited victorious warriors. Again and again each, when he could make himself heard, recounted his own heroic exploits, none of which lost dramatic value in the retelling. A statistician overhearing them might have computed the enemy dead at fully two thousand.

Their reminiscences were interrupted by the appearance of a giant figure among them. It appeared to have materialized from thin air. It had not been there one moment; the next it had. It was he whom they had known as Muzimo; it was Tarzan of the Apes. Upon his shoulder he bore the bound figure of a man.

"Tarzan of the Apes!" cried some.

"Muzimo!" cried other.

"What have you brought us?" demanded Orando.

Tarzan threw the bound figure to the ground. "I have brought back your witch-doctor," he replied. "I have brought back Sobito, who is also a priest of the Leopard God."

"It is a lie!" screamed Sobito.

"See the leopard skin upon him," exclaimed a warrior.

"And the curved claws of the Leopard Men!" cried another.

"No, Sobito is not a Leopard Man!" jeered a third.

"I found him in the temple of the Leopard Men," explained Tarzan. "I thought you would like to have your witch-doctor back to make strong medicine for you that would preserve you from the Leopard Men."

"Kill him!" screamed a warrior.

"Kill Sobito! Kill Sobito!" was taken up by four score throats.

Angry men advanced upon the witch-doctor.

"Wait!" commanded Orando. "It will be better to take Sobito back to Tumbai, for there are many there who would like to see him die. It will give him time to think about the bad things he has done; it will make him suffer longer, as he has made others suffer; and I am sure that the parents of Nyamwegi would like to see Sobito die."

"Kill me now," begged Sobito. "I do not wish to go back to Tumbai."

"Tarzan of the Apes captured him," suggested a warrior. "Let him tell us what to do with Sobito."

"Do as you please with him," replied the apeman; "he is

not my witch-doctor. I have other business to attend to. I go now. Remember Tarzan of the Apes, if you do not see him again, and because of him treat white men kindly, for Tarzan is your friend and you are his."

As silently as he had come, he disappeared; and with him went little Nkima, whom the warriors of the Watenga country knew as The Spirit of Nyamwegi.

15

The Little Men

BOBOLO and Kapopa dragged Kali Bwana along the narrow forest trails away from the great river that was life artery of the district, back into the dense, dismal depth of the jungle, where great beasts prowled and the little men lived. Here there were no clearings nor open fields; they passed no villages.

The trails were narrow and little used and in places very low, for the little men do not have to clear their trails to the same height that others must.

Kapopa went ahead, for he knew the little men better than Bobolo knew them; though both knew their methods, knew how they hid in the underbrush and speared unwary passers-by or sped poisoned arrows from the trees above. They would recognize Kapopa and not molest them. Behind Kapopa came Kali Bwana. There was a fiber rope around her fair neck. Behind her was Bobolo, holding the rope's end.

The girl was in total ignorance of their destination or of what fate awaited her there. She moved in a dumb lethargy of despair. She was without hope, and her only regret was that she was also without the means of ending her tragic sufferings. She saw the knife at the hip of Kapopa as he walked ahead of her and coveted it. She thought of the dark river and the crocodiles and regretted them. In all respects her situation appeared to her worse than it had ever been before. Perhaps it was the depressing influence of the somber forest or the mystery of the unknown into which she was being led like some dumb beast to the slaughter. Slaughter! The word fascinated her. She knew that Bobolo was a cannibal. Perhaps they were taking her somewhere into the depths of the grim wood to slaughter and devour her. She wondered why the idea no longer revolted her, and then she guessed the truth—it postulated death. Death! Above all things now she craved death.

How long they plodded that seemingly endless trail she did not know, but after an eternity of dull misery a voice hailed them. Kapopa halted.

"What do you want in the country of Rebega?" demanded the voice.

"I am Kapopa, the witch-doctor," replied Kapopa. "With me are Bobolo, the chief, and his wife. We come to visit Rebega."

"I know you, Kapopa," replied the voice, and a second later a diminutive warrior stepped into the trail ahead of them from the underbrush at its side. He was about four feet tall and stark naked except for a necklace and some anklets and arm bands of copper and iron.

His eyes were small and close set, giving his unpleasant countenance a crafty appearance. His expression denoted surprise and curiosity as he regarded the white girl, but he asked no questions. Motioning them to follow him, he continued along the crooked trail. Almost immediately two other warriors, apparently materializing from thin air, fell in behind them; and thus they were escorted to the village of Rebega, the chief.

It was a squalid village of low huts, bisected ovals with a door two or three feet in height at each end. The huts were arranged about the periphery of an ellipse, in the center of which was the chief's hut. Surrounding the village was a crude boma of pointed sticks and felled timber with an opening at either end to give ingress and egress.

Rebega was an old, wrinkled man. He squatted on his haunches just outside one of the entrances to his hut, surrounded by his women and children. As the visitors approached him he gave no sign of recognition, his small, beady eyes regarding them with apparent suspicion and malice. His was indeed a most repellent visage.

Kapopa and Bobolo greeted him, but he only nodded once and grunted. To the girl his whole attitude appeared antagonistic, and when she saw the little warriors closing in about them from every hut she believed that Kapopa and Bobolo had placed themselves in a trap from which they might have difficulty in escaping. The thought rather pleased her. What the result would be for her was immaterial; nothing could be worse than the fate that Bobolo had intended for her. She had never seen pygmies before; and, notwithstanding her mental perturbation, her normally active mind found interest in observing them. The women were smaller than the men, few of them being over three feet in height; while the children seemed incredibly tiny. Among them all, however, there was not a prepossessing countenance nor a stitch of clothing, and they were obviously filthy and degraded.

There was a moment's silence as they halted before Rebega, and then Kapopa addressed him. "You know us, Rebega—Kapopa, the witch-doctor, and Bobolo, the chief!"

Rebega nodded. "What do you want here?" he demanded.

"We are friends of Rebega," continued Kapopa, ingratiatingly.

"Your hands are empty," observed the pygmy; "I see no presents for Rebega."

"You shall have presents if you will do what we ask," promised Bobolo.

"What do you want Rebega to do?"

"Bobolo has brought his white wife to you," explained Kapopa. "Keep her here in your village for him in safety; let no one see her; let no one know that she is here."

"What are the presents?"

"Meal, plantain, fish; every moon enough for a feast for all in your village," replied Bobolo.

"It is not enough," grunted Rebega. "We do not want a white woman in our village. Our own women make us enough trouble."

Kapopa stepped close to the chief and whispered rapidly into his ear. The sullen expression on Rebega's countenance deepened, but he appeared suddenly nervous and fearful. Perhaps Kapopa, the witch-doctor, had threatened him with the malign attentions of ghosts and demons if he did not accede to their request. At last he capitulated.

"Send the food at once," he said. "Even now we have not enough for ourselves, and this woman will need as much food as two of us."

"It shall be sent tomorrow," promised Bobolo. "I shall come with it myself and remain over night. Now I must return to my village. It is getting late, and it is not well to be out after night has fallen. The Leopard Men are everywhere."

"Yes," agreed Rebega, "the Leopard Men are everywhere. I shall keep your white woman for you if you bring food. If you do not I shall send her back to your village."

"Do not do that!" exclaimed Bobolo. "The food shall be sent you."

It was with a feeling of relief that Kali Bwana saw Bobolo and Kapopa depart. During the interview with Rebega no one had once addressed her, just as no one would have addressed a cow he was arranging to stable. She recalled the plaints of American Negroes that they were not treated with equality by the whites. Now that conditions were reversed, she could not see that the Negroes were more magnanimous than the whites. Evidently it all depended upon which was the more powerful and had nothing whatsoever to do with innate gentleness of spirit or charity.

When Bobolo and Kapopa had disappeared in the forest, Rebega called to a woman who had been among the interested spectators during the brief interview between him and his visitors. "Take the white woman to your hut," he commanded. "See that no harm befalls her. Let no stranger see her. I have spoken."

"What shall I feed her?" demanded the woman. "My man was killed by a buffalo while hunting, and I have not enough food for myself."

"Let her go hungry, then, until Bobolo brings the food he has promised. Take her away."

The woman seized Kali Bwana by the wrist and led her toward a miserable hut at the far end of the village. It seemed to the girl to be the meanest hut of all the squalid village. Filth and refuse were piled and strewn about the doorway through which she was conducted into its gloomy, windowless interior.

A number of other women had followed her guardian,

and now all these crowded into the hut after them. They jabbered excitedly and pawed her roughly in their efforts to examine and finger her garments and her ornaments. She could understand a little of their language, for she had been long enough now with the natives to have picked up many words, and the pygmies of this district used a dialect similar to that spoken in the villages of Gato Mgungu and Bobolo. One of them, feeling of her body, remarked that she was tender and that her flesh should be good to eat, at which they all laughed, exposing their sharp-filed, yellow teeth.

"If Bobolo does not bring food for her, she will be too thin," observed Wlala, the woman who was her guardian.

"If he does not bring food, we should eat her before she becomes too thin," advised another. "Our men hunt, but they bring little meat. They say the game has gone away. We must have meat."

They remained in the small, ill-smelling hut until it was time to go and prepare the evening meal for their men. The girl, exhausted by physical exertion and nervous strain, sickened by the close air and the stench of the hut's interior, had lain down in an effort to secure the peace of oblivion in sleep; but they had prodded her with sticks, and some of them had struck her in mere wanton cruelty. When they had gone she lay down again, but immediately Wlala struck her a sharp blow.

"You cannot sleep while I work, white woman," she cried. "Get to work!" She pressed a stone pestle into the girl's hand and indicated a large stone at one side of the hut. In a hollow worn in the stone was some corn. Kali Bwana could not understand all that the woman said, but enough to know that she was to grind the corn. Wearily she commenced the work, while Wlala, just outside the hut, built her cooking fire and prepared her supper. When it was ready the woman gobbled it hungrily, offering none to the girl. Then she came back into the hut.

"I am hungry," said Kali Bwana. "Will you not give me food?"

Wlala flew into a frenzy of rage. "Give you food!" she screamed. "I have not enough food for myself. You are the wife of Bobolo; let him bring you food."

"I am not his wife," replied the girl. "I am his prisoner. When my friends discover how you have treated me, you will all be punished."

Wlala laughed. "Your friends will never know," she taunted. "No one comes to the country of the Betetes. In my life I have seen only two other white-skinned people; those two we ate. No one came and punished us. No one will punish us after we have eaten you. Why did Bobolo not keep you in his own village? Were his women angry? Did they drive you out?"

"I guess so," replied the girl.

"Then he will never take you back. It is a long way from the village of Bobolo to the village of Rebega. Bobolo will soon tire of coming so far to see you while he has plenty of wives in his own village; then he will give you to us." Wlala licked her thick lips.

The girl sat dejectedly before the stone mortar. She was very tired. Her hands had dropped to her sides. "Get to work, you lazy sow!" cried Wlala and struck her across the head with the stick she kept ever ready at hand. Wearily, Kali Bwana resumed her monotonous chore. "And see that you grind it fine," added Wlala; then she went out to gossip with the other women of the village.

As soon as she was gone the girl stopped working. She was so tired that she could scarcely raise the stone pestle, and she was very hungry. Glancing fearfully through the doorway of the hut, she saw that no one was near enough to see her, and then, quickly, she gathered a handful of the raw meal and ate it. She dared not eat too much, lest Wlala discover the theft; but even that little was better than nothing. Then she added some fresh corn to the meal in the mortar and ground that to the same consistency as the other.

When Wlala returned to the hut, the girl was fast asleep beside the mortar. The woman kicked her into wakefulness; but as by now it was too dark to work and the woman herself lay down to sleep, Kali Bwana was at last permitted undisturbed slumber.

Bobolo did not return the following day, nor the second day, nor the third; neither did he send food. The pygmies were very angry. They had been anticipating a feast. Perhaps Wlala was the angriest, for she was the hungriest; also, she had commenced to suspect the theft of her meal. Not being positive, but to be on the safe side, she had beaten Kali Bwana unmercifully while she accused her of it. At least she started to beat her; then suddenly something quite unexpected had happened. The white girl, leaping to her feet, had seized the pygmy, torn the stick from her hand, and struck her repeatedly with it before Wlala could run from the hut. After that Wlala did not again strike Kali Bwana. In fact, she treated her with something approximating respect, but her voice was raised loudly in the village against the hated alien and against Bobolo.

In front of Rebega's hut was a concourse of women and warriors. They were all angry and hungry. "Bobolo has not brought the food," cried one, repeating for the hundredth time what had been said by each.

"What do we want of meal, or plantain, or fish when we have flesh here for all?" The speaker jerked a thumb meaningly in the direction of Wlala's hut.

"Bobolo would bring warriors and kill us if we harmed his white wife," cautioned another.

"Kapopa would cast a spell upon us, and many of us would die."

"He said he would come back with food the next day."

"Now it has been three days, and he has not returned."

"The flesh of the white girl is good now," argued Wlala. "She has been eating my meal, but I have stopped that. I have taken the meal from the hut and hidden it. If she does not have food soon, her flesh will not be so good as now. Let us eat her."

"I am afraid of Kapopa and Bobolo," admitted Rebega.

"We do not have to tell them that we ate her," urged Wlala.

"They will guess it," insisted Rebega.

"We can tell them that the Leopard Men came and took her away," suggested a rat-faced little fighting man; "and if they do not believe us we can go away. The hunting is not good here, anyway. We should go elsewhere and hunt."

For a long time Rebega's fears outweighed his natural inclination for human flesh, but at last he told them that if the food Bobolo had promised did not arrive before dark they would have a dance and a feast that night.

In the hut of Wlala, Kali Bwana heard the loud shouts of approval that greeted Rebega's announcement and thought that the food Bobolo had promised had arrived. She hoped that they would give her some of it, for she was weak from hunger. When Wlala came she asked her if the food had arrived.

"Bobolo has sent no food, but we shall eat tonight," replied the woman, grinning. "We shall eat all that we wish; but it will not be meal, nor plaintain, nor fish." She came over to the girl then and felt of her body, pinching the flesh slightly between her fingers. "Yes, we shall eat," she concluded.

To Kali Bwana the inference was obvious, but the strange chemistry of emotion had fortunately robbed her of the power to feel repugnance for the idea that would have so horribly revolted her a few short weeks ago. She did not think of the grisly aftermath; she thought only of death, and welcomed it.

The food from Bobolo did not come, and that night the Betetes gathered in the compound before Rebega's hut. The women dragged cooking pots to the scene and built many fires. The men danced a little; but only for a short time, for they had been too long on short rations. Their energy was at low ebb.

At last a few of them went to the hut of Wlala and dragged Kali Bwana to the scene of the festivities. There was some dispute as to who was to kill her. Rebega was frankly afraid of the wrath of Kapopa, though he was not so much concerned about Bobolo. Bobolo could only follow them with warriors whom they could see and kill; but Kapopa could remain in his village and send demons and ghosts after them. At last it was decided that the women should kill her; and Wlala, remembering the blows that the white girl had struck her, volunteered to do the work herself.

"Tie her hands and feet," she said, "and I will kill her." She did not care to risk a repetition of the scene in her hut at the time she had attempted to beat the girl.

Kali Bwana understood, and as the warriors prepared to bind her she crossed her hands to facilitate their work. They threw her to the ground and secured her feet; then she closed her eyes and breathed a prayer. It was for those she had left behind in that far away country and for "Jerry."

THE night that Tarzan had brought Sobito to their
camp the Utengas had celebrated the event in beer sal-
vaged from the loot of Gato Mgungu's village before they
had burned it. They had celebrated late into the night, stopping only when the last of the beer had been consumed; then
they had slept heavily and well. Even the sentries had dozed at
their posts, for much beer poured into stomachs already filled
with food induces a lethargy difficult to combat.

And while the Utenga warriors slept, Sobito was not idle.
He pulled and tugged at the bonds that held his wrists, with
little fear that his rather violent efforts would attract attention.
At last he felt them gradually stretching. Sweat poured from
his tough old hide; beads of it stood out upon his wrinkled
forehead. He was panting from the violence of his exertions.
Slowly he dragged one hand farther and farther through the
loop; just a hair's breadth at a time it moved, but eventually it slipped out—free!

For a moment the old witch-doctor lay still, recouping the
energy that he had expended in his efforts to escape his bonds.
Slowly his eyes ranged the camp. No one stirred. Only the
heavy, stertorous breathing of the half-drunk warriors disturbed the silence of the night. Sobito drew his feet up within
reach of his hands and untied the knots of the cords that
confined them; then very quietly and slowly he arose and
slipped, bent half-doubled, down toward the river. In a moment the darkness had swallowed him, and the sleeping camp
slept on.

On the shore he found the canoes that the Utengas had
captured from the forces of Gato Mgungu; with considerable
difficulty he pushed one of the smaller of them into the river,
after satisfying himself that there was at least one paddle in
it. As he leaped into it and felt it glide out into the current,

he felt like one snatched from the jaws of death by some unexpected miracle.

His plans were already made. He had had plenty of time
while he was lying working with his bonds to formulate them.
He might not with safety return to the temple of the
Leopard God, that he knew full well; but down the river lay
the village of his old friend Bobolo, who by the theft of the
white priestess was doubtless as much anathema in the eyes of
the Leopard Men as he. To Bobolo's village, therefore, he
would go. What he would do afterward was in the laps of
the gods.

*   *   *   *   *   *   *

Another lone boatman drifted down the broad river toward
the village of Bobolo. It was Old Timer. He, too, had determined to pay a visit to the citadel of *his* old friend; but it
would be no friendly visit. In fact, if Old Timer's plans were
successful, Bobolo would not be aware that a visit was being
paid him, lest his hospitality wax so mightily that the guest
might never be permitted to depart. It was the white girl,
not Bobolo, who lured Old Timer to this rash venture. Something within him more powerful than reason told him that
he must save her, and he knew that if any succor was to
avail it must come to her at once. As to how he was to accomplish it he had not the most remote conception; all that
must depend upon his reconnaissance and his resourcefulness.

As he drifted downward, paddling gently, his mind was
filled with visions of the girl. He saw her as he had first seen
her in her camp: her blood-smeared clothing, the dirt and
perspiration, but, over all, the radiance of her fair face, the
haunting allure of her blond hair, dishevelled and falling in
wavy ringlets across her forehead and about her ears. He
saw her as he had seen her in the temple of the Leopard
God, garbed in savage, barbaric splendor, more beautiful
than ever. It thrilled him to live again the moments during
which he had talked to her, touched her.

Forgotten was the girl whose callous selfishness had made
him a wanderer and an outcast. The picture of her that he
had carried constantly upon the screen of memory for two
long years had faded. When he thought of her now he
laughed; and instead of cursing her, as he had so often done

before, he blessed her for having sent him here to meet and know this glorious creature who now filled his dreams.

Old Timer was familiar with this stretch of the river. He knew the exact location of Bobolo's village, and he knew that day would break before he came within sight of it. To come boldly to it would be suicidal; now that Bobolo was aware that the white man knew of his connection with the Leopard Men, his life would not be safe if he fell into the hands of the crafty old chief.

For a short time after the sun rose he drifted on down stream, keeping close to the left bank; and shortly before he reached the village he turned the prow of his craft in to shore. He did not know that he would ever need the canoe again; but on the chance that he might he secured it to the branch of a tree, and then clambered up into the leafy shelter of the forest giant.

He planned to make his way through the forest toward the village in the hope of finding some vantage point from which he might spy upon it; but he was confident that he would have to wait until after darkness had fallen before he could venture close, when it was in his plan to scale the palisade and search the village for the girl while the natives slept. A mad scheme—but men have essayed even madder when spurred on by infatuation for a woman.

As Old Timer was about to leave the tree and start toward the village of Bobolo, his attention was attracted toward the river by a canoe which had just come into sight around a bend a short distance up stream. In it was a single native. Apprehending that any movement on his part might attract the attention of the lone paddler and wishing above all things to make his way to the village unseen, he remained motionless. Closer and closer came the canoe, but it was not until it was directly opposite him that the white man recognized its occupant as that priest of the Leopard God whom his rescuer had demanded should be delivered into his hands.

Yes, it was Sobito; but how had Sobito come here? What was the meaning of it? Old Timer was confident that the strange white giant who had rescued him had not demanded Sobito for the purpose of setting him free. Here was a mystery. Its solution was beyond him, but he could not see that it materially concerned him in any way; so he gave it no further thought after Sobito had drifted out of sight beyond the next turning of the river below.

Moving cautiously through the jungle the white man came at last within sight of the village of Bobolo. Here he climbed a tree well off the trail where he could overlook the village without being observed. He was not surprised that he did not see the girl who he was confident was there, knowing that she was doubtless a prisoner in one of the huts of the chief's compound. All that he could do was wait until darkness had fallen—wait and hope.

Two days' march on the opposite side of the river lay his own camp. He had thought of going there first and enlisting the aid of his partner, but he dared not risk the four days' delay. He wondered what The Kid was doing; he had not had much time to think about him of late, but he hoped he had been more successful in his search for ivory than he had.

The tree in which Old Timer had stationed himself was at the edge of a clearing. Below him and at a little distance women were working, hoeing with sharpened sticks. They were chattering like a band of monkeys. He saw a few warriors set out to inspect their traps and snairs. The scene was peacefully pastoral. He had recognized most of the warriors and some of the women, for Old Timer was well acquainted in the village of Bobolo. The villagers had been friendly, but he knew that he dared no longer approach the village openly because of his knowledge of Bobolo's connection with the Leopard Men. Because of that fact and his theft of the white girl the chief could not afford to let him live; he knew too much.

He had seen the village many times before, but now it had taken on a new aspect. Before, it had been only another native village inhabited by savage natives; today it was glorified in his eyes by the presence of a girl. Thus does imagination color our perceptions. How different would the village of Bobolo have appeared in the eyes of the watcher had he known the truth, had he known that the girl he thought so near him was far away in the hut of Wlala, the Betete pygmy, grinding corn beneath the hate-filled eyes of a cruel taskmaster, suffering from hunger!

In the village Bobolo was having troubles of his own. So-

bito had come! The chief knew nothing of what had befallen
the priest of the Leopard God. He did not know that he had
been discredited in the eyes of the order; nor did Sobito plan
to enlighten him. The wily old witch-doctor was not sure that
he had any plans at all. He could not return to Tumbai, but
he had to live somewhere. At least he thought so; and he
needed, if not friends, allies. He saw in Bobolo a possible
ally. He knew that the chief had stolen the white priestess,
and he hoped that this knowledge might prove of advantage
to him; but he said nothing about the white girl. He believed
that she was in the village and that sooner or later he would
see her. They had talked of many things since his arrival,
but they had not spoken of the Leopard Men nor of the
white girl. Sobito was waiting for any turn of events that
would give him a cue to his advantage.

Bobolo was nervous. He had been planning to take food
to Rebega this day and visit his white wife. Sobito had upset
his plans. He tried to think of some way by which he could
rid himself of his unwelcome guest. Poison occurred to him;
but he had already gone too far in arousing the antagonism of
the Leopard Men, and knowing that there were loyal members of the clan in his village, he feared to add the poisoning
of a priest to his other crime against the Leopard God.

The day dragged on. Bobolo had not yet discovered why
Sobito had come to his village; Sobito had not yet seen the
white girl. Old Timer was still perched in the tree overlooking
the village. He was hungry and thirsty, but he did not dare
desert his post lest something might occur in the village that
it would be to his advantage to see. Off and on all day
he had seen Bobolo and Sobito. They were always talking.
He wondered if they were discussing the fate of the girl. He
wished that night would come. He would like to get down
and stretch his legs and get a drink. His thirst annoyed him
more than his hunger; but even if he had contemplated de-
serting his post to obtain water, it could not be done now.
The women in the field had worked closer to his tree. Two of
them were just beneath its overhanging branches. They
paused in the shade to rest, their tongues rattling ceaselessly.

Old Timer had overheard a number of extremely intimate
anecdotes relating to members of the tribe. He learned that
if a certain lady were not careful her husband was going

to catch her in an embarrassing situation, that certain charms are more efficacious when mixed with nail parings, that the young son of another lady had a demon in his belly that caused him intense suffering when he overate. These things did not interest Old Timer greatly, but presently one of the women asked a question that brought him to alert attention.

"What do you think Bobolo did with his white wife?"

"He told Ubooga that he had sent her back to the Leopard Men from whom he says that he stole her," replied the other.

"Bobolo has a lying tongue in his head," rejoined the first woman; "it does not know the truth."

"I know what he did with her," volunteered the other. "I overheard Kapopa telling his wife."

"What did he say?"

"He said that they took her to the village of the little men."

"They will eat her."

"No, Bobolo has promised to give them food every moon if they keep her for him."

"I would not like to be in the village of the little men no matter what they promised. They are eaters of men, they are always hungry, and they are great liars." Then the women's work carried them away from the tree, and Old Timer heard no more; but that which he had heard had changed all his plans.

No longer was he interested in the village of Bobolo; once again it was only another native village.

17

Charging Lions

WHEN Tarzan of the Apes left the camp of the Utengas, he appropriated one of the canoes of the defeated Leopard Men, as Sobito was to do several hours later, and paddled across the broad river to its opposite shore. His destination was the village of Bobolo; his mission, to question the chief relative to the white girl. He felt no keen personal interest in her and was concerned only because of racial ties, which, after all, are not very binding. She was a white woman and he was a white man, a fact that he sometimes forgot, since, after all, he was a wild beast before everything else.

He had been very active for several days and nights, and he was tired. Little Nkima also was tired, nor did he let Tarzan forget it for long; so when the ape-man leaped ashore from the canoe he sought a comfortable place among the branches of a tree where they might lie up for a few hours.

The sun was high in the heavens when Tarzan awoke. Little Nkima, snuggling close to him, would have slept longer; but the ape-man caught him by the scruff of the neck and shook him into wakefulness. "I am hungry," said Tarzan; "let us find food and eat."

"There is plenty to eat in the forest," replied Nkima; "let us sleep a little longer."

"I do not want fruit or nuts," said the ape-man. "I want meat. Nkima may remain here and sleep, but Tarzan goes to kill."

"I shall go with you," announced Nkima. "Strong in this forest is the scent of Sheeta, the leopard. I am afraid to remain alone. Sheeta is hunting, too; he is hunting for little Nkima."

The shadow of a smile touched the lips of the ape-man, one of those rare smiles that it was vouch-safed but few to see. "Come," he said, "and while Tarzan hunts for meat Nima can rob birds' nests."

The hunting was not good, for though the apeman ranged far through the forest his searching nostrils were not rewarded with the scent of flesh that he liked. Always strong was the scent of Sheeta, but Taran liked not the flesh of the carnivores. Driven to it by the extremity of hunger, he had eaten more than once of Sheeta and Numa and Sabor; but it was the flesh of the herbivores that he preferred.

Knowing that the hunting was better farther from the river, where there were fewer men, he swung deeper and deeper into the primeval forest until he was many miles from the river. This country was new to Tarzan, and he did not like it; there was too little game. This thought was in his mind when there came to his nostrils the scent of Wappi, the antelope. It was very faint, but it was enough. Straight into the wind swung Tarzan of the Apes, and steadily the scent of Wappi grew stronger in his nostrils. Mingling with it were other scents: the scent of Pacco, the zebra, and of Numa, the lion; the fresh scent of open grassland.

On swung Tarzan of the Apes and little Nkima. Stronger grew the scent spoor of the quarry in the nostrils of the hunter, stronger the hunger-craving growing in his belly. His keen nostrils told him that there was not one antelope ahead but many. This must be a good hunting ground that he was approaching! Then the forest ended; and a rolling, grassy plain, tree-dotted, stretched before him to blue mountains in the distance.

Before him, as he halted at the forest's edge, the plain was rich with lush grasses; a mile away a herd of antelope grazed, and beyond them the plain was dotted with zebra. An almost inaudible growl rumbled from his deep chest; it was the anticipatory growl of the hunting beast that is about to feed.

Strong in his nostrils was the scent of Numa, the lion. In those deep grasses were lions; but in such rich hunting ground, they must be well fed, he knew, and so he could ignore them. They would not bother him, if he did not bother them, which he had no intention of doing.

To stalk the antelope amid the concealment of this tall grass was no difficult matter for the apeman. He did not have to see them; his nose would guide him to them. First he noted carefully the terrain, the location of each tree, an out-cropping of rock that rose above the grasses. It was likely that the lions would be lying up there in the shadow of the rocks.

He beckoned to Nkima, but Nkima held back. "Numa is there," complained the monkey, "with all his brothers and sisters. They are waiting there to eat little Nkima. Nkima is afraid."

"Stay where you are, then; and when I have made my kill I will return."

"Nkima is afraid to remain."

Tarzan shook his head. "Nkima is a great coward," he

said. "He may do what he pleases. Tarzan goes to make his kill."

Silently he slid into the tall grasses, while Nkima crouched high in a great tree, choosing the lesser of two evils. The little monkey watched him go out into the great plain where the lions were; and he shivered, though it was very warm.

Tarzan made a detour to avoid the rocks; but even where he was, the lion scent was so strong that he almost lost the scent of Wappi. Yet he felt no apprehension. Fear he did not know. By now he had covered half the distance to the quarry, which was still feeding quietly, unmindful of danger.

Suddenly to his left he heard the angry coughing growl of a lion. It was a warning growl that the ape-man knew might presage a charge. Taran sought no encounter with Numa. All that he wished was to make his kill and depart. He moved away to the right. Fifty feet ahead of him was a tree. If the lion charged, it might be necessary to seek sanctuary there, but he did not believe that Numa would charge. He had given him no reason to do so; then a cross current of wind brought to his nostrils a scent that warned him of his peril. It was the scent of Sabor, the lioness. Now Tarzan understood; he had nearly stumbled upon a mating lion, which meant that a charge was almost inevitable, for a mating lion will charge anything without provocation.

Now the tree was but twenty-five feet away. A roar thundered from the grasses behind him. A quick backward glance, showing the grass tops waving tumultuously, revealed the imminence of his danger; Numa was charging!

Up to that time he had seen no lion, but now a massive head framed by a dark brown mane burst into view. Tarzan of the Apes was angry. It galled him to flee. A dignified retreat prompted by caution was one thing; abject flight, another. Few creatures can move with the swiftness of Tarzan, and he had a start of twenty-five feet. He could have reached the tree ahead of the lion, but he did not attempt to do so—not at once. Instead he wheeled and faced the roaring, green-eyed monster. Back went his spear arm, his muscles rolling like molten steel beneath his bronzed skin; then forward with all the weight of his powerful frame backed by those mighty thews. The heavy Utenga war spear shot from his hand. Not until then did Tarzan of the Apes turn and fly; but he did not run from the lion that was pursuing him. Behind Numa he had seen Sabor coming, and behind her the grasses waved in many places above the rushing bodies of charging lions. Tarzan of the Apes fled from certain and sudden death.

The spear momentarily checked the charge of the nearest lion, and in that fraction of a split second that spelled the difference between life and death the ape-man swarmed up the tree that had been his goal, while the raking talons of Numa all but grazed his heel.

Safe out of reach Tarzan turned and looked down. Below him a great lion in his death throes was clawing at the haft of the spear that was buried in his heart. Behind the first lion a lioness and six more males had burst into view. Far out across the plain the antelopes and the zebras were disappearing in the distance, startled into flight by the roars of the charging lion.

The lioness, never pausing in her charge, ran far up the bole of the tree in her effort to drag down the man-thing. She had succeeded in getting one forearm across a lower branch, and she hung there a moment in an effort to scramble farther upward; but she could not get sufficient footing for her hind feet to force her heavy weight higher, and presently she slipped back to the ground. She sniffed at her dead mate and then circled the tree, growling. The six males paced to and fro, adding their angry roars to the protest of Sabor, while from above them the ape-man looked down and through snarling lips growled out his own disappointment and displeasure. In a tree top half a mile away a little monkey screamed and scolded.

For half an hour the lioness circled the tree, looking up at Tarzan, her yellow-green eyes blazing with rage and hatred; then she lay down beside the body of her fallen mate, while the six males squatted upon their haunches and watched now Sabor, now Tarzan, and now one another.

Tarzan of the Apes gazed ruefully after his departed quarry and back toward the forest. He was hungrier now than ever. Even if the lions went away and permitted him to descend, he was still as far from a meal as he had been when he awoke in the morning. He broke twigs and branches from the tree and hurled them at Sabor in an attempt to drive her away, knowing that wherever she went the males would follow; but she only growled the more ferociously and remained in her place beside the dead lion.

Thus passed the remainder of the day. Night came, and still the lioness remained beside her dead mate. Tarzan upbraided himself for leaving his bow and arrows behind in the forest. With them he could have killed the lioness and the lions and escaped. Without them he could do nothing but throw futile twigs at them and wait. He wondered how long he would have to wait. When the lioness waxed hungry enough she would go away; but when would that be? From the size of her belly and the smell of her breath the man-beast squatting above her knew that she had eaten recently and well.

Tarzan had long since resigned himself to his fate. When he had found that hurling things at Sabor would not drive her away, he had desisted. Unlike man he did not continue to annoy her merely for the purpose of venting his displeasure. Instead he curled himself in a crotch of the tree and slept.

In the forest, at the edge of the plain, a terrified little monkey rolled himself into the tiniest ball that he could achieve and suffered in silence. If he were too large or too noisy, he feared that he might sooner attract the attention of Sheeta, the leopard. That Sheeta would come eventually and eat him he was certain. But why hasten the evil moment?

When the sun rose and he was still alive, Nkima was surprised but not wholly convinced. Sheeta might have overlooked him in the dark, but in the daylight he would be sure to see him; however, there was some consolation in knowing that he could see Sheeta sooner and doubtless escape him. With the rising sun his spirits rose, but he was still unhappy because Tarzan had not returned. Out on the plain he could see him in the tree, and he wondered why he did not come down and return to little Nkima. He saw the lions, too; but it did not occur to him that it was they who prevented Tarzan returning. He could not conceive that there might be any creature or any number of creatures which his mighty master could not overcome.

Tarzan was irked. The lioness gave no sign that she was ever going away. Several of the males had departed to hunt during the night, and one that had made a kill near by lay on it not far from the tree. Tarzan hoped that Sabor would be attracted by it; but though the odor of the kill was strong in the ape-man's nostrils, the lioness was not tempted away by it.

Noon came. Tarzan was famished and his throat was dry. He was tempted to cut a club from a tree branch and attempt to battle his way to liberty; but he knew only too well what the outcome would be. Not even he, Tarzan of the Apes, could hope to survive the onslaught of all those lions, which was certain to follow immediately he descended from the tree if the lioness attacked him. That she would attack him if he approached that close to her dead mate was a foregone conclusion. There was nothing to do but wait. Eventually she would go away; she could not remain there forever.

Nor did she. Shortly after noon she arose and slunk toward the kill that one of the males had made. As she disappeared in the tall grass, the other males followed her. It was fortunate for the ape-man that the kill lay beyond the tree in which he had taken refuge, away from the forest. He did not wait after the last male disappeared among the waving grasses, but dropped from the tree, recovered his spear from the carcass of Numa, and started at a brisk walk toward the forest. His keen ears took note of every sound. Not even softpadded Numa could have stalked him without his being aware of it, but no lion followed him.

Nkima was frantic with joy. Tarzan was only hungry and thirsty. He was not long in finding the means for quenching his thirst, but it was late before he made a kill and satisfied his hunger; then his thoughts returned to the object of his excursion. He would go to the village of Bobolo and reconnoiter.

He had gone far inland from the river, and his hunting had taken him down the valley to a point which he guessed was about opposite the village where he hoped to find the girl. He had passed a band of great apes led by Zu-tho, whom he had thought far away in his own country; and he had stopped to talk with them for a moment; but neither the great apes nor Tarzan, who was reared among them, are loquacious, so that he soon left them to pursue the purpose

he had undertaken. Now he swung through the trees directly toward the river, where he knew that he could find land-
marks to assure him of his position.

It was already dark; so Nkima clung to the back of his
master, his little arms about the bronzed neck. By day he
swung through the trees with Tarzan; but at night he clung
tightly to him, for by night there are terrible creatures
abroad in the jungle; and they are all hunting for little
Nkima.

The scent spoor of man was growing stronger in the nostrils of Tarzan, so that he knew that he was approaching a
village of the Gomangani. He was certain that it could not
be the village of Bobolo; it was too far from the river. Furthermore, there was an indication in the odors wafted to his
nostrils that the people who inhabited it were not of the
same tribe as Bobolo. The mere presence of Gomangani
would have been sufficient to have caused Tarzan to investigate, for it was the business of the Lord of the Jungle to
have knowledge of all things in his vast domain; but there
was another scent spoor faintly appreciable among the varied
stenches emanating from the village that in itself would have
been sufficient to turn him from his direct path to the
river. It was but the faintest suggestion of a scent, yet the
ape-man recognized it for what it was; and it told him that
the girl he sought was close at hand.

Silently he approached the village, until from the outspread-
ing branches of a great tree he looked down upon the compound before the hut of Rebega, the chief.

18

Arrows Out of the Night

THE KID had returned to his camp after a fruitless
search for elephants. He hoped that Old Timer had
been more successful. At first he thought that the other's
protracted absence indicated this, but as the days passed

and his friend did not return he became anxious. His position was not an enviable one. The faith and loyalty of his three retainers had been sorely shaken. Only a genuine attachment for the two white men had kept them with them during the recent months of disappointment and ill fortune. How much longer he could expect to hold them, he did not know. He was equally at a loss to imagine what he would do if they deserted him, yet his chief concern was not for himself but for his friend.

Fortunately he had been able to keep the camp well supplied with fresh meat, and the natives, therefore, reasonably contented; but he knew that they longed to return to their own village now that they could not see any likelihood of profiting by their connection with these two poverty-stricken white men.

Such thoughts were occupying his mind late one afternoon upon his return from a successful hunt for meat when his reveries were interrupted by the shouts of his *boys*. Glancing up, he saw two of the men who had accompanied Old Timer entering the camp. Leaping to his feet, he went forward to meet them, expecting to see his friend and the third following closely behind them; but when he was close enough to see the expressions upon their faces he realized that something was amiss.

"Where are your bwana and Andereya?" he demanded.

"They are both dead," replied one of the returning natives.

"Dead!" ejaculated The Kid. It seemed to him that the bottom had suddenly dropped from his world. Old Timer dead! It was unthinkable. Until now he had scarcely realized how much he had depended upon the older man for guidance and support, nor to what extent this friendship had become a part of him. "How did it happen?" he inquired dully. "Was it an elephant?"

"The Leopard men, Bwana," explained the native who had made the announcement.

"The Leopard Men! Tell me how it happened."

With attention to minute details and with much circumlocution the two boys told all they knew; and when at last they had finished, The Kid saw a suggestion of a ray of hope. They had not actually seen Old Timer killed. He might still be a prisoner in the village of Gato Mgungu.

"He said that if he had not returned to us by the time the shadow of the forest had left the palisade in the morning we should know that he was dead," insisted the native.

The youth mentally surveyed his resources: five discontented natives and himself—six men to march upon the stronghold of the Leopard Men and demand an accounting of them. And five of these men held the Leopard Men in such awe that he knew that they would not accompany him. He raised his eyes suddenly to the waiting natives. "Be ready to march when the sun rises tomorrow," he snapped.

There was a moment's hesitation. "Where do we march?" demanded one, suspiciously.

"Where I lead you," he replied, shortly; then he returned to his tent, his mind occupied with plans for the future and with the tragic story that the two *boys* had narrated.

He wondered who the girl might be. What was Old Timer doing pursuing a white woman? Had he gone crazy, or had he forgotten that he hated all white women? Of course, he reflected, there was nothing else that his friend might have done. The girl had been in danger, and that of course would have been enough to have sent Old Timer on the trail of her abductors; but how had he become involved with her in the first place? The *boys* had not been explicit upon this point. He saw them now, talking with their fellows. All of them appeared excited. Presently they started across the camp toward his tent.

"Well, what is it now?" he asked as they stopped before him.

"If you are going to the village of the Leopard Men, Bwana," announced the spokesman, "we will not follow you. We are few, and they would kill us all and eat us."

"Nonsense!" exclaimed The Kid. "They will do nothing of the sort. They would not dare."

"That is what the old bwana said," replied the spokesman, "but he did not return to us. He is dead."

"I do not believe that he is dead," retorted The Kid. "We are going to find out."

"You, perhaps, but not we," rejoined the man.

The Kid saw that he could not shake them in their decision. The outlook appeared gloomy, but he was determined to go if he had to go alone. Yet what could he accomplish without them? A plan occurred to him.

"Will you go part way with me?" he asked.

"How far?"

"To the village of Bobolo. I may be able to get help from him."

For a moment the natives argued among themselves in low voices; then their spokesman turned again to the white man. "We will go as far as the village of Bobolo," he said.

"But no farther," added another.

*   *   *   *   *   *   *

Old Timer waited until the women hoeing in the field had departed a little distance from the tree in which he was hiding; then he slipped cautiously to the ground on the side opposite them. He had never been to the village of the little men. He had often heard the natives of Bobolo's village speak of them and knew in a general way the direction in which they pygmy village lay, but there were many trails in this part of the forest. It would be easy to take the wrong one.

He knew enough of the Betetes to know that he might have difficulty in entering their village. They were a savage, warlike race of Pygmies and even reputed to be cannibals. The trails to their village were well guarded, and the first challenge might be a poisoned spear. Yet, though he knew these things to be true, the idea of abandoning his search for the girl because of them did not occur to him. He did not hesitate in reaching a decision, but the very fact that she was there hastened it instead.

Dark soon overtook him, but he stopped only because he could not see to go on. At the first break of dawn he was away again. The forest was dense and gloomy. He could not see the sun, and he was haunted by the conviction that he was on the wrong trail. It must have been about mid-afternoon when he came to a sudden halt, baffled. He had recognized his own footprints in the trail ahead of him; he had walked in a great circle.

Absolutely at a loss as to which direction to take, he struck out blindly along a narrow, winding trail that intercepted the one he had been traversing at the point at which

he had made his harrowing discovery. Where the trail led
or in what direction he could not know, nor even whether it
led back toward the river or farther inland: but he must be
moving, he must go on.

Now he examined carefully every trail that crossed or
branched from the one he was following. The trails, some of
them at least, were well-worn; the ground was damp; the
spoor of animals was often plain before his eyes. But he saw
nothing that might afford him a clue until shortly before
dark; then careful scrutiny of an intersecting trail revealed
the tiny footprint of a pygmy. Old Timer was elated. It
was the first sense of elation that he had experienced during
all that long, dreary day. He had come to hate the forest. Its
sunless gloom oppressed him. It had assumed for him the
menacing personality of a powerful, remorseless enemy that
sought not only to thwart his plans but to lure him to his
death. He longed to defeat it—to show it that he was more
cunning, if less powerful than it.

He hastened along the new trail, but darkness overtook
him before he learned whether or not it led to his goal. Yet
now he did not stop as he had the previous night. So long
had the forest defeated and mocked him that perhaps he was
a little mad. Something seemed to be calling to him out of the
blackness ahead. Was it a woman's voice? He knew better,
yet he listened intently as he groped his way through the
darkness.

Presently his tensely listening ears were rewarded by a
sound. It was not the voice of a woman calling to him, but
it was still the sound of human voices. Muffled and indistinct,
it came to him out of that black void ahead. His heart beat a
little faster; he moved more cautiously.

When he came at last within sight of a village he could
see nothing beyond the palisade other than the firelight playing upon the foliage of overspreading trees and upon the
thatched roofs of huts, but he knew that it was the village of
the little men. There, behind that palisade, was the girl he
sought. He wanted to cry aloud, shouting words of encouragement to her. He wanted her to know that he was near
her, that he had come to save her; but he made no sound.

Cautiously he crept nearer. There was no sign of sentry.
The little men do not need sentries in the dark forest at

night, for few are the human enemies that dare invite the dangers of the nocturnal jungle. The forest was their protection by night.

The poles that had been stuck in the ground to form the palisade were loosely bound together by lianas; there were spaces between them through which he glimpsed the firelight. Old Timer moved cautiously forward until he stood close against the palisade beside a gate and, placing an eye to one of the apertures, looked into the village of Rebega. What he saw was not particularly interesting: a group of natives gathered before a central hut which he assumed to be the hut of the chief. They appeared to be arguing about something, and some of the men were dancing. He could see their heads bobbing above those of the natives who shut off his view.

Old Timer was not interested in what the little men were doing. At least he thought he was not. He was interested only in the girl, and he searched the village for some evidence of her presence there, though he was not surprised that he did not see her. Undoubtedly she was a prisoner in one of the huts. Had he known the truth he would have been far more interested in the activities of that little group of pygmies, the bodies of some of which hid from his sight the bound girl at its center.

Old Timer examined the gate and discovered that it was crudely secured with a fiber rope. From his breeches' pocket he took the pocket knife that the Leopard Men had overlooked and began cutting the fastening, congratulating himself upon the fact that the villagers were occupied to such an extent with something over by the chief's hut that he could complete his work without fear of detection.

He planned only to prepare a way into the village, when he undertook his search for the girl after the natives had retired to their huts for the night, and a way out when he had found her. For some unaccountable reason his spirits were high; success seemed assured. Already he was anticipating his reunion with the girl; then there was a little break in the circle of natives standing between him and the center of the group, and through that break he saw a sight that turned him suddenly cold with dread.

It was the girl, bound hand and foot, and a savage-faced devil-woman wielding a large knife. As Old Timer saw the

hideous tableau revealed for a moment to his horrified gaze,
the woman seized the girl by the hair and forced her head
back, the knife flashed in the light of the cooking fires that
had been prepared against the coming feast, and Old Timer,
unarmed save for a small knife, burst through the gates and
ran toward the scene of impending murder.

A cry of remonstrance burst from his lips that sounded
in the ears of the astonished pygmies like the war cry of
attacking natives, and at the same instant an arrow passed
through the body of Wlala from behind, transfixing her
heart. Old Timer's eyes were on the executioner at the moment, and he saw the arrow, as did many of the pygmies; but
like them he had no idea from whence it had come—whether
from friend or foe.

For a moment the little men stood in stupid astonishment,
but the white man realized that their inactivity would be brief
when they discovered that they had only a lone and unarmed
man to deal with; it was then that there flashed to his fertile
brain a forlorn hope.

Half turning, he shouted back toward the open gate, "Surround the village! Let no one escape, but do not kill unless
they kill me." He spoke in a dialect that he knew they would
understand, the language of the people of Bobolo's tribe;
and then to the villagers, "Stand aside! Let me take the white
woman, and you will not be harmed." But he did not wait
for permission.

Leaping to the girl's side, he raised her in his arms; and
then it was that Rebega seemed to awaken from his stupor.
He saw only one man. Perhaps there were others outside
his village, but did he not have warriors who could fight?
Kill the white man!" he shouted, leaping forward.

A second arrow passed through the body of Rebega; and
as he sank to the ground, three more, shot in rapid succession,
brought down three warriors who had sprung forward to do
his bidding. Instantly terror filled the breasts of the remaining
pygmies, sending them scurrying to the greater security of
their huts.

Throwing the girl across his shoulder, Old Timer bolted
for the open gate and disappeared in the forest. He heard a
rending and a crash behind him, but he did not know what
had happened, nor did he seek to ascertain.

19

"The Demons Are Coming!"

THE sight that met the eyes of Tarzan of the Apes as he looked down into the compound of the village of Rebega, the Betete chief, gave him cause for astonishment. He saw a white girl being bound. He saw the cooking pots and the fires, and he guessed what was to transpire. He was on his way to the village of Bobolo in search of a white girl imprisoned there. Could there be two white girls captives of natives in this same district? It scarcely seemed probable. This, therefore, must be the white girl whom he had supposed in the village of Bobolo; but how had she come here?

The question was of less importance than the fact that she *was* here or the other still more important fact that he must save her. Dropping to the ground, he scaled the palisade and crept through the village from the rear, keeping well in the shadow of the huts; while little Nkima remained behind in the tree that the ape-man had quitted, his courage having carried him as far as it could.

When the pygmies had cleared a space for their village they had left a few trees within the enclosure to afford them shade, and one of these grew in front of the hut of Rebega. To this tree Tarzan made his way, keeping the bole of it between him and the natives assembled about the fires; and into its branches he swung just in time to see Wlala seize the girl by the hair and lift her blade to slash the fair throat.

There was no time for thought, barely time for action. The muscles of the ape-man responded almost automatically to the stimulus of necessity. To fit an arrow to his bow and to loose the shaft required but the fraction of a split second. Simultaneously he heard the noise at the gate, saw the white man running forward, heard him yell. Even had he not recognied him, he would have known instinctively that he was here for but one purpose—the rescue of the girl. And when he heard Rebega's command, knowing the danger that the white man faced, he shot the additional arrows that brought down those most closely menacing him and frightened the rest of the pygmies away for the short time that was necessary to permit the removal of the captive from the village.

Tarzan of the Apes had no quarrel with the little men. He had accomplished that for which he had come and was ready to depart, but as he turned to descend from the tree there was a rending of wood, and the limb upon which he was standing broke suddenly from the stem of the tree and crashed to the ground beneath, carrying the ape-man with it.

The fall stunned him momentarily, and when he regained consciousness he found his body overrun by pygmy warriors who were just completing the act of trussing his arms and legs securely. Not knowing that they had completed their job, nor how well they had done it, the ape-man surged heavily upon his bonds, the effort sending the pygmies in all directions; but the cords held and the Lord of the Jungle knew that he was the captive of as cruel and merciless a people as the forests of the great river basin concealed.

The Betetes were still nervous and fearful. They had refastened the gates that Old Timer had opened, and a force of warriors was guarding this entrance as well as the one at the opposite end of the village. Poison-tipped spears and arrows were in readiness for any enemy who might approach, but the whole village was in a state of nervous terror bordering upon panic. Their chief was dead; the white girl whom they had been about to devour was gone; a gigantic white man had dropped from the heavens into their village and was now their prisoner. All these things had happened within a few seconds; it was little wonder that they were nervous.

As to their new captive there was a difference of opinion. Some thought that he should be slain at once, lest he escape. Others, impressed by the mysterious manner of his entrance into the village, were inclined to wait, being fearful because of their ignorance of his origin, which might easily be supernatural.

The possible danger of an attack by an enemy beyond their gates finally was a reprieve for the ape-man, for the simple reason that they dared not distract their attention from the defense of the village to indulge in an orgy of eating. Tomorrow night would answer even better, their leaders argued; and so a score of them half carried, half dragged the great body of their prisoner into an unoccupied hut, two of their number remaining outside the entrance on guard.

Swaying upon the topmost branch of a tree, Nkima hugged himself in grief and terror, but principally terror; for in many respects he was not greatly unlike the rest of us who, with Nkima, have descended from a common ancestor. His own troubles affected him more than the troubles of another, even though that other was a loved one.

This seemed a cruel world indeed to little Nkima. He was never long out of one trouble before another had him in its grip, though more often than not the troubles were of his own making. This time, however, he had been behaving perfectly (largely through the fact that he was terror-stricken in this strange forest); he had not insulted a single creature all day nor thrown missiles at one; yet here he was alone in the dark, the scent of Sheeta strong in his nostrils, and Tarzan a prisoner in the hands of the little Gomangani.

He wished that Muviro and the other Waziri were here, or Jad-bal-ja, the Golden Lion. Either of these would come to the rescue of Tarzan and save him, too; but they were far away. So far away were they that Nkima had long since given up hope of seeing any of them again. He wanted to go into the village of the little Gomangani that he might be near his master, but he dared not. He could only crouch in the tree and wait for Sheeta or Kudu. If Sheeta came first, as he fully expected him to do, that would be the last of little Nkima. But perhaps Kudu, the sun, would come first, in which event there would be another day of comparative safety before hideous night settled down again upon an unhappy world.

As his thoughts dwelt upon such lugubrious prophecies, there rose from the village below him the uncanny notes of a weird cry. The natives in the village were startled and terrified, because they only half guessed what it was. They had heard it before occasionally all during their lives, sounding mysterious and awe-inspiring from the dark distances of the jungle; but they had never heard it so close to them before. It sounded almost in the village. They had scarcely had time to think these thoughts when they learned that the terrible cry had been voiced from one of their own huts.

Two terrified warriors apprised them of this, the two warriors who had been placed on guard over their giant captive. Wide-eyed and breathless, they fled from their post of duty. "It is no man that we have captured," cried one of them, "but a demon. He has changed himself into a great ape. Did you not hear him?"

The other natives were equally frightened. They had no chief, no one to give orders, no one to whom they might look for advice and protection in an emergency of this nature. "Did you see him?" inquired one of the sentries. "What does he look like?"

"We did not see him, but we heard him."

"If you did not see him, how do you know that he has changed himself into a great ape?"

"Did I not say that I heard him?" demanded a sentry. "When the lion roars, do you have to go out into the forest to look at him to know that he is a lion?"

The skeptic scratched his head. Here was logic irrefutable. However, he felt that he must have the last word. "If you had looked, you would have known for sure," he said. "Had I been on guard I should have looked in the hut. I should not have run away like an old woman."

"Go and look, then," cried one of the sentries. The skeptic was silenced.

Nkima heard the weird cry from the village of the little men. It thrilled him, too, but it did not frighten him. He listened intently, but no sound broke the silence of the great forest. He became uneasy. He wished to raise his voice, too, but he dared not, knowing that Sheeta would hear. He wished to go to the side of his master, but fear was stronger than love. All he could do was wait and shiver; he did not dare whimper for fear of Sheeta.

Five minutes passed—five minutes during which the Betetes did a maximum of talking and a minimum of thinking. However, a few of them had almost succeeded in screwing up their courage to a point that would permit them to investigate the hut in which the captive was immured, when again the weird cry shattered the silence of the night; where-upon the investigation was delayed by common consent.

Now, faintly from afar sounded the roar of a lion; and a moment later out of the dim distance came an eerie cry that seemed a counterpart of that which had issued from the hut. After that, silence fell again upon the forest, but only for a short time. Now the wives of Rebega and the wives of the warriors who had been killed commenced their lamentations. They moaned and howled and smeared themselves with ashes.

An hour passed, during which the warriors held a council and chose a temporary chief. It was Nyalwa, who was known as a brave warrior. The little men felt better now; there was a recrudescence of courage. Nyalwa perceived this and realized that he should take advantage of it while it was hot. He also felt that, being chief, he should do something important.

"Let us go and kill the white man," he said. "We shall be safer when he is dead."

"And our bellies will be fuller," remarked a warrior. "Mine is very empty now."

"But what if he is not a man but a demon?" demanded another.

This started a controversy that lasted another hour, but at last it was decided that several of them should go to the hut and kill the prisoner; then more time was consumed deciding who should go. And during this time little Nkima had experienced an accession of courage. He had been watching the village all the time; and he had seen that no one approached the hut in which Tarzan was confined and that none of the natives were in that part of the village, all of them being congregated in the open space before the hut of the dead Rebega.

Fearfully Nkima descended from the tree and scampered to the palisade, which he scaled at the far end of the village where there were no little men, even those who had been guarding the rear gate having deserted it at the first cry of the prisoner. It took him but a moment to reach the hut in which Tarzan lay. At the entrance he stopped and peered into the dark interior, but he could see nothing. Again he grew very much afraid.

"It is little Nkima," he said. "Sheeta was there in the forest waiting for me. He tried to stop me, but I was not afraid. I have come to help Tarzan."

The darkness hid the smile that curved the lips of the ape-man. He knew his Nkima—knew that if Sheeta had been within a mile of him he would not have moved from the safety of the slenderest high-flung branch to which no Sheeta could pursue him. But he merely said, "Nkima is very brave."

The little monkey entered the hut and leaped to the broad chest of the ape-man. "I have come to gnaw the cords that hold you," he announced.

"That you cannot do," replied Tarzan; "otherwise I should have called you long ago."

"Why can I not?" demanded Nkima. "My teeth are very sharp."

"After the little men bound me with rope," explained Tarzan, "they twisted copper wire about my wrists and ankles. Nkima cannot gnaw through copper wire."

"I can gnaw through the cords," insisted Nkima, "and then I can take the wire off with my fingers."

"You can try," replied Tarzan, "but I think that you cannot do it."

Nyalwa had at last succeeded in finding five warriors who would accompany him to the hut and kill the prisoner. He regretted that he had suggested the plan, for he had found it necessary, as candidate for permanent chieftainship, to volunteer to head the party.

As they crept slowly toward the hut, Tarzan raised his head. "They come!" his whispered to Nkima. "Go out and meet them. Hurry!"

Nkima crept cautiously through the doorway. The sight that first met his eyes was of six warriors creeping stealthily toward him. "They come!" he screamed to Tarzan. "The little Gomangani come!" And then he fled precipitately.

The Betetes saw him and were astonished. They were also not a little fearful. "The demon has changed himself into a little monkey and escaped," cried a warrior.

Nyalwa hoped so, but it seemed almost too good to be true; however, he grasped at the suggestion. "Then we may go back," he said. "If he has gone we cannot kill him."

"We should look into the hut," urged a warrior who

had hoped to be chief and who would have been glad to demonstrate that he was braver than Nyalwa.

"We can look into it in the morning when it is light," argued Nyalwa; "it is very dark now. We could see nothing."

"I will go and get a brand from the fire," said the warrior, "and then if Nyalwa is afraid I will go into the hut. I am not afraid."

"I am not afraid," cried Nyalwa. "I will go in without any light." But he had no more than said it than he regretted it. Why was he always saying things first and thinking afterward!

"Then why do you stand still?" demanded the warrior. "You cannot get into the hut by standing still."

"I am not standing still," remonstrated Nyalwa, creeping forward very slowly.

While they argued, Nkima scaled the palisade and fled into the dark forest. He was very much afraid, but he felt better when he had reached the smaller branches of the trees, far above the ground. He did not pause here, however, but swung on through the darkness, for there was a fixed purpose in the mind of little Nkima. Even his fear of Sheeta was submerged in the excitation of his mission.

Nyalwa crept to the doorway of the hut and peered in. He could see nothing. Prodding ahead of him with his spear he stepped inside. The five warriors crowded to the entrance behind him. Suddenly there burst upon Nyalwa's startled ears the same weird cry that had so terrified them all before. Nyalwa wheeled and bolted for the open air, but the five barred his exit. He collided with them and tried to claw his way over or through them. He was terrified, but it was a question as to whether he was any more terrified than the five. They had not barred his way intentionally, but only because they had not moved as quickly as he. Now they rolled out upon the ground and, scrambling to their feet, bolted for the opposite end of the village.

"He is still there," announced Nyalwa after he had regained his breath. "That was what I went into the hut to learn. I have done what I said I would."

"We were going to kill him," said the warrior who would be chief. "Why did you not kill him? You were in there with him and you had your spear. He was bound and helpless. If you had let me go in, I would have killed him."

"Go in and kill him then," growled Nyalwa, disgusted.

"I have a better way," announced another warrior.

"What is it?" demanded Nyalwa, ready to jump at any suggestion.

"Let us all go and surround the hut; then when you give the word we will hurl our spears through the walls. In this way we shall be sure to kill the white man."

"That is just what I was going to suggest," stated Nyalwa. "We will all go; follow me!"

The little men crept again stealthily toward the hut. Their numbers gave them courage. At last they had surrounded it and were waiting the signal from Nyalwa. The spears with their poisoned tips were poised. The life of the ape-man hung in the balance, when a chorus of angry growls just beyond the palisade stilled the word of command on the lips of Nyalwa.

"What is that?" he cried.

The little men glanced toward the palisade and saw dark forms surmounting it. "The demons are coming!" shrieked one.

"It is the hairy men of the forest," cried another.

Huge, dark forms scaled the palisade and dropped into the village. The Betetes dropped back, hurling their spears. A little monkey perched upon the roof of a hut screamed and chattered. "This way!" he cried. "This way, Zu-tho! Here is Tarzan of the Apes in this nest of the Gomangani."

A huge, hulking form with great shoulders and long arms rolled toward the hut. Behind him were half a dozen enormous bulls. The Betetes had fallen back to the front of Rebega's hut.

"Here!" called Tarzan. "Tarzan is here, Zu-tho!"

The great ape stooped and peered into the dark interior of the hut. His enormous frame was too large for the small doorway. With his great hands he seized the hut by its door posts and tore it from the ground, tipping it over upon its back, as little Nkima leaped, screaming, to the roof of an adjacent hut.

"Carry me out into the forest," directed the ape-man.

Zu-tho lifted the white man in his arms and carried

him to the palisade, while the pygmies huddled behind the hut of Rebega, not knowing what was transpiring in that other part of their village. The other bulls followed, growling angrily. They did not like the scent of the man-things. They wished to get away. As they had come, they departed; and a moment later the dark shadows of the jungle engulfed them.

20

"I Hate You!"

AS Old Timer carried the girl out of the village of the Betetes into the forest, every fiber of his being thrilled to the contact of her soft, warm body. At last he held her in his arms. Even the danger of their situation was forgotten for the moment in the ecstasy of his gladness. He had found her! He had saved her! Even in the excitement of the moment he realized that no other woman had ever aroused within him such an overpowering tide of emotion.

She had not spoken; she had not cried out. As a matter of fact she did not know into whose hands she had now fallen. Her reaction to her rescue had been anything but a happy one, for she felt that she had been snatched from merciful death to face some new horror of life. The most reasonable explanation was that Bobolo had arrived in time to snatch her from the hands of the pygmies, and she preferred death to Bobolo.

A short distance from the village Old Timer lowered her to the ground and commenced to cut away her bonds. He had not spoken either. He had not dared trust his voice to speak, so loudly was his heart pounding in his throat. When the last bond was cut he helped her to her feet. He wanted to take her in his arms and crush her to him, but something stayed him. Suddenly he felt almost afraid of her. Then he found his voice.

"Thank God that I came in time," he said.

The girl voiced a startled exclamation of surprise. "You are a white man!" she cried. "Who are you?"

"Who did you think I was?"

"Bobolo."

He laughed. "I am the man you don't like," he explained.

"Oh! And you risked your life to save me. Why did you do it? It was obvious that you did not like me; perhaps that was the reason I did not like you."

"Let's forget all that and start over."

"Yes, of course," she agreed; "but you must have come a long way and faced many dangers to save me. Why did you do it?"

"Because I—" He hesitated. "Because I couldn't see a white woman fall into the hands of these devils."

"What are we going to do now? Where can we go?"

"We can't do much of anything before morning," he replied. "I'd like to get a little farther away from that village; then we must rest until morning. After that we'll try to reach my camp. It's two days' march on the opposite side of the river—if I can find the river. I got lost today trying to locate Rebega's village."

They moved on slowly through the darkness. He knew that they were starting in the right direction, for when he had come to the clearing where the village stood he had noted the constellations in the sky; but how long they could continue to hold their course in the blackness of the forest night where the stars were hidden from their view, he did not know.

"What happened to you after Bobolo dragged me from the canoe at the mouth of that frightful river?" she asked.

"They took me back to the temple."

The girl shuddered. "That terrible place!"

"They were going to—to prepare me for one of their feasts," he continued. "I imagine I'll never be so close to death as that again without dying. The priestesses were just about to mess me up with their clubs."

"How did you escape?"

"It was nothing short of a miracle," he replied. "Even now I cannot explain it. A voice called down from the rafters of the temple, claiming to be the *muzimo* of some native.

A *muzimo,* you know, is some kind of ghost; I think each one of them is supposed to have a *muzimo* that looks after him. Then the finest looking white man I ever saw shinned down one of the pillars, grabbed me right out from under the noses of the priests and priestesses, and escorted me to the river where he had a canoe waiting for me."

"Hadn't you ever seen him before?"

"No. I tell you it was a modern miracle, not unlike one that happened in the pygmy village just as I had busted in to head off that bloodthirsty, old she-devil who was going to knife you."

"The only miracle that I am aware of was your coming just when you did; if there was another I didn't witness it. You see I had my eyes closed, waiting for Wlala to use her knife, when you stopped her."

"I didn't stop her."

"What?"

"That was the miracle."

"I do not understand."

"Just as the woman grabbed you by the hair and raised her knife to kill you, an arrow passed completely through her body, and she fell dead. Then as I rushed in and the warriors started to interfere with me, three or four of them fell with arrows through them, but where the arrows came from I haven't the slightest idea. I didn't see anyone who might have shot them. I don't know whether it was someone trying to aid us, or some natives attacking the Betete village."

"Or some one else trying to steal me," suggested the girl. "I have been stolen so many times recently that I have come to expect it; but I hope it wasn't that, for they might be following us."

"Happy thought," commented Old Timer; "but I hope you're wrong. I think you are, too, for if they had been following us to get you, they would have been on us before. There is no reason why they should have waited."

They moved on slowly through the darkness for about half an hour longer; then the man stopped. "I think we had better rest until morning," he said, "though I don't know just how we are going to accomplish it. There is no place to lie down but the trail, and as that is used by the leopards at night it isn't exactly a safe couch."

"We might try the trees," she suggested.

"It is the only alternative. The underbrush is too thick here—we couldn't find a place large enough to lie down. Can you climb?"

"I may need a little help."

"I'll go up first and reach down and help you up," he suggested.

A moment later he had found a low branch and clambered onto it. "Here," he said, reaching down, "give me your hand." Without difficulty he swung her to his side. "Stay here until I find a more comfortable place."

She heard him climbing about in the tree for a few minutes, and then he returned to her. "I found just the place," he announced. "It couldn't have been better if it had been made to order." He helped her to her feet, and then he put an arm about her and assisted her from branch to branch as they climbed upward toward the retreat he had located.

It was a great crotch where three branches forked, two of them laterally and almost parallel. "I can fix this up like a Pullman," he observed. "Just wait a minute until I cut some small branches. How I ever stumbled on it in the dark gets me."

"Another miracle, perhaps," she suggested.

Growing all about them were small branches, and it did not take Old Timer long to cut as many as he needed. These he laid close together across the two parallel branches. Over them he placed a covering of leaves.

"Try that," he directed. "It may not be a feather bed, but it's better than none."

"It's wonderful." She had stretched out on it in the first utter relaxation she had experienced for days—relaxation of the mind and nerves even more than of the body. For the first time in days she did not lie with terror at her side.

He could see her only dimly in the darkness; but in his mind's eyes he visualized the contours of that perfect form, the firm bosom, the slender waist, the rounded thigh; and again passion swept through him like a racing torrent of molten gold.

"Where are you going to sleep?" she asked.

"I'll find a place," he replied huskily. He was edging closer to her. His desire to take her in his arms was almost maniacal.

"I am so happy," she whispered sleepily. "I didn't expect ever to be happy again. It must be because I feel so safe with you."

The man made no reply. Suddenly he felt very cold, as though his blood had turned to water; then a hot flush suffused him. "What the devil did she say that for?" he soliloquized. It angered him. He felt that it was not fair. What right had she to say it? She was *not* safe with him. It only made the thing that he contemplated that much harder to do—took some of the pleasure from it. Had he not saved her life at the risk of his own? Did she not owe him something? Did not all women owe him a debt for what one woman had done to him?

"It seems so strange," she said drowsily.

"What?" he asked.

"I was so afraid of you after you came to my camp, and now I should be afraid if you were not here. It just goes to show that I am not a very good judge of character, but really you were not very nice then. You seem to have changed."

He made no comment, but he groped about in the darkness until he had found a place where he could settle himself, not comfortably, but with a minimum of discomfort. He felt that he was weak from hunger and exhaustion. He would wait until tomorrow. He thought that it might be easier then when her confidence in him was not so fresh in his mind, but he did not give up his intention.

He wedged himself into a crotch where a great limb branched from the main bole of the tree. He was very uncomfortable there, but at least there was less danger that he might fall should he doze. The girl was a short distance above him. She seemed to radiate an influence that enveloped him in an aura at once delicious and painful. He was too far from her to touch her, yet always he felt her. Presently he heard the regular breathing that denoted that she slept. Somehow it reminded him of a baby—innocent, trusting, confident. He wished that it did not. Why was she so lovely? Why did she have hair like that? Why had God given her such eyes and lips? Why— Tired nature would be denied no longer. He slept.

Old Timer was very stiff and sore when he awoke. It was daylight. He glanced up toward the girl. She was sitting up looking at him. When their eyes met she smiled. Little things, trivial things often have a tremendous effect upon our lives. Had Kali Bwana not smiled then in just the way that she did, the lives of two people might have been very different.

"Good morning," she called, as Old Timer smiled back at her. "Did you sleep in that awful position all night?"

"It wasn't so bad," he assured her; "at least I slept."

"You fixed such a nice place for me; why didn't you do the same for yourself?"

"You slept well?" he asked.

"All night. I must have been dead tired; but perhaps what counted most was the relief from apprehension. It is the first night since before my men deserted me that I have felt free to sleep."

"I am glad," he said; "and now we must be on the move; we must get out of this district."

"Where can we go?"

"I want to go west first until we are below Bobolo's stamping grounds and then cut across in a northerly direction toward the river. We may have a little difficulty crossing it, but we shall find a way. At present I am more concerned about the Betetes than about Bobolo. His is a river tribe. They hunt and trap only a short distance in from the river, but the Betetes range pretty well through the forest. Fortunately for us they do not go very far to the west."

He helped her to the ground, and presently they found a trail that seemed to run in a westerly direction. Occasionally he saw fruits that he knew to be edible and gathered them; thus they ate as they moved slowly through the forest. They could not make rapid progress because both were physically weak from abstinence from sufficient food; but necessity drove them, and though they were forced to frequent rests they kept going.

Thirst had been troubling them to a considerable extent when they came upon a small stream, and here they drank and rested. Old Timer had been carefully scrutinizing the trail that they had been following for signs of the pygmies; but he had discovered no spoor of human foot and was convinced that this trail was seldom used by the Betetes.

The girl sat with her back against the stem of a small tree, while Old Timer lay where he could gaze at her profile surreptitiously. Since that morning smile he looked upon her out of new eyes from which the scales of selfishness and lust had fallen. He saw now beyond the glittering barrier of her physical charms a beauty of character that far transcended the former. Now he could appreciate the loyalty and the courage that had given her the strength to face the dangers of this savage world for—what?

The question brought his pleasant reveries to an abrupt conclusion with a shock. For what? Why, for Jerry Jerome, of course. Old Timer had never seen Jerry Jerome. All that he knew about him was his name, yet he disliked the man with all the fervor of blind jealousy. Suddeny he sat up.

"Are you married?" He shot the words as though from a pistol.

The girl looked at him in surprise. "'Why, no," she replied.

"Are you engaged?"

"Aren't your questions a little personal?" There was just a suggestion of the total frigidity that had marked her intercourse with him that day that he had come upon her in her camp.

Why shouldn't he be personal, he thought. Had he not saved her life; did she not owe him everything? Then came a realization of the caddishness of his attitude. "I am sorry," he said.

For a long time he sat gazing at the ground, his arms folded across his knees, his chin resting on them. The girl watched him intently; those level, grey eyes seemed to be evaluating him. For the first time since she had met him she was examining his face carefully. Through the unkempt beard she saw strong, regular features, saw that the man was handsome in spite of the dirt and the haggard look caused by deprivation and anxiety. Neither was he as old as she had thought him. She judged that he must still be in his twenties.

"Do you know," she remarked presently, "that I do not even know your name?"

He hesitated a moment before replying and then said, "The Kid calls me Old Timer."

"That is not a name," she remonstrated, "and you are not old."

"Thank you," he acknowledged, "but if a man is as old as he feels I am the oldest living man."

"You are tired," she said soothingly, her voice like the caress of a mother's hand; "you have been through so much, and all for me." Perhaps she recalled the manner in which she had replied to his recent question, and regretted it. "I think you should rest here as long as you can."

"I am all right," he told her; "it is you who should rest, but it is not safe here. We must go on, no matter how tired we are, until we are farther away from the Betete country." He rose slowly to his feet and offered her his hand.

Across the stream, through which he carried her despite her objections that he must not overtax his strength, they came upon a wider trail along which they could walk abreast. Here he stopped again to cut two staffs. "They will help us limp along," he remarked with a smile; "we are getting rather old, you know." But the one that he cut for himself was heavy and knotted at one end. It had more the appearance of a weapon than a walking stick.

Again they took up their weary flight, elbow to elbow. The feel of her arm touching his occasionally sent thrills through every fiber of his body; but recollection of Jerry Jerome dampened them. For some time they did not speak, each occupied with his own thoughts. It was the girl who broke the silence.

"Old Timer is not a name," she said; "I cannot call you that—it's silly."

"It is not much worse than my real name," he assured her. "I was named for my grandfather, and grandfathers so often have peculiar names."

"I know it," she agreed, "but yet they were good old substantial names. Mine was Abner."

"Did you have only one?" he bantered.

"Only one named Abner. What was yours, the one you were named for?"

"Hiram; but my friends call me Hi," he added hastily.

"But your last name? I can't call you Hi."

"Why not? We are friends, I hope."

"All right," she agreed; "but you haven't told me your last name."

"Just call me Hi," he said a little shortly.

"But suppose I have to introduce you to some one?"

"To whom, for instance?"

"Oh, Bobolo," she suggested, laughingly.

"I have already met the gentleman; but speaking about names," he added, "I don't know yours."

"The natives called me Kali Bwana."

"But I am not a native," he reminded her.

"I like Kali," she said; "call me Kali."

"It means woman. All right, Woman."

"If you call me that, I shan't answer you."

"Just as you say, Kali." Then after a moment, "I rather like it myself; it makes a cute name for a girl."

As they trudged wearily along, the forest became more open, the underbrush was not so dense, and the trees were farther apart. In an open space Old Timer halted and looked up at the sun; then he shook his head.

"We've been going east instead of south," he announced.

"How hopeless!"

"I'm sorry; it was stupid of me, but I couldn't see the sun because of the damned trees. Oftentimes inanimate objects seem to assume malign personalities that try to thwart one at every turn and then gloat over his misfortunes."

"Oh, it wasn't your fault," she cried quickly. "I didn't intend to imply that. You've done all that anyone could have."

"I'll tell you what we can do," he announced.

"Yes, what?"

"We can go on to the next stream and follow that to the river; it's bound to run into the river somewhere. It's too dangerous to go back to the one we crossed back there. In the meantime we might as well make up our minds that we're in for a long, hard trek and prepare for it."

"How? What do you mean?"

"We must eat; and we have no means of obtaining food other than the occasional fruits and tubers that we may find, which are not very strengthening food to trek on. We must have meat, but we have no means for obtaining it. We need weapons."

"And there is no sporting goods house near, not even a hardware store." Her occasional, unexpected gaieties heartened him. She never sighed or complained. She was often serious, as became their situation; but even disaster, added to all the trials she had endured for weeks, could not dampen her spirits entirely nor destroy her sense of humor.

"We shall have to be our own armorers," he explained. "We shall have to make our own weapons."

"Let's start on a couple of Thompson machine guns," she suggested. "I should feel much safer if we had them."

"Bows and arrows and a couple of spears are about all we rate," he assured her.

"I imagine I could make a machine gun as readily," she admitted. "What useless things modern women are!"

"I should scarcely say that. I don't know what I should do without you." The involuntary admission slipped out so suddenly that he scarcely realized what he had said—he, the woman-hater. But the girl did, and she smiled.

"I thought you didn't like women," she remarked, quite seriously. "It seems to me that I recall quite distinctly that you gave me that impression the afternoon that you came to my camp."

"Please don't," he begged. "I did not know you then."

"What a pretty speech! It doesn't sound at all like the old bear I first met."

"I am not the same man, Kali." He spoke the words in a low voice seriously.

To the girl it sounded like a confession and a plea for forgiveness. Impulsively she placed a hand on his arm. The soft, warm touch was like a spark to powder. He wheeled and seized her, pressing her close to him, crushing her body to his as though he would make them one; and in the same instant, before she could prevent it, his lips covered hers in a brief, hot kiss of passion.

She struck at him and tried to push him away. "How— how dared you!" she cried. "I hate you!"

He let her go and they stood looking at one another, panting a little from exertion and excitement.

"I hate you!" she repeated.

He looked into her blazing eyes steadily for a long moment. "I love you, Kali," he said, "my Kali!"

21

Because Nsenene Loved

ZU-THO, the great ape, had quarrelled with To-yat, the king. Each had coveted a young she just come into maturity. To-yat was a mighty bull, the mightiest of the tribe, for which excellent reason he was king; therefore Zu-tho hesitated to engage him in mortal combat. However, that did not lessen his desire for the fair one; so he ran away with her, coaxing some of the younger bulls who were dissatisfied with the rule of To-yat to accompany them. They came and brought their mates. Thus are new tribes formed. There is always a woman at the bottom of it.

Desiring peace, Zu-tho had moved to new hunting grounds far removed from danger of a chance meeting with To-yat. Ga-yat, his life-long friend, was among those who had accompanied him. Ga-yat was a mighty bull, perhaps mightier than To-yat himself; but Go-yat was of an easy-going disposition. He did not care who was king as long as he had plenty to eat and was not disturbed in the possession of his mates, a contingency that his enormous size and his great strength rendered remote.

Ga-yat and Zu-tho were good friends of Tarzan, perhaps Ga-yat even more than the latter, for Ga-yat was more inclined to be friendly; so when they saw Tarzan in the new jungle they had chosen for their home they were glad, and when they heard his cry for help they hastened to him, taking all but the two that Zu-tho left to guard the shes and the balus.

They had carried Tarzan far away from the village of the Gomangani to a little open glade beside a stream. Here they laid him on soft grasses beneath the shade of a tree,

but they could not remove the wires that held his wrists
and ankles. They tried and Nkima tried; but all to no avail,
though the little monkey finally succeeded in gnawing
the ropes which had also been placed around both his wrists
and his ankles.

Nkima and Ga-yat brought food and water to Tarzan,
and the great apes were a protection to him against the
prowling carnivores; but the ape-man knew that this could
not last for long. Soon they would move on to some other
part of the forest, as was their way, nor would any considerations of sympathy or friendship hold them. Of the former they
knew little or nothing, and of the latter not sufficient to make
them self-sacrificing.

Nkima would remain with him; he would bring him
food and water, but he would be no protection. At the first
glimpse of Dango, the hyaena, or Sheeta, the leopard,
little Nkima would flee, screaming, to the trees. Tarzan
racked his fertile brain for a solution to his problem. He
thought of his great and good friend, Tantor, the elephant,
but was forced to discard him as a possibility for escape
as Tantor could no more remove his bonds than the apes.
He could carry him, but where? There was no friend within
reach to untwist the confining wire. Tantor would protect him,
but of what use would protection be if he must lie here
bound and helpless. Better death than that.

Presently, however, a solution suggested itself; and he
called Ga-yat to him. The great bull came lumbering to his
side. "I am Ga-yat," he announced, after the manner of the
great apes. It was a much shorter way of saying, "You called
me, and I am here. What do you want?"

"Ga-yat is not afraid of anything," was Tarzan's manner of
approaching the subject he had in mind.

"Ga-yat is not afraid," growled the bull. "Ga-yat kills."

"Ga-yat is not afraid of the Gomangani," continued the
ape-man.

"Ga-yat is not afraid," which was a much longer way of
saying no.

"Only the Tarmangani or the Gomangani can remove the
bonds that keep Tarzan a prisoner."

"Ga-yat kills the Tarmangani and the Gomangani."

"No," objected Tarzan. "Ga-yat will go and fetch one to take the wires from Tarzan. Do not kill. Bring him here."

"Ga-yat understands," said the bull after a moment's thought.

"Go now," directed the ape-man, and with no further words Ga-yat lumbered away and a moment later had disappeared into the forest.

*   *   *   *   *   *   *

The Kid and his five followers arrived at the north bank of the river opposite the village of Bobolo, where they had no difficulty in attracting the attention of the natives upon the opposite side and by means of signs appraising them that they wished to cross.

Presently several canoes put out from the village and paddled up stream to make the crossing. They were filled with warriors, for as yet Bobolo did not know either the identity or numbers of his visitors and was taking no chances. Sobito was still with him and had given no intimation that the Leopard Men suspected that he had stolen the white priestess, yet there was always danger that Gato Mgungu might lead an expedition against him.

When the leading canoe came close to where The Kid stood, several of the warriors in it recognized him, for he had been often at the village of Bobolo; and soon he and his men were taken aboard and paddled across to the opposite bank.

There was little ceremony shown him, for he was only a poor elephant poacher with a miserable following of five Negroes; but eventually Bobolo condescended to receive him; and he was led to the chief's hut, where Bobolo and Sobito, with several of the village elders, were seated in the shade.

The Kid's friendly greeting was answered with a surly nod. "What does the white man want?" demanded Bobolo.

The youth was quick to discern the altered attitude of the chief; before, he had always been friendly. He did not relish the implied discourtesy of the chief's salutation, the omission of the deferential *bwana;* but what was he to do? He fully realized his own impotency, and though it galled him to do so he was forced to overlook the insulting inflection that Boblolo had given the words "white man."

"I have come to get you to help me find my friend, the old bwana," he said. "My *boys* say that he went into the village of Gato Mgungu, but that he never came out."

"Why do you come to me, then," demanded Bobolo; "why do you not go to Gato Mgungu?"

"Because you are our friend," replied The Kid; "I believed that you would help me."

"How can I help you? I know nothing about your friend."

"You can send men with me to the village of Gato Mgungu," replied The Kid, "while I demand the release of the old bwana."

"What will you pay me?" asked Bobolo.

"I can pay you nothing now. When we get ivory I will pay."

Bobolo sneered. "I have no men to send with you," he said. "You come to a great chief and bring no presents; you ask him to give you warriors and you have nothing to pay for them."

The Kid lost his temper. "You lousy old scoundrel!" he exclaimed. "You can't talk that way to me and get away with it. I'll give you until tomorrow morning to come to your senses." He turned on his heel and walked down the village street, followed by his five retainers; then he heard Bobolo yelling excitedly to his men to seize him. Instantly the youth realized the predicament in which his hot temper had placed him. He thought quickly, and before the warriors had an opportunity to arrest him he turned back toward Bobolo's hut.

"And another thing," he said as he stood again before the chief; "I have already dispatched a messenger down river to the station telling them about this affair and my suspicions. I told them that I would be here waiting for them when they came with soldiers. If you are thinking of harming me, Bobolo, be sure that you have a good story ready, for I told them that I was particularly suspicious of you."

He waited for no reply, but turned again and walked toward the village gate, nor was any hand raised to stay him. He grinned to himself as he passed out of the village, for he had sent no messenger, and no soldiers were coming.

As a gesture of contempt for the threats of Bobolo, The Kid made camp close to the village; but his men were not a little perturbed. Some of the villagers came out with food, and from his almost exhausted stores the white extracted enough cloth to purchase a day's rations for himself and his men. Among his callers was a girl whom he had known for some time. She was a happy, good-natured creature; and The Kid had found amusement in talking to her. In the past he had given her little presents, which pleased her simple heart, as did the extravagant compliments that The Kid amused himself by paying her.

Bring a girl presents often and tell her that she is the most beautiful girl in the village, and you may be laying the foundation for something unpleasant in the future. You may be joking, but the girl may be in earnest. This one was. That she had fallen in love with The Kid should have worked to his detriment as a punishment for his thoughtlessness, but it did not.

At dusk the girl returned, sneaking stealthily through the shadows. The Kid was startled by her abrupt appearance before his tent, where he sat smoking.

"Hello there, Nsenene!" he exclaimed. "What brings you here?" He was suddenly impressed by the usually grave demeanor of the girl and her evident excitement.

"Hush!" cautioned the girl. "Do not speak my name. They would kill me if they knew I had come here."

"What's wrong?"

"Much is wrong. Bobolo is going to send men with you tomorrow. He will tell you that they are going to the village of Gato Mgungu with you, but they will not. When they get you out in the river, out of sight of the village, they will kill you and all your men and throw you to the crocodiles. Then when the white men come, they will tell them that they left you at the village of Gato Mgungu; and the white men will go and they will find no village, because it has been burned by the Utengas. There will be no one there to tell them that Bobolo lied."

"Gato Mgungu's village burned! What became of the old bwana?"

"I know nothing about him, but he is not at the village of Gato Mgungu, because there is no village there. I think he is dead. I heard it said that the Leopard Men killed him.

Bobolo is afraid of the Leopard Men because he stole their white priestess from them."

"White priestess! What do you mean?" demanded The Kid.

"They had a white priestess. I saw her here when Bobolo brought her to be his wife, but Ubooga would not have her around and made Bobolo send her away. She was a white woman, very white, with hair the color of the moon."

"When was this?" demanded the astonished youth.

"Three days ago, maybe four days. I do not remember."

"Where is she now? I should like to see her."

"You will never see her," replied Nsenene; "no one will ever see her."

"Why not?"

"Because they sent her to the village of the little men."

"You mean the Betetes?"

"Yes, the Betetes. They are eaters of men."

"Where is their village?" asked The Kid.

"You want to go there and get the white woman?" demanded Nsenene suspiciously.

There was something in the way the girl asked the question that gave The Kid his first intimation that her interest was prompted by more than friendship for him, for there was an unquestionable tinge of jealous suspicion in her tone. He leaned forward with a finger on his lips. "Don't tell anybody, Nsenene," he cautioned in a whisper; "but the white woman is my sister. I must go to her rescue. Now tell me where the village is, and next time I come I'll bring you a fine present." If he had felt any compunction about lying to the girl, which he did not, he could easily have salved his conscience with the knowledge that he had done it in a good cause; for if there was any truth in the story of the white priestess, captive of the Betetes, then there was but one course of procedure possible for him, the only white man in the district who had knowledge of her predicament. He had thought of saying that the woman was his mother or daughter, but had compromised on sister as appearing more reasonable.

"Your sister!" exclaimed Nsenene. "Yes, now that I remember, she looked like you. Her eyes and her nose were like yours."

The Kid suppressed a smile. Suggestion and imagination were potent powers. "We do look alike," he admitted; "but tell me, where is the village?"

As well as she could Nsenene described the location of the village of Rebega. "I will go with you, if you will take me," she suggested. "I do not wish to stay here any longer. My father is going to sell me to an old man whom I do not like. I will go with you and cook for you. I will cook for you until I die."

"I cannot take you now," replied The Kid. "Maybe some other time, but this time there may be fighting."

"Some other time then," said the girl. "Now I must go back to the village before they close the gates."

At the first break to dawn The Kid set out in search of the village of Rebega. He told his men that he had given up the idea of going to the village of Gato Mgungu, but that while they were here he was going to look for ivory on this side of the river. If he had told them the truth, they would not have accompanied him.

22

In the Crucible of Danger

FOR a long time Old Timer and the girl walked on in silence. There were no more interchanges of friendly conversation. The atmosphere was frigid. Kali Bwana walked a little behind the man. Often her eyes were upon him. She was thinking seriously, but what her thoughts were she did not reveal.

When they came to a pleasant open stretch through which a small stream wound, Old Timer stopped beneath a great tree that grew upon the bank of the stream. "We shall remain here for a while," he said.

The girl made no comment, and he did not look at her but started at once to make camp. First he gathered dead branches of suitable size, for a shelter, cutting a few green ones to give it greater strength. These he formed into a frame-work resembling that of an Indian wicki-up, covering the whole with leafy branches and grasses.

While he worked, the girl assisted him, following his example without asking for directions. Thus they worked in silence. When the shelter was finished he gathered wood for a fire. In this work she helped him, too.

"We shall be on short rations," he said, "until I can make a bow and some arrows."

This elicited no response from the girl; and he went his way, searching for suitable material for his weapon. He never went far, never out of sight of the camp; and presently he was back again with the best that he could find. With his knife he shaped a bow, rough but practical; and then he strung it with the pliable stem of a slender creeper that he had seen natives use for the same purpose in an emergency. This done, he commenced to make arrows. He worked rapidly, and the girl noticed the deftness of his strong fingers. Sometimes she watched his face, but on the few occasions that he chanced to look up she had quickly turned her eyes away before he could catch them upon him.

There were other eyes watching them from the edge of a bit of jungle farther up the stream, close-set, red-rimmed, savage eyes beneath beetling brows; but neither of them was aware of this; and the man continued his work, and the girl continued to study his face contemplatively. She still felt his arms about her; his lips were still hot upon hers. How strong he was! She had felt in that brief moment that he could have crushed her like an egg shell, and yet in spite of his savage impulsiveness he had been tender and gentle.

But these thoughts she tried to put from her and remember only that he was a boor and a cad. She scanned his clothing that now no longer bore even a resemblance to clothing, being nothing but a series of rags held together by a few shreds and the hand of Providence. What a creature to dare take her in his arms! What a thing to dare kiss her! She flushed anew at the recollection. Then she let her eyes wander again to his face. She tried to see only the unkempt beard, but through it her eyes persisted in seeing the contours of his fine features. She became almost angry with herself and turned her eyes away that she might not longer entertain this line of thought; and as she did so she stifled a scream and leaped to her feet.

"God!" she cried; "look!"

At her first cry the man raised his eyes. Then he, too, leaped to his feet. "Run!" he cried to the girl. "For God's sake, Kali, run!"

But she did not run. She stood there waiting, in her hand the futile staff he had cut for her that she had seized as she leaped to her feet; and the man waited, his heavier cudgel ready in his hand.

Almost upon them, rolling toward them in his awkward gait, was an enormous bull ape, the largest that Old Timer had ever seen. The man glanced quickly sideways and was horrified to see the girl still standing there near him.

"Please run away, Kali," he implored. "I cannot stop him; but I can delay him, and you must get away before he can get you. Don't you understand, Kali? It is you he wants." But the girl did not move, and the great beast was advancing steadily. "Please!" begged the man.

"You did not run away when I was in danger," she reminded him.

He started to reply; but the words were never spoken, for it was then that the ape charged. Old Timer struck with his club, and the girl rushed in and struck with hers. Utter futility! The beast grasped the man's weapon, tore it from his hand, and flung it aside. With his other hand he sent Kali Bwana spinning with a blow that might have felled an ox had not the man broken its force by seizing the shaggy arm; then he picked Old Timer up as one might a rag doll and rolled off toward the jungle.

When the girl, still half dazed from the effect of the blow, staggered to her feet she was alone; the man and the beast had disappeared. She called aloud, but there was no reply. She thought that she had been unconscious, but she did not know; so she could not know how long it had been since the beast had carried the man away. She tried to follow, but she did not know in which direction they had gone; she would have followed and fought for the man—her man. The words formed in her mind and brought no revulsion of feeling. Had he not called her "my Kali"—my woman?

What a change this brief episode had wrought in her!

A moment before, she had been trying to hate him, trying to seek out everything disgusting about him—his rags, his beard, the dirt upon him. Now she would have given a world to have him back, nor was it alone because she craved protection. This she realized. Perhaps she realized the truth, too; but if she did she was not ashamed. She loved him, loved this nameless man of rags and tatters.

*   *   *   *   *   *   *

Tarzan of the Apes stoically awaited his fate, whatever it might be. He neither wasted his strength in useless efforts to break bonds that he had found unbreakable, nor dissipated his nervous energy in futile repining. He merely lay still. Nkima squatted dejectedly beside him. There was always something wrong with the world; so Nkima should have been accustomed to that, but he liked to feel sorry for himself. Today he was in his prime; he could scarcely have been more miserable if Sheeta had been pursuing him.

The afternoon was waning as Tarzan's keen ears caught the sound of approaching footsteps. He heard them before either Nkima or the great apes heard them, and he voiced a low growl that apprised the others. Instantly the great, shaggy beasts were alert. The shes and the balus gathered nearer the bulls; all listened in absolute silence. They sniffed the air; but the wind blew from them toward whatever was approaching, so that they could detect no revealing spoor. The bulls were nervous; they were prepared either for instant battle or for flight.

Silently, notwithstanding its great weight, a mighty figure emerged from the forest. It was Ga-yat. Under one arm he carried a man-thing. Zu-tho growled. He could see Ga-yat; but he could not smell him, and one knows that one's eyes and ears may deceive one, but never one's nose. "I am Zu-tho," he growled, baring his great fighting fangs. "I kill!"

"I am Ga-yat," answered the other, as he lumbered toward Tarzan.

Presently the others caught his scent spoor and were satisfied, but the scent of the man-thing annoyed and angered them. They came forward, growling. "Kill the Tarmangani!" was on the lips of many.

Ga-yat carried Old Timer to where Tarzan lay and threw him unceremoniously to the ground. "I am Ga-yat," he said; "here is a Tarmangani. Ga-yat saw no Gomangani."

The other bulls were crowding close, anxious to fall upon the man-thing. Old Timer had never seen such a concourse of great apes, had never known that they grew so large. It was evident that they were not gorillas, and they were more man-like than any apes he had seen. He recalled the stories that natives had told of these hairy men of the forest, stories that he had not believed. He saw the white man lying bound and helpless among them, but at first he did not recognize him. He thought that he, too, was a prisoner of these man-like brutes. What terrible creatures they were! He was thankful that his captor had taken him rather than Kali. Poor Kali! What would become of her now?

The bulls were pressing closer. Their intentions were evident even to the man. He thought the end was near. Then, to his astonishment, he heard savage growls burst from the lips of the man near him, saw his lip curl upward, revealing strong, white teeth.

"The Tarmangani belongs to Tarzan," growled the ape-man. "Do not harm that which is Tarzan's."

Ga-yat and Zu-tho turned upon the other bulls and drove them back, while Old Timer looked on in wide-eyed astonishment. He had not understood what Tarzan said; he could scarcely believe that he had communicated with the apes, yet the evidence was such that he was convinced of it against his better judgment. He lay staring at the huge, hairy creatures moving slowly away from him; even they seemed unreal.

"You are no sooner out of one difficulty than you find yourself in another," said a deep, low voice in English.

Old Timer turned his eyes toward the speaker. The voice was familiar. Now he recognized him. "You are the man who got me out of that mess in the temple!" he exclaimed.

"And now I am in a 'mess,'" said the other.

"Both of us," added Old Timer. "What do you suppose they will do with us?"

"Nothing," replied the ape-man.

"Then why did they bring me here?"

"I told one of them to go and get me a man," replied Tarzan. "Evidently you chanced to be the first man he came upon. I did not expect a white man."

"You sent that big brute that got me? They do what you ask? Who are you, and why did you send for a man?"

"I am Tarzan of the Apes, and I wanted someone who could untwist these wires that are around my wrists; neither the apes nor Nkima could do it."

"Tarzan of the Apes!" exclaimed Old Timer. "I thought you were only a part of the folklore of the natives." As he spoke he started to work on the wires that confined the ape-man's wrists—copper wires that untwisted easily.

"What became of the white girl?" asked the latter. "You got her out of the Betete village, but I couldn't follow you because the little devils got me."

"You were there! Ah, now I see; it was you who shot the arrows."

"Yes."

"How did they get you, and how did you get away from them?"

"I was in a tree above them. The branch broke. I was stunned for a moment. Then they bound me."

"That was the crash I heard as I was leaving the village."

"Doubtless," agreed the ape-man. "I called the great apes," he continued, "and they came and carried me here. Where is the white girl?"

"She and I were on our way toward my camp when the ape got me," explained Old Timer. "She is alone back there now. When I get these wires off, may I go back to her?"

"I shall go with you. Where was the place? Do you think you can find it?"

"It cannot be far, not more than a few miles, yet I may not be able to find it."

"I can," said Tarzan.

"How?" inquired Old Timer.

"By Ga-yat's spoor. It is still fresh."

The white man nodded, but he was not convinced. He thought it would be a slow procedure picking out the foot-

prints of the beast all the way back to the spot at which
he had been seized. He had removed the wires from Tarzan's wrists and was working upon those of his ankles; a
moment later the ape-man was free. He leaped to his feet.

"Come!" he directed and started at a trot toward the spot
at which Ga-yat had emerged from the jungle.

Old Timer tried to keep up with him, but discovered that
he was weak from hunger and exhaustion. "You go ahead,"
he called to the ape-man. "I cannot keep up with you, and
we can't waste any time. She is there alone."

"If I leave you, you will get lost," objected Tarzan. "Wait,
I have it!" He called to Nkima, who was swinging through
the trees above them, and the monkey dropped to his shoulder. "Stay near the Tarmangani," he directed, "and show him
the trail that Tarzan follows."

Nkima objected; he was not interested in the Tarmangani,
but at last he understood that he must do as Tarzan wished.
Old Timer watched them chattering to one another. It
seemed incredible that they were conversing, yet the illusion
was perfect.

"Follow Nkima," said Tarzan; "he will guide you in the
right direction." Then he was off at a swinging trot along
a track that Old Timer could not see.

*   *   *   *   *   *   *

Kali Bwana was stunned by the hopelessness of her position. After the brief sense of security she had enjoyed since
the man had taken her from the village of the pygmies her
present situation seemed unbearable by contrast, and in addition she had suffered a personal loss. To the burden of her
danger was added grief.

She gazed at the crude shelter he had built for her, and
two tears rolled down her cheeks. She picked up the bow
he had made and pressed her lips against the insensate wood.
She knew that she would never see him again, and the
thought brought a choking sob to her throat. It had been
long since Kali Bwana had wept. In the face of privation,
adversity, and danger she had been brave; but now she crept
into the shelter and gave herself over to uncontrolled grief.

What a mess she had made of everything! Thus ran her thoughts. Her ill-conceived search for Jerry had ended in failure; but worse, it had embroiled a total stranger and led him to his death, nor was he the first to die because of her. There had been the faithful Andereya, whom the Leopard Men had killed when they captured her; and there had been Wlala, and Rebega, and his three warriors—all these lives snuffed out because of her stubborn refusal to understand her own limitations. The white officers and civilians along the lower stretch of the river had tried to convince her, but she had refused to listen. She had had her own way, but at what price! She was paying now in misery and remorse.

For some time she lay there, a victim of vain regrets; and then she realized the futility of repining, and by an effort of the will seized control of her shaken nerves. She told herself that she must not give up, that even this last, terrible blow must not stop her. She still lived, and she had not found Jerry. She would go on. She would try to reach the river; she would try in some way to cross it, and she would find Old Timer's camp and enlist the aid of his partner. But she must have food, strength-giving flesh. She could not carry on in her weakened condition. The bow that *he* had made, and that she had hugged to her breast as she lay in the shelter, would furnish her the means to secure meat; and with this thought in mind she arose and went out to gather up the arrows. It was still not too late to hunt.

As she emerged from the frail hut she saw one of the creatures that she had long feared inwardly, knowing that this forest abounded in them—a leopard. The beast was standing at the edge of the jungle looking toward her. As its yellow eyes discovered her, it dropped to its belly, its face grimacing in a horrid snarl. Then it started to creep cautiously toward her, its tail weaving sinuously. It could have charged and destroyed her without these preliminaries; but it seemed to be playing with her, as a cat plays with a mouse.

Nearer and nearer it came. The girl fitted an arrow to the bow. She knew how futile a gesture it would be to launch that tiny missile at this great engine of destruction; but she was courageous, and she would not give up her life without defending it to the last.

The beast was coming closer. She wondered when it would charge. Many things passed through her mind, but clear and outstanding above all the rest was the image of a man in rags and tatters. Then, beyond the leopard, she saw a figure emerge from the jungle—a giant white man, naked but for a loin cloth.

He did not hesitate. She saw him running quickly forward toward the leopard; and she saw that the beast did not see him, for its eyes were upon her. The man made no sound as he sprang lightly across the soft turf. Suddenly, to her horror, she saw that he was unarmed.

The leopard raised its body a little from the ground. It gathered its hind feet beneath it. It was about to start the swift rush that would end in death for her. Then she saw the running man launch himself through the air straight for the back of the grim beast. She wanted to close her eyes to shut out the horrid scene that she knew must ensue as the leopard turned and tore his rash antagonist to ribbons.

What followed after the bronzed body of the white man closed with that of the great cat defied her astonished eyes to follow. There was a swift intermingling of spotted hide and bronzed skin, of arms and legs, of talons and teeth; and above all rose the hideous growls of two blood-mad beasts. To her horror she realized that not the cat alone was the author of them; the growls of the man were as savage as those of the beast.

From the midst of the whirling mass she saw the man suddenly rise to his feet, dragging the leopard with him. His powerful fingers encircled the throat of the carnivore from behind. The beast struck and struggled to free itself from that grip of death, but no longer did it growl. Slowly its struggles lessened in violence, and at last it went limp; then the man released one hand and twisted its neck until the vertebrae snapped, after which he cast the carcass to the ground. For a moment he stood over it. He seemed to have forgotten the girl; then he placed a foot upon it, and the forest re-echoed to the victory cry of the bull ape.

Kali Bwana shuddered. She felt her flesh turn cold. She

thought to flee from this terrible wild man of the forest; then he turned toward her, and she knew that it was too late. She still held the bow and arrow ready in her hands. She wondered if she could hold him off with these. He did not appear an easy man to frighten.

Then he spoke to her. "I seem to have arrived just in time," he said quietly. "Your friend will be here presently," he added, for he saw that she was afraid of him. That one should fear him was no new thing to Tarzan of the Apes. There were many who had feared him, and perhaps for this reason he had come to expect it from every stranger. "You may put down your bow. I shall not harm you."

She lowered the weapon to her side. "My friend!" she repeated. "Who? Whom do you mean?"

"I do not know his name. Have you many friends here?"

"Only one, but I thought him dead. A huge ape carried him away."

"He is safe," the ape-man assured her. "He is following behind me."

Kali Bwana sank limply to the ground. "Thank God!" she murmured.

Tarzan stood with folded arms watching her. How small and delicate she looked! He wondered that she had been able to survive all that she had passed through. The Lord of the Jungle admired courage, and he knew what courage this slender girl must possess to have undergone what she had undergone and still be able to face a charging leopard with that puny weapon lying on the grass beside her.

Presently he heard some one approaching and knew it was the man. When he appeared he was breathing hard from his exertion, but at sight of the girl he ran forward. "You are all right?" he cried. He had seen the dead leopard lying near her.

"Yes," she replied.

To Tarzan, her manner seemed constrained, and so did that of the man. He did not know what had passed between them just before they had been separated. He could not guess what was in the heart of each, nor could Old Timer guess what was in the heart of the girl. Being a girl, now that the man was safe, she sought to hide her true emotions from him. And Old Timer was ill at ease. Fresh in his mind were the events of the afternoon; ringing in his ears her bitter cry, "I hate you!"

Briefly he told her all that had occurred since the ape had carried him away, and then they planned with Tarzan for the future. He told them that he would remain with them until they had reached the man's camp, or that he would accompany them down river to the first station; but to Old Timer's surprise the girl said that she would go to his camp and there attempt to organize a new safari, either to accompany her down river or in the further prosecution of her search for Jerry Jerome.

Before night fell Tarzan had brought meat to the camp, using the bow and arrows that Old Timer had made, and the man and the girl cooked theirs over a fire while the ape-man sat apart tearing at the raw flesh with his strong, white teeth. Little Nkima, perched upon his shoulder, nodded sleepily.

23

Converging Trails

EARLY the next morning they started for the river, but they had not gone far when the wind veered into the north, and Tarzan halted. His delicate nostrils questioned the tell-tale breeze.

"There is a camp just ahead of us," he announced. "There are white men in it."

Old Timer strained his eyes into the forest. "I can see nothing," he said.

"Neither can I," admitted Tarzan; "but I have a nose."

"You can smell them?" asked Kali.

"Certainly, and because my nose tells me that there are white men there I assume that it is a friendly camp; but we will have a look at it before we go too close. Wait here."

He swung into the trees and was gone, leaving the man and the girl alone together; yet neither spoke what was in his heart. The constraint of yesterday still lay heavily upon him. He wanted to ask her forgiveness for having taken her into his arms, for having dared to kiss her. She wanted him to take her into his arms again and kiss her. But they stood there in silence like two strangers until Tarzan returned.

"They are all right," announced the ape-man. "It is a company of soldiers with their white officers and one civilian. Come! They may prove the solution of all your difficulties."

The soldiers were breaking camp as Tarzan and his companions arrived. The surprised shouts of the black soldiers attracted the attention of the white men—two officers and a civilian—who came forward to meet them. As his eyes fell upon the civilian, Old Timer voiced an exclamation of surprise.

"The Kid!" he exclaimed, and the girl brushed past him and ran forward, a glad cry upon her lips.

"Jerry! Jerry!" she cried as she threw herself into The Kid's arms.

Old Timer's heart sank. Jerry! Jerry Jerome, his best friend! What cruel tricks fate can play.

When the greetings and the introductions were over, the strange combination of circumstances that had brought them together thus unexpectedly were explained as the story of each was unfolded.

"Not long ago," the lieutenant in command of the expedition explained to Kali, "we heard rumors of the desertion of your men. We arrested some of them in their villages and got the whole story. Then I was ordered out to search for you. We had come as far as Bobolo's yesterday when we got an inkling of your whereabouts from a girl named Nsenene. We started for the Betete village at once and met this young man wandering about, lost, just as we were going into camp here. Now you have assured the success of my mission by walking in on me this morning. There remains nothing now but to take you back to civilization."

"There is one other thing that you can do while you are here," said Old Timer.

"'And that?" inquired the lieutenant.

"There are two known Leopard Men in the village of Bobolo. Three of us have seen them in the temple of the Leopard God taking active parts in the rites. If you wish to arrest them it will be easy."

"I certainly do," replied the officer. "Do you know them by sight?"

"Absolutely," stated Old Timer. "One of them is an old witch-doctor named Sobito, and the other is Bobolo himself."

"Sobito!" exclaimed Tarzan. "Are you sure?"

"He is the same man you carried away from the temple, the man you called Sobito. I saw him drifting down the river in a canoe the morning after I escaped."

"We shall arrest them both," said the officer, "and now as the men are ready to march, we will be off."

"I shall leave you here," said the ape-man. "You are safe now," he added, turning to the girl. "Go out of the jungle with these men and do not come back; it is no place for a white girl alone."

"Do not go yet," exclaimed the officer. "I shall need you to identify Sobito."

"You will need no one to identify Sobito," replied the ape-man, and swinging into a tree, he vanished from their sight.

"And that is that," commented The Kid.

On the march toward Bobolo's village the girl and The Kid walked close together, while Old Timer followed dejectedly behind. Finally The Kid turned and addressed him. "Come on up here, old man, and join us; I was just telling Jessie about a strange coincidence in something I said in Bobolo's village last night. There is a girl there named Nsenene. You probably remember her, Old Timer. Well, she told me about this white girl who was a captive in the pygmy village; and when I showed interest in her and wanted to know where the village was so that I could try to get the girl away from them, the little rascal got jealous I discovered that she had a crush on me; so I had to think quickly to explain my interest in the white girl, and the first thing that entered my head was to tell her that the girl was my sister. Wasn't that a mighty strange coincidence?"

"Where's the coincidence?" demanded Old Timer.

The Kid looked at him blankly. "Why, didn't you know," he exclaimed. "Jessie *is* my sister."

Old Timer's jaw dropped. "Your sister!" Once again the sun shone and the birds sang. "Why didn't you tell me you were looking for your brother?" he demanded of Kali.

"Why didn't you tell me that you knew Jerry Jerome?" she countered.

"I didn't know that I knew him," he explained. "I never knew The Kid's name. He didn't tell me and I never asked."

"There was a reason why I couldn't tell you," said The Kid; "but it's all right now. Jessie just told me."

"You see,—" she hesitated.

"Hi," prompted Old Timer.

The girl smiled and flushed slightly. "You see, Hi," she commenced again, "Jerry thought that he had killed a man. I am going to tell you the whole story because you and he have been such close friends.

"Jerry was in love with a girl in our town. He learned one night that an older man, a man with a vile reputation, had enticed her to his apartment. Jerry went there and broke in. The man was furious, and in the fight that followed Jerry shot him. Then he took the girl home, swearing her to secrecy about her part in the affair. That same night he ran away, leaving a note saying that he had shot Sam Berger, but giving no reason.

"Berger did not die and refused to prosecute; so the case was dropped. We knew that Jerry had run away to save the girl from notoriety, more than from fear of punishment; but we did not know where he had gone. I didn't know where to look for him for a long time.

"Then Berger was shot and killed by another girl, and in the meantime I got a clue from an old school friend of Jerry's and knew that he had come to Africa. Now there was absolutely no reason why he should not return home; and I started out to look for him."

"And you found him," said Old Timer.

"I found something else," said the girl, but he did not catch her meaning.

It was late when they arrived at the village of Bobolo, which they found in a state of excitement. The officer marched his men directly into the village and formed them so that they could command any situation that might arise.

At sight of The Kid and Old Timer and the girl Bobolo appeared frightened. He sought to escape from the village, but the soldiers stopped him, and then the officer informed him that he was under arrest. Bobolo did not ask why. He knew.

"Where is the witch-doctor called Sobito?" demanded the officer.

Bobolo trembled. "He is gone," he said.

"Where?" demanded the officer.

"To Tumbai," replied Bobolo. "A little while ago a demon came and carried him away. He dropped into the village from the sky and took Sobito up in his arms as though he had no weight at all. Then he cried, 'Sobito is going back to the village of Tumbai!', and he ran through the gateway and was gone into the forest before anyone could stop him."

"Did anyone try?" inquired Old Timer with a grin.

"No," admitted Bobolo. "Who could stop a spirit?"

*   *   *   *   *   *   *

The sun was sinking behind the western forest, its light playing upon the surging current of the great river that rolled past the village of Bobolo. A man and a woman stood looking out across the water that was plunging westward in its long journey to the sea down to the trading posts and the towns and the ships, which are the frail links that connect the dark forest with civilization.

"Tomorrow you will start," said the man. "In six or eight weeks you will be home. Home!" There was a world of wistfulness in the simple, homely word. He sighed. "I am so glad for both of you."

She came closer to him and stood directly in front of him,

looking straight into his eyes. "You are coming with us," she said.

"What makes you think so?" he asked.

"Because I love you, you will come."